HIS CURVY SURPRISE

A SMALL TOWN CURVY GIRL ROMANCE

BOOK BOYFRIENDS WANTED
BOOK 16

MARY E THOMPSON

BOOK BOYFRIENDS WANTED

It's a beautiful day... maybe not. A storm is brewing in the neighborhood, and Chelsea and Derek are right at the center of it. All they want is to find a place where they belong, but it's not so easy when her existence makes him crazy. In more ways than one! Get to know all the characters in MacKellar Cove and fall in love with your favorite new book boyfriend. This small town is a truly special place to be.

Never miss a thing when you sign up for Mary's newsletter. *Romancing the Curves* comes with subscriber exclusive freebies, sneak peeks, and a first look at everything Mary has to offer. Be the first to know about new releases and sales and all the curves ahead!

SUBSCRIBE NOW AT MARYETHOMPSON.COM

Happy reading!

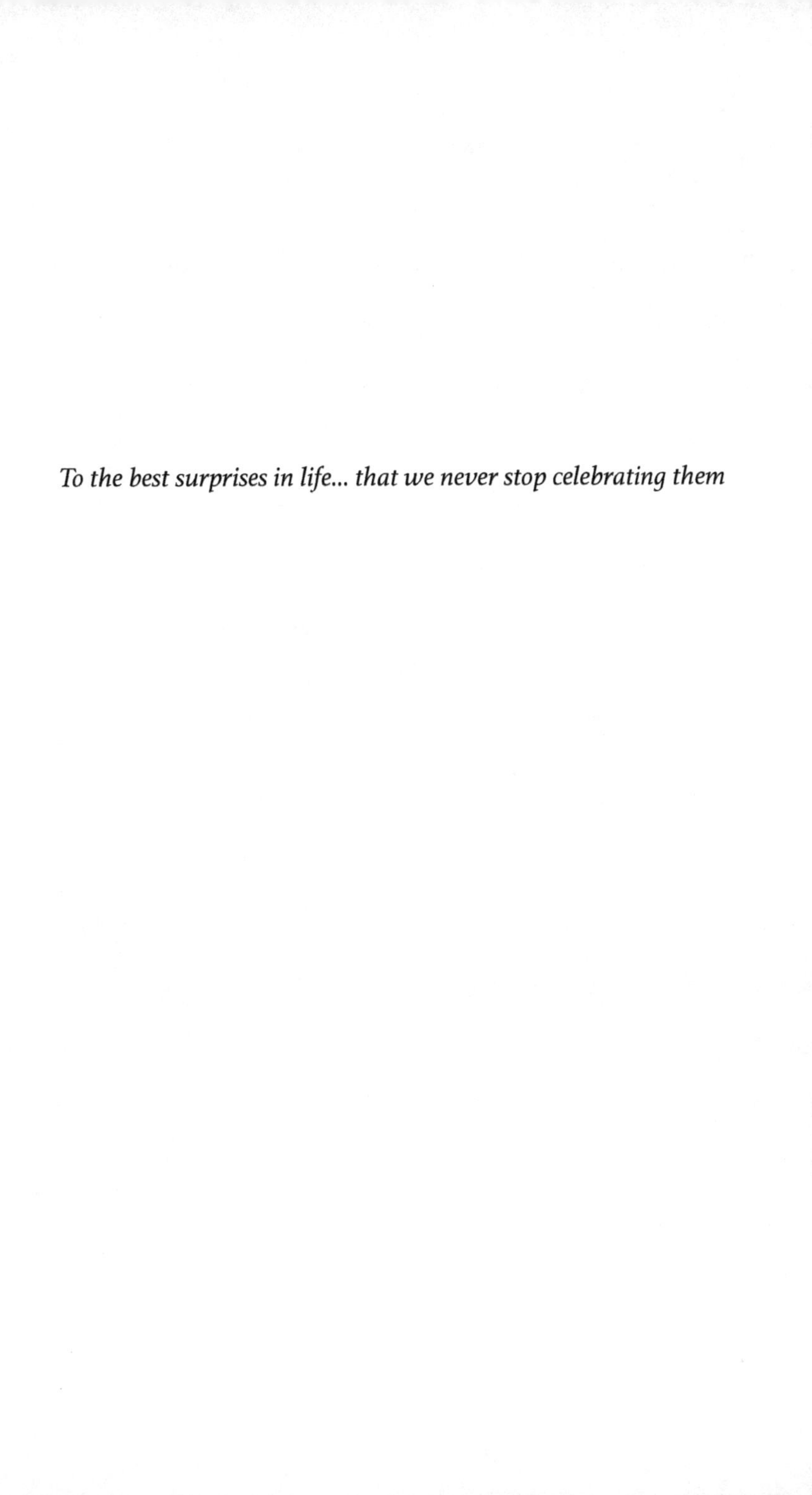

To the best surprises in life... that we never stop celebrating them

1

CHELSEA

I MIXED A DRINK AND CARRIED IT OUT TO THE BACK PATIO. Summer was coming to an end, and I was going to get as much out of my backyard as possible. School started the day before for the local kids, and that always told me fall was coming. But not just yet.

"Thank you," Sofia said, accepting the drink I made for her. She took a sip and groaned. "So good."

"This was a great idea," Haley said.

Haley and Sofia were my two closest friends and the first two I thought of when I decided to throw open the back door and have fun. My yard was perfect for it. I considered inviting more people, but after a long day at work, Haley and Sofia were enough for me.

And surprisingly, they were both available and not with their boyfriends for the evening. Definitely a miracle.

"I'm glad you guys could come. Ever since I moved in, I've been wanting to do something out here again," I told them.

"That was a good party," Haley said.

I nodded with her. The party was fun. Haley, Sofia, and my cousin, Elise, invited all their friends to help me move in. It seemed like half the town ended up in my little house, bringing food and drinks and moving all my furniture and belongings inside. Some of them even brought new and new-to-me gifts to help me get settled in.

After the move, we turned up the music and enjoyed my backyard. It was a great time. Until the next morning when I found a note on my door from my neighbor telling me I needed to keep it down in the future.

It was a Saturday night. And there were police officers at the party. We didn't violate any rules. They made sure of it.

But my neighbor didn't care. Obviously.

"Have you met your neighbor yet?" Haley asked, as if reading my mind.

I shook my head and sipped my drink. Water after the last two heavy pours I'd treated myself to. "I don't know if I want to."

"Have you gotten more notes?" Sofia asked.

I shook my head again. "I've been afraid to invite people over. This is the first time I've done anything since then."

"We should crank up the music and be really obnoxious," Haley said, a mischievous grin on her face.

"Please don't," I said.

Sofia was with me, pushing Haley back into her chair. "We don't want Chelsea to have trouble with her neighbors."

Haley scowled. "You guys are no fun."

"Getting arrested wouldn't be fun either," I said.

Haley waved her hand. "You wouldn't get arrested. A noise complaint would be a pain, but I don't think they can actually do anything to you for it."

"In MacKellar Cove? I'd be willing to bet something

would happen. My neighbors would hate me, if nothing else." I looked at my house and dreaded the idea of having to leave. I'd worked a long time to get to where I could buy my own place. Apartment living was not something I was willing to go back to. Not after my last apartment ended up being more like a smoker's paradise instead of my personal retreat.

"Have you met any of your neighbors?" Sofia asked, changing the subject to take Haley away from the violence she was no doubt planning.

"There's a lady across the street who's really nice. Mrs. Walsh. She adores Dozer."

My dopey dog lifted his head at his name. He smiled at me, his tongue hanging out the side of his mouth.

"You can go back to sleep," I told him.

Of course, addressing him directly meant he had to get involved in the conversation. He got to his feet and bounced over to me, dropping his head onto my lap.

"I said you can go back to sleep."

Dozer barked a happy, loud sound, no doubt alerting half the neighborhood to his presence.

"Maybe Mrs. Walsh will be on your side and you won't have to worry about the one who left you the note," Sofia said.

I rubbed Dozer's head and shrugged. "I hope so."

"Let's talk about happy things. What about the guy you've been talking to on Book Boyfriends Wanted?" Sofia asked. "Have you asked him to meet yet?"

I shook my head. "No. I'm not ready for that."

"Why not? It's just a date," Haley said.

"Dating is painful. Either he's not who he says he is and is boring or weird or creepy, or he takes one look at me and decides he's not interested." I sighed heavily and sipped my water. "This guy is sweet and funny, and I'm not ready to ruin that yet."

"I think you should, because you need someone good in your life. Instead of your obnoxious neighbor," Haley said. "He's making you miserable for no good reason. This guy makes you happy."

I shrugged. "For now. Eventually I'll meet him. Probably."

"Has he asked?" Sofia asked.

I shook my head. "No. When we started talking, he was friendly and talkative. It's gotten deeper and more personal. It's like we know each other, even though we don't."

"I wonder if you do. Knox and I met the night before our first date. You never know if this guy is someone you know," Haley said.

Sofia groaned. "We all know about your one-night stand with Knox."

"I wasn't saying anything about that!" Haley argued, her laughter betraying her words.

"Sure," Sofia and I said together.

Haley stood and shook her head. "I was just thinking you need some joy in your life. And a few orgasms never hurt." Haley winked and went inside.

"Should I be worried about her?" I asked Sofia.

"About?"

"Causing trouble for me with my neighbor?"

Sofia chuckled and shook her head. "Haley's a little crazy, but she won't do anything to risk your comfort or safety. She knows what it's like to share walls with people, and this is not much different. If you're not respectful of your neighbors, they won't be respectful of you."

"I wasn't trying to be disrespectful," I said, feeling like I did something wrong.

Sofia smiled. "I never said you did. I know you, Chelsea. I know you're not going to intend harm. Melody knows your neighbor, right? Did you ask her about him? You're sure it's that one?" Sofia pointed to the house next door.

It was a cute house with dark blue siding and a porch on the front. I couldn't see the backyard because of the fence between our homes, but the house was two stories and well-maintained. The single dad who lived there with his son took care of his place.

I nodded in answer to Sofia's question about the man who left the note coming from that house. "My doorbell camera caught him leaving. It didn't pick up where he came from, but it saw him going back that way. It could have been someone farther down, but I doubt they would cut across the driveway."

"Doubtful. What did Melody say?"

I wrinkled my nose. "I haven't asked her. I don't want to put her in the middle and make her feel like she has to choose sides between us."

"You're not the one doing it. The single dad with a notepad is the one causing problems," Sofia said.

I wasn't sure I completely agreed. We were loud that first night, but I really thought there would be more flexibility on my first day. Especially since it was a weekend. I wasn't up late or making noise on a weeknight.

"Yes, he is," Haley said loudly, joining us again with a bottle of water in her hand. "And we're not gonna take it!"

"Haley!" Sofia hissed.

"It's crap," Haley said, again, not lowering her voice. "He has no right to tell Chelsea she can't enjoy a night in her own backyard well before any noise ordinances begin. What the hell?"

"If you don't sit down, we're leaving," Sofia threatened.

Haley gasped. "What? Why?"

"Because Chelsea wants to live here. She wants to get along with her neighbors. Just because the guy next door knows Melody and has a son doesn't mean things won't escalate."

Haley dropped onto a chair. "You think he'd be dangerous?"

Sofia shook her head. "I hope not, but I don't know him. You can't assume anything."

"Shit." Haley swung her gaze to me. "I'm sorry, Chelsea. I never thought..."

"It's okay," I assured her. "I don't think he's dangerous, but I don't want to piss him off either. Or anyone else on my street."

"Maybe we should go," Haley said, her cheeks red and her eyes regretful.

Sofia downed the last of her drink and stood. "Probably a good idea."

They helped me clean up and bring everything inside. I assured them leaving the dishes would be fine and said goodbye as they headed out the front door.

Thankfully, they were quiet getting into Haley's car. I waited until her headlights turned to face the road before going to the backyard and double checking we'd gotten everything, then locking up my house for the night.

"Just you and me, Dozer," I told my dog.

He barked, then scratched at the back door.

"Really? We were just outside for hours, and now you have to pee."

He barked again. The little shit.

I sighed and opened the back door. He took off, disappearing into the darkness in seconds. I searched the yard, trying to spot him and make sure he didn't destroy anything else back there. He wasn't the best trained dog around. Or even a little trained.

"Dozer!" I called, wondering why he wasn't back. He rarely took long when it was dark outside.

I waited, listening for the jangle of his collar, but heard nothing.

I took a few steps into the yard and called him again.

Still nothing.

"Where the hell are you? Dozer!" I shouted, knowing it was going to piss off my neighbor, but he would have to get over it.

Finally, the jangle of his collar met my ears. He was near the fence to the neighbor's house.

"What are you doing?" I snapped at my dog when he finally came into view.

His head was covered in dirt. One ear was flopped over on top of his head. His collar was closer to his jaw than his neck.

"You need to leave that fence alone or we're going to be in even more trouble," I scolded Dozer.

Not that he understood me, but it made me feel better.

We went inside, and then he shook the dirt from his face and body, sending it flying all over my house.

"Dozer!" I shouted.

It didn't stop the chaos. Or the madness.

He looked up at me, a sweet smile on his face.

"You need a bath. Then I need to clean this place."

So much for sleep.

I STRETCHED AS I WOKE, stopping when I felt a lump next to me. I lifted my head and laughed.

"Dozer, what are you doing in my bed?" I asked him. My dog was less of a morning person than I was. Person? Dog? Could a dog be a morning person? Morning animal?

Whatever it was, he was not it. He wanted to sleep in until noon and nothing was going to get him up. Even getting a lecture for sleeping in my bed, when he had a perfectly good doggy bed five feet away.

"Dozer," I groaned, swinging my legs from my bed and walking to his bed. I leaned down, my gaze locked on my stubborn dog, and patted the bed.

"What the..." My gaze went right back to the doggy bed. The wet doggy bed. The wet doggy bed I just put my hand in. "Oh, gross! Dozer!"

He gave me those eyes that said he was sorry and wouldn't do it again.

Liar.

I held my hand up like the offending thing it was and hurried to the bathroom. I scrubbed my skin, twice, then dragged my lazy-ass dog off my bed before he decided mine was good enough for a bathroom, too.

"You need to figure out this bathroom thing or one of us isn't going to survive," I said with a scowl.

Dozer pranced ahead of me, going straight to the door and waiting for me to open it for him. He refused to use the doggy door. He tried it the first day we moved in, and he got stuck. Almost ripped the entire door off the hinges. One day I'd have a bigger one installed, but that was a future problem when money was less tight.

Nope, I was just going to waste money on new doggy beds when he used them as his toilet.

After Dozer and I both did our business, mine inside,

thank you very much, I tossed his bed into the wash and started on breakfast. I turned on the TV for noise while I made eggs and sausage. Dozer sat quietly, patiently waiting for his treat, happily chomping down the sausage after catching it midair.

With breakfast done and the kitchen cleaned up from last night's impromptu party, I changed into a pair of shorts and threw on a sweatshirt. The local veterinarian, Dr. Harris, told me Dozer needed to be walked daily, sometimes twice a day. He warned me a forty-to-fifty pound dog like Dozer would have a lot of energy.

"Who's a good boy?" I cooed at my sweet dog. He wasn't perfect, but neither was I, and I damn sure wasn't about to send him back just because of a few adjustments.

I clipped on Dozer's leash as he jumped around, excited to go for a walk. We stepped out onto the porch, and as I turned to lock the door, I saw a note taped to the window next to my door.

"What the...?" I grabbed it, struggling to keep Dozer from taking off down the steps for our walk. "Sit, Dozer," I snapped.

He listened. For long enough that I could open the note.

Dear Neighbor,

I'd hoped you would have realized by now that this is a family neighborhood. All night parties are not the way to make friends. Neither is letting your dog damage the fence between our yards. I'd appreciate it if you would be more respectful of the rest of us sharing this area

for our home in the future.
Thank you.

What. The. Fuck?

All night parties? The dog destroying the fence? It was half destroyed when I moved in. What the hell was he talking about?

Knowing I couldn't do anything about it at the moment, I pocketed the note and scowled at my neighbor's house. He wasn't home, but it didn't matter. Dozer needed a walk, and I liked the exercise it gave me to walk him around the block.

We walked down the driveway and turned toward the neighbor from hell's house. I tried to peer down his driveway to where he said the fence was destroyed, but it looked fine to me. What a liar!

"Good morning," a voice said from across the street.

I looked over and saw Mrs. Walsh getting her mail.

"Good morning, Mrs. Walsh. How are you today?"

"Oh, I'm good. How are you, Ms. Chelsea? And Dozer?"

Dozer barked and pulled at the leash, desperate to get to his new friend. Mrs. Walsh liked to give Dozer full-body rubdowns, and he was happy to accept the treatment.

"Dozer!" I snapped, trying to keep a hold of his leash before he ran across the street and tackled the woman.

He jumped and pranced around me, realizing I was going to let him see his favorite person. I looked both ways down our quiet street, then hurried across so he didn't rip my arm from the socket. He wasn't even that big of a dog, but he was strong. Especially when he saw Mrs. Walsh.

"Who's a good boy?" Mrs. Walsh cooed at my dog. She crouched next to him, laughing when Dozer flopped on the ground and rolled over onto her feet.

"I am so sorry," I told her.

Mrs. Walsh shook her head. "Nothing to be sorry for. We used to foster dogs, so I've had dozens in and out of my home over the years. He's a good one. Sweetest thing ever."

"He doesn't know he's a dog," I told her.

"They usually don't." Mrs. Walsh rubbed Dozer's belly, smiling like it made her entire day to do it.

She was the first, and only, of my neighbors to welcome me to the street. She showed up the first week I moved in with a chocolate cream pie and her phone number, asking me to call her if I ever needed anything. The older woman confessed her life was too quiet for her since she lost her husband two years earlier and her kids had their own lives. We talked for hours, the time passing like it was nothing.

She realized she knew my parents and my aunt and uncle, not a surprise since MacKellar Cove was fairly small. Her kids were all older than me, so I didn't know them, but she declared we were family, anyway.

"Have you met anymore of the neighbors?" she asked when Dozer fell asleep, snoring loudly on the sidewalk with himself exposed, not a care in the world.

I shook my head. "No, I haven't." A part of me wanted to tell her about my rude next-door neighbor who left notes for me, but I didn't feel right badmouthing a man I'd never met.

"You have the perfect yard for a gathering. Maybe you should have everyone over while the weather is holding out. I'd be happy to help you take care of things."

"That's a great idea, Mrs. Walsh."

She beamed under my praise. "You don't have to, of course. We can also plan a street party, where everyone participates and we block off the street. My Walter always told me my ideas were too big for most people to handle."

"Not for me," I told her. "I like parties and getting together with others. And I'd love to know my neighbors."

"Then it's settled. Let me know what I can do, and when you want to do it. Nothing fancy, just casual so people can meet, I would guess."

I nodded. "Sounds perfect."

And then I could meet my new neighbor. And find out why he was so rude.

2

DEREK

I signed my name and handed over my license to the woman who ran the afterschool program at MacKellar Cove Community Center. Would she ask for my license every day for the full school year, or was it just because we were only a week in and everyone was new?

"How was today?" I asked her.

"Good," she said with forced cheer. "Everyone had a great day!"

I tried to figure out if it was the blanket lie she told all parents or if there was a problem specifically with my kid.

As soon as I saw Jude, I knew the answer.

He dragged his feet toward me, staring at the ground and sulking the entire way.

Shit.

"Hey, bud. You ready to go home?" I asked my eleven-year-old.

He shrugged, the preteen years already showing up.

"Well, it's time to go, so no choice. Let's get something to eat. What are you in the mood for tonight?"

Another shrug told me it was going to be a rough night.

Was he tired? I clenched my jaw at the thought. My new neighbor was not respectful at all of the fact that not everyone had the freedom in their schedules to be up all night long. Her parties were keeping both Jude and me up past our bedtimes and now, they were affecting his school.

I stayed silent until we made it to my truck. If he wouldn't talk to me with others around, there was no reason to push for it. He climbed up in the backseat and buckled his seatbelt, then crossed his arms and scowled at me.

"What's going on? Why are you grumpy? Are you tired?"

"No. I just hate going there."

"Where? To school?"

"No! To that afterschool thing. Why can't I just go home?"

"You're too young, Jude. We had this conversation."

"None of my friends go there. They go home after school."

"Alone? Or do they have a parent waiting for them?"

Jude's silence answered the question for me.

I warred with myself. Sixth grade was middle school, and the district allowed the kids to get off the bus alone. To go home without an adult present. But I wasn't comfortable with it. Not when Jude would be home alone for three or four hours every afternoon. I'd barely started leaving him home for an hour, and three or four was way beyond me.

We drove home without another word. Being a single parent came with countless questions about what I was doing, and if my choices were the right ones. The way Jude dragged his backpack inside told me this decision was not one he agreed with. At all.

I let Jude go inside, then turned back to the street to get the mail. It was nice out, Upstate New York still holding on to the last warm days of summer before fall officially took over.

"Good evening, Derek," Mrs. Walsh said, calling from across the street. "How's the school year starting so far?"

I bypassed my mailbox and checked both ways before crossing the dead quiet street. When Sasha and I bought the house, the neighborhood feel and quiet street were the biggest selling points. They still were, as long as my new neighbor wasn't having a party and her dog wasn't trying to knock down the fence that separated our yards.

"Hi, Mrs. Walsh. How are you?"

"I'm doing real well, Derek. And you know I told you to call me Faith."

"I'll try, but you know it's not in me to do that."

Mrs. Walsh laughed, the sound a balm on my battered soul. She was a bright spot in my day. Between work and home, I didn't have a lot of things that made me smile.

"What has Jude so unhappy today?" Mrs. Walsh asked, her keen eye not missing the attitude my son dragged into the house with his backpack.

I glanced back to make sure Jude wasn't outside, then shook my head. "He doesn't want to go to the afterschool care program. He said none of his friends are there."

"Where are they?"

"Home. Sixth graders are allowed to get off the bus without an adult."

Mrs. Walsh sighed, shaking her head. "I know the strings need to be cut eventually, but it seems like we're trying to cut them younger and younger. When my kids were young, I'm sure it was the same, but I was home. Everyone I knew was the same. Families don't operate the same way now."

"No, they don't," I agreed, thinking of the easy way my ex

walked away, without a second thought about her son and what it would do to him to know his mother didn't want him enough to stay in the area where she could be in his life at all.

"In my day, we also watched out for each other. Why don't you let Jude come to my house?"

"I couldn't," I said before she could even finish her question.

"You could. Or I could come to your house so he's at home and comfortable."

"It's too much to ask."

"Then it's a good thing I'm offering," Mrs. Walsh said. "Middle school is hard enough on a kid. What do you say we give it a try? See how the first few weeks go and evaluate from there?"

"I don't know, Mrs. Walsh." I was not going to agree. I couldn't. Jude was my responsibility. Making sure he was safe was up to me. I couldn't leave him in the care of someone who wasn't family, even if Mrs. Walsh felt like it at times.

"I know you don't do well asking for help, Derek. You don't like to count on others—"

"It's not—"

"It is. And I understand that. I didn't let anyone else take care of my kids when they were little. But I'm home, Derek. I'm just a lonely old woman who's trying to make sure this neighborhood is what it was when my kids were the young ones. Safe and friendly."

She was good. Damn good. Because the more she talked, the more I wanted to agree with her.

"Start with a week, Derek. Go from there. I bet others would help if you asked, too." Mrs. Walsh's nod toward my next-door neighbor didn't go unnoticed.

I snorted. "Not everyone who lives in this neighborhood is going to be reliable and helpful."

"She's having a party this weekend," Mrs. Walsh said.

"That's not a surprise."

"A neighborhood party. She wants to get to know everyone. I think it's a great idea. Too many people have moved onto the street and never gotten to know each other. Hopefully you and Jude can come."

I shook my head. "I'm working all weekend. The shop is open Saturday and Sunday."

"You need some time off, Derek. If you work every day, you're going to drive yourself mad."

I nodded. She was right, but it was the only option. I couldn't leave the shop in the hands of the guys. They were capable, but something always came up. Something I needed to handle. Something they didn't have time to handle if they were going to do the jobs assigned to them. "I'm okay."

Mrs. Walsh's look was pointed. She knew I was lying, but she didn't call me on it. "How about I take Jude to the party? It's on Saturday afternoon. Starts at two and runs through dinner. Probably over around seven."

I shook my head the whole time she spoke. "Jude comes to the shop with me on Saturdays."

Mrs. Walsh didn't push, but the desire to do so was in her eyes. "If you change your mind..."

"Thanks, Mrs. Walsh. Enjoy your evening."

"You, too, Derek. Think about my offer."

I waved to her and jogged back across the street. I grabbed my mail, peeling the folded piece of neon orange paper from under the flag on the side of the box. I opened the orange paper as I walked up the driveway, rolling my eyes when I saw the invitation from my next-door neighbor to get to know each other at her block party Saturday afternoon.

"Not happening," I muttered under my breath.

I walked into my house, cringing when I heard the TV blaring from the living room.

"Can you turn that down?" I called to Jude.

The indecipherable grumble was the only answer I got before the volume dropped.

"Thank you!"

More grumbling.

Yay.

I climbed the stairs to my room, grabbing clean clothes before I went to the bathroom for a shower. I didn't like cooking dinner when I was covered in grease and smelled like an engine.

I rushed through my shower, not liking to leave Jude alone after leaving him in afterschool care. When I opened the bathroom door, the TV was once more cranked to full volume.

I sighed. It was the one and only thing he could control. I didn't like it, but I understood it. Sort of.

I stomped down the stairs, making sure he knew I was coming. The volume quickly dropped to a normal volume before I returned to the living room.

"What do you want for dinner?" I asked him.

He shrugged, not offering any ideas.

"How about burgers?" I asked, knowing it was his favorite food and something he'd likely be happy about.

"Sure," he said, showing zero enthusiasm.

I closed my eyes and counted to ten. We would not survive the entire school year if he was so unhappy. I hated it. And maybe I was being too overprotective.

"Mrs. Walsh was outside. She said you could go to her house instead of the community center after school."

"Really?" He turned to look at me, his brown eyes skeptical but curious.

"Yeah. Or she said she could come here so you're comfortable."

"I could come home?" It was the most excited he'd been since I picked him up.

"Maybe. We have to talk about it."

"I'll do anything. I'll clean my room and pack my lunch and... and... and anything else."

"Help me with dinner?" I asked.

Jude jumped up and hurried to the kitchen.

I smiled and followed him, running my hand over his short hair. My heart squeezed. I'd do anything for my son. Anything to make him happy. Just one offer had him excited. How could I say no?

SATURDAY MORNING, Jude dragged himself downstairs for breakfast. He rested his head on his hand and ate his cereal while I drank a very large cup of coffee.

The neighbor had people over again the night before, and we were dragging.

Barking outside drew my attention to the window. Her dog was running around the backyard, barking like it was chasing something. Not that anything was there. The dog was a wild menace.

"Damn dog," I muttered.

Then *she* walked outside. My new neighbor wore a tiny light blue tank top that barely contained her full breasts. No bra, clearly. Her nipples pressed against the tight fabric. She crossed her arms over her chest and rubbed her hands down her arms.

I looked down at her shorts. How they qualified as shorts, I didn't know. I'd seen panties that covered more skin than those shorts. Thick, lush thighs and endless creamy skin. My dick thickened at the thought of wrapping those thighs around my shoulders and diving into the treasure between.

"Dad?" Jude asked, bumping into me. "What's going on?"

I swallowed my groan. "Nothing." I cleared my throat. "Nothing. Just watching that pain in the patootie dog next door run around like a crazy animal."

"I think he looks funny. He's always smiling."

"When did you see the dog?"

"I was outside once when he jumped up on the fence. He stopped when he saw me, like he was surprised I was there. I think he was scared, but I held out my hand and he licked it. Then he smiled and barked and went back to running around his yard."

"When was this? I didn't know. That dog could be dangerous."

Jude rolled his eyes and dumped the milk from his bowl into the sink. "He's funny, Dad. He's not dangerous." Jude put his bowl and spoon in the sink, then spotted the stack of mail with the flyer I never tossed on top. "What's this?"

I reached to grab it from him. "Nothing."

"It says it's a party," Jude said, spinning out of my reach. "Can we go?"

"No."

"Why? It's next door. And it's today!"

"And I have to work."

"You always have to work," Jude grumbled. His shoulders slumped, the gray tee he wore outlining the childhood shape of his body. He looked younger when he pouted, a leftover note from a less than ideal upbringing.

God, I did my fucking best. But it was never going to be good enough. Not when he didn't have the childhood his friends had.

"I agreed to start letting you come home after school next week. I'm not going to ask Mrs. Walsh to take you to a party at a stranger's house."

"We could meet her. Talk to her. Then she wouldn't be a stranger."

"No," I said immediately. "She's always having parties, and that dog is going to knock down that fence and get someone hurt. She's not someone we need to know."

"You always say we should get to know our neighbors. That we live here so we have friends and people we can count on."

"Not people like her," I said, my tone offering no room for argument.

Jude glared at me for a long moment, but he finally sighed and let it go.

He was silent on the drive to my shop. Stone Auto Repair was a dream come true for me. When Mr. Stone retired and offered the business for sale to his employees, I jumped at the chance. I was the only one who wanted to buy it, and it became mine.

Not that it was easy to be the boss. Going from coworker to boss was a bigger hurdle than I expected. I itched to get my hands dirty most days and spent more hours on paperwork and the phone than I ever wanted, but I was proud of the shop and the guys who worked for me.

Ricky, one of the older guys in the shop, walked out when he saw me pull up. He headed to Jude's door and high-fived him when he jumped out of the truck. Ricky raised his brows at me, silently asking if everything was good.

I rolled my eyes, letting him know things were not great, and he took over, distracting Jude and letting me off the hook.

Like I said, the guys were the best.

A dozen hours later, Jude was less miserable and actually smiling when he got back in the truck to go home. He talked about the vehicles Ricky worked on and what Ricky let Jude help with. He was excited and happy and pleasant.

Until we turned into the driveway and saw the party was still going on next door. The party that was supposed to have been over an hour ago.

"People are still there. Can we go, Dad?" Jude asked, his excited face pressed against the window.

"I'm tired. It's been a long day. And the party is supposed to be over. People will be going home soon."

"But Dad..."

"No, Jude." His face fell, and I added, "Maybe next time."

He opened his door with a grumble, his words lost in the noise outside as soon as the door was open.

I didn't move for a minute. Every day, since my new neighbor moved in, just when I thought I was having a good day, something would happen that would change that. The dog would push the fence over just a little more, threatening a collapse. He would bark and interrupt the quiet neighborhood. Jude would get mad about something. Always.

Things were different since she arrived. The couple who lived there before were quiet. They were respectful. They didn't keep us up. But she was loud all night, and now all day. She made it impossible to sleep. Her dog was a pain, and she was a temptation I did not need in my life.

Or want. I'd been through losing one mother to my son. I wasn't looking to lose another one. Ever. Which meant staying single was my best and only option.

That app I downloaded? That was to take the edge off once in a while. Not love. Not romance. Not permanent.

Which was why the one woman I was talking to was going to stay on the app. I wanted to meet her, but she was someone I enjoyed talking to. I couldn't risk meeting her and losing that connection. There was no chance it would be more than what it was.

I had one love in my life. And he was glaring at me from the front porch. He was all that mattered. He was all I cared about. And giving him a life that was good was all I wanted.

Even if it was a little lonely for me. I didn't matter as much as Jude did.

3

CHELSEA

I was so happy I chose my house. I knew it was meant to be when I first saw it, but after the notes, I doubted my instinct. Now, I knew my instinct was right and my jerk of a neighbor wasn't like the rest of them.

My other neighbors were amazing. Welcoming and friendly and kind. Mrs. Walsh introduced me to everyone who came to the party, and they were all so excited to be there.

Many of them were familiar. Between walking Dozer through the neighborhood and growing up and living almost all of my life in MacKellar Cove, I knew most of the people who showed up. Friends of my parents arrived with a house-warming gift and an invitation to dinner. A lot came to say hi and introduce themselves. Other neighbors were just excited to get out of the house and meet each other. As friendly and welcoming as everyone was, I got the feeling they didn't do much together.

And thanks to Mrs. Walsh, I was helping to change that. It was a good feeling.

As things were winding down, I saw my next-door

neighbor pull in. It was late. The sun was low on the horizon, setting soon. The lights I strung around the fence made the backyard glow. I watched as my neighbor looked over at my yard and shook his head.

My chest tightened. I'd hoped he would walk over. Say hello. Be nice and neighborly and maybe not hate me.

But he went inside instead of joining us. He shuffled his son into the house and never came back out.

Dammit.

"I'm going to head out, Ms. Chelsea," Mrs. Walsh said, coming up from behind me and startling me from my disappointment.

I turned to her and hugged the older woman. "Thank you for suggesting this. It's been so great to meet so many people."

"I feel bad leaving you to deal with the rest of this event."

I shook my head. "Not at all. I had a great time, and I appreciate you introducing me to everyone who showed up."

She pursed her lips at the house next door. "I'm sorry he didn't come over. I spoke to him the other day and mentioned it. He said he was working, but I suggested he come after. Derek is a nice man, but he's busy."

"I understand," I said, even though I didn't. I didn't know anyone who wasn't busy. Every single person who showed up was busy. But they were all willing to be considerate and friendly.

Mrs. Walsh grinned. "I know you don't, but that's okay."

I laughed, not arguing with her.

"I think most of these people are going to head out soon. If they don't, come get me and I'll shoo them all away."

I smiled, knowing she would do exactly that. "Thank

you. I think things are winding down. I'll start cleaning up. That usually gets people moving."

Mrs. Walsh chuckled. "Very true. Thank you again for hosting, Ms. Chelsea. It was good for me to get out of the house and enjoy an evening with others. I look forward to doing it again. A few people said they want this to be a regular thing and are looking to host in the future."

"That would be a lot of fun."

She patted my hand, then turned and walked down the driveway. I watched her walk away, my heart full of joy. Even though the man I'd hoped to meet didn't show up, others did. And it was a good night. A very good night.

Within an hour, everyone had left. I let Dozer run around in the backyard while I collected the trash and carried things inside. The food was all gone, and the yard was a bit trashed, but it was worth it.

I collapsed onto my couch with a smile and turned on the TV, letting the movie lull me to sleep.

A WEEK AFTER THE PARTY, Dozer and I were up early Saturday morning before I had to go to work. It was the last official day of summer, and I was trying to enjoy it. I drank my coffee while Dozer sniffed every inch of the yard. He barked at a bird that swooped low and settled on top of the fence.

"Dozer!" I shouted when he jumped up, front paws on the fence as close as he could get to the bird. The fence leaned, bending over much farther than I thought was safe.

The bird flew off, and Dozer raced across the yard after it, stopping at the other side and barking like crazy before I shouted at him again.

"Dozer, get over here. Now!"

Dozer dropped his head, looking up at me like he was sorry.

A door slammed behind me at the house next door. I ignored the house, and whoever slammed the door, and stayed focused on my obnoxious dog.

I kept my face stern until he trudged into the house and hunched next to the sink, where his treats were stored.

"Good boys get treats. Were you a good boy?" I demanded.

He barked softly, adding a howl like he was begging.

"Really?"

He did it again.

I groaned. There was no way I could say anything against him. I grabbed a treat and tossed it to him.

He caught it mid-air, chomping down on it and swallowing the whole thing in less than two seconds. He looked up at me like he should get a second one.

"Not a chance, buddy," I said, crossing my arms.

He huffed at me, then pranced to his bed in the living room. He curled up on it and was snoring within seconds.

I shook my head and went to get ready for work.

Two hours later, I was waving goodbye to my first client of the day and took a breath. I was already worn out.

"Are you okay?" Haley asked. As my friend and business partner, she was more aware of my moods than anyone else ever had been.

I shook my head. "I don't know. I just feel off."

"Why? What's going on?"

I shrugged as the door dinged with the arrival of our next clients. The next two hours passed quickly, the town drama and chatter of clients keeping me focused on the day instead of worrying about anything else.

When Haley said goodbye to her last client before lunch, she locked the front door and met me in the back. We both packed a lunch that day, and I was already warming mine up when she joined me. The ladies who worked part time went to lunch most weekends and were all gone, leaving Haley and me alone.

I sat at the table and tried to think through my anxiety, searching for the cause of it.

"Okay, spill. What is going on? You seem really off today. What was the note today?" Haley sat down next to me.

"No note today. Yesterday I had one, but I know Dozer woke him up this morning. A door slammed when I was outside." My chest squeezed at the memory.

"Maybe because you left early. He didn't have time to put one on your door?"

I shrugged. "Possible. Something to look forward to when I get home."

"Why does he get to you so badly?"

I shook my head. "I don't know. I really wanted to get along with my neighbors, but he's just not willing to get to know me."

"I still can't believe he left a note after you had a party for the entire neighborhood."

"I can't believe he's leaving notes at all. I mean, who does that? I'd go ring the doorbell and ask my neighbor to be quieter."

"Would you? I wouldn't."

"Really?"

Haley nodded and took a bite of her sandwich. "Absolutely. The world is a little crazy. You never know what is going on with people. Someone could just as easily smile and say sure as they could shoot you dead on their front step."

I shivered at the thought. "I can't see him doing that."

Haley shrugged. "I can't either. Not with the way Melody and Knox talk about him. Both of them are big fans of his. Always going on and on about how nice Derek is."

"Lucky me, I'm the only one in town he hates."

Haley laughed softly. "I'm sure that's not true, but I wish there was an explanation for why he seems to have it out for you."

I shook my head. "It's obvious it's the noise, but I'm not violating any ordinances. He has no grounds."

"It'll be better through the winter. You won't be outside as much."

"I'll still have to let Dozer out."

"How could anyone not love that adorable oaf?"

I snorted a laugh. Haley was right. My dog was a menace, but I adored him and couldn't imagine anyone not feeling the same. "I just have to figure out what he likes. Something that will make him like me."

"If he's a good father, he likes his kid. It sounds like he is. Maybe something with the kid."

"Yeah, I'm not sure that's a good idea."

"Why not? Kids love you."

"Sure, but it will not go over well if I draw the kid closer with candy and my dog. People get arrested for things like that."

Haley cackled. "I didn't mean something like that. That would definitely be bad. I meant something like... Hell, I don't know. What do kids like?"

I chuckled. "Again, not a path we should be going down. I think I need to do something different than trying to manipulate a child."

"When you put it like that..."

Haley and I laughed and shook our heads, but I felt a

little better about my situation knowing she was trying to help. Maybe one day I'd figure out how to get my neighbor to like me.

I WAS off Tuesday and had big plans for the day. I was going to sleep in and catch up on shows I'd missed and be lazy. It was going to be glorious.

Except for Bulldozer. My dog was up at the crack of damn dawn to go outside. It was better than peeing in his bed, or mine, but I was not thrilled. I trudged to the back door, where the doggy door was still too small, and let him out. He took off like a shot, racing around before he found the perfect spot to do his business.

It was freezing outside, and I didn't grab a jacket. I bounced on my toes and shivered, hoping Dozer would hurry. My breasts bounced under my tiny tank, which was fine for sleeping but not so great for late September in Upstate New York.

Dozer wandered around the yard and took his time sniffing every blade of grass before he wandered back my way. I turned to let us inside and swore I saw my neighbor at his window.

I looked back, but no one was there. I was losing my mind.

Dozer waited at the sink for his treats, and since he didn't bark and wake up everyone else in the neighborhood, I gave him two.

Then I went back to bed.

A few hours later, Bulldozer did what he did best and dragged me out of bed. He laid down next to me and worked his way closer and closer and closer until I nearly fell off the other side.

"What the hell?" I asked him.

He stood on the mattress and barked happily, like he thought the whole thing was a game. Then he turned in circles and pawed at the comforter.

"Nope. Nope." I stood and grabbed his collar. "You are not using my bed as a bathroom. Come on. If you can hold it, I'll get changed and we can go for a walk."

He took off to the front door, barking the whole time as he raced down the stairs. His nails tapped on the hardwood floors, his excitement evident in the way he paced, barking at the stairs before going back to the door.

I dressed quickly, throwing on a sweatshirt and a pair of sweatpants over the clothes I slept in. I tied my hair up and grabbed a pair of socks, hopping on one foot to put them on, stopping when I got to the top of the stairs.

Dozer saw me at the top of the stairs and let out another excited bark.

"I'm coming," I told him. I pulled my sock on, then went down the stairs to take him out.

"Sit," I said, smiling when he actually listened so I could attach the leash to his collar.

We walked outside, and I let Dozer's leash extend while I locked the front door. I was surprised when I saw a note taped to my window.

> Dear neighbor,
> Yet again, your late night meant no one else could sleep. You are inconsiderate and selfish. Next time, I will call the police. Please don't make me do that.

Please.

My mouth opened and closed, searching for words and an explanation. He was threatening me? Calling the police?

What the hell?

I was done. I was done ignoring him and his notes. I was done sitting back and letting him make me feel bad for existing. I was fucking done.

"Come on, Dozer," I snarled, pulling my dog away from my flowerbed and toward my neighbor's house.

I let my temper guide me up his front walk to the porch hidden behind tall hedges. Dozer barked as we drew closer to the house, and a sound had me pulling him back before we reached the house.

"Hello?" I called.

"Hello?" a voice answered. Small, scared, and not adult.

Dozer's tail dropped. He pressed himself to my side. We walked together toward the porch and came face-to-face with the kid who lived in the house.

His eyes went wide when he saw me, but they lit up when he saw Dozer.

"Hi. I'm Chelsea, and this is Bulldozer."

The boy looked up at me, then back to Dozer. A red backpack sat on the ground next to him. "Can I pet him?"

I nodded and released the tension on Dozer's leash just enough to let him know he could approach. My sweet dog ducked his head and approached the kid like he understood how scared the child was.

He laughed when Dozer got close enough. Dozer flopped down next to the boy and rolled over.

"What's your name?" I asked him.

"Jude," he told Dozer more than me.

"Jude. It's nice to meet you. Why are you outside?"

"No one's here. Mrs. Walsh is supposed to meet my bus, but she's not here. We had a half day. My dad works late. I don't have a key. I'm locked out."

I drew a breath and nodded. Fall brought much cooler temperatures, and it was chilly. Sitting outside all day was not good for anyone. "I live right next door. Do you want to come to my house and we can make some phone calls? Get you out of the cold?"

Jude nodded, staring at Dozer the entire time. He threw his backpack over his shoulder and kept one hand on the dog while we cut across the yards. I unlocked my front door and let us in, kicking off my shoes and unhooking Dozer's leash.

Dozer didn't move from Jude's side. He stayed right with the kid, guiding him into the kitchen and sitting next to him when Jude sat at the table.

My first call was to Mrs. Walsh. She answered on the first ring, then told me she had no idea it was a half day and was two hours away on her way to a doctor's appointment. She told me Derek, Jude's dad, owned Stone Auto Repair and to call there to see if Derek could leave work early.

The man who answered the phone at Stone Auto Repair said Derek wasn't available, but he'd leave Derek a message to call me. I made sure he had my name and phone number, but I was on my own with a kid.

"So, Jude. Mrs. Walsh isn't home, and your dad isn't available, but someone's going to get a message to him. Until then, it seems you're stuck with us."

Jude shrugged. "That's okay. I always wanted a dog. My dad said no. Is it okay if I play with him?"

I nodded. "Of course. Do you guys want to go in the backyard? I was going to take Dozer for a walk when we saw you. He needs the exercise if you want to run around with him a little."

Jude jumped up, nodding happily.

I opened the back door for the two of them to go outside. I stuck my phone in my pocket and followed them out the door. I sat down to watch them run around, smiling at the easy friendship they developed.

We went back inside when Dozer and Jude came back to the patio, both puffing exhausted breaths.

"How about some water and maybe something to eat? Did you have lunch yet, Jude?"

He shook his head. "Do you have macaroni and cheese?"

I smiled. A kid after my own heart. "I sure do. Want me to make some for us?"

He nodded.

We went inside, and I showed Jude where the treats were for Dozer. Jude laughed when Dozer caught the first one out of mid-air.

I'd always wanted kids. I'd forced the thought away for so many years that the overwhelming desire for a kid slammed harder into my chest than I expected and brought tears to my eyes.

Jude wasn't mine. He never would be mine. But dammit, I still wanted kids. One day.

4

WE SAT AT THE TABLE TOGETHER AND ATE MACARONI AND cheese. I asked Jude about school and his friends and made small talk with him. After we finished lunch, he asked if he could go outside with Bulldozer again.

"Of course. He's going to be spoiled with all this play time."

"I can come over again. I mean, if you want. If that's okay."

"Dozer would love that. I would, too. It's been fun hanging out with you."

Jude nodded and followed Dozer outside. Their excited noises made me smile.

I cleaned the kitchen, keeping an eye on the backyard the whole time. Dozer was careful with Jude, like he could tell Jude was still young. I wasn't sure how old he was, but my guess was pre-teen. Old enough to be smart and thoughtful and respectful, but young enough to still be scared when he was alone on his porch.

Before I walked outside to join them, I tried to call his

dad again. It had only been a couple of hours, but I was surprised I hadn't heard anything back.

"Stone Auto Repair," a man said into the phone.

"Hi, my name is Chelsea Moss."

"Okay, what vehicle do you have?"

"I'm not calling to make an appointment."

"Uh, okay. How can I help you?"

"I called earlier. I'm looking for Derek Bailey."

"Uh…" The guy went quiet for a minute. A door closed on his end. "Listen, the boss isn't looking for a relationship. I'm not trying to be a dick or anything, but he's—"

"Oh, my God, stop talking. Why in the hell would you think I'm looking for a relationship?"

"You wouldn't be the first."

I choked on my next words and struggled to get a breath out. I exhaled slowly. "Okay, um, listen, I'm his next-door neighbor. I was walking my dog earlier and found his son on his doorstep. He was locked out and alone and scared."

"What the hell?" the man barked.

"Jude said Mrs. Walsh usually gets him off the bus, but it was a half-day, and she didn't know, I guess, and she's at a doctor's appointment. I called a while ago and left a message for Derek to call me back, but I haven't heard anything, so I wanted to call again."

"Jesus. Fuck. Is Jude okay?"

"He's fine. He's a great kid. And he's safe here with me. I'm a local. I own Serenity Salon on Grace Street. I'm home today, so Jude is fine here."

"I know that place. You said you're Chelsea?"

"Yeah."

"My wife's a client of yours. Emily says you're a magician and always makes her vision come to life. I'm a fan, too, because my wife is gorgeous and you always make her feel like it."

"Thank you. I appreciate that. Emily Martinez?"

"That's her."

"She's great to work with."

"I'll tell her you said that. Sorry. Sorry. Jude. How is Jude? You said he's okay?"

"Yeah, he's good. He was scared when we found him. He was locked out and didn't know what was going on. Right now, he's playing with my dog in my backyard. I am looking at them. We had lunch, and he's been outside, but I was surprised I hadn't heard from anyone."

"I'll let Derek know right now. He'll be there soon to get Jude. Thank you, Chelsea. Thank you. And I apologize for my—"

"Don't worry about it. I'm just glad I reached you instead of the other guy. I gave him my name and number and said Jude was with me, but I don't think he realized Jude wasn't supposed to be with me."

"Yeah. I'll take care of that, too."

"Thanks. Jude really is okay here. I don't mind keeping him. But I wanted to make sure his dad knew where he was."

"He'll be relieved. I don't think he has any idea Jude isn't in school right now. I'll let him know. Thanks, Chelsea. I'll make sure Emily has an extra big tip for you next time she comes in."

"Oh, no. That's not necessary."

"Maybe not, but it is deserved. Thanks. I'll give you a call back once I talk to Derek. Shouldn't be long."

"Thank you."

"Yep."

He hung up, and I realized I never got his name. *Emily's husband* probably wasn't it.

I walked outside with water and sat at the table. Jude ran over and took a swig from the cup I brought outside for him, and Dozer lapped up his water from the bowl on the ground.

Jude collapsed onto the chair next to mine and let out a breath. Dozer curled up in the sunshine next to Jude, keeping an eye on the boy.

As both boys huffed exhausted breaths, I thought it might be a good idea to do something a little quieter. And out of the chilly afternoon air.

"Do you have any homework, Jude?"

"Yeah," he grumbled.

"What do you say you get started on it and we can let Dozer rest for a few minutes? He looks tired."

Jude looked at the dog. Dozer, God love him, panted harder, like he really was exhausted from running around in the yard. Jude nodded. "Yeah, he does look tired."

"If you get your homework done, then you don't have to worry about it when your dad gets home."

"Okay," Jude mumbled. But he followed me inside and grabbed his backpack.

We sat at the table again. I went through my phone, accepting new appointments requests and deleting emails. I scrolled social media for a bit, and before I knew it, Jude was jumping up from the table and announcing he was done with homework.

"Already?"

He nodded. "Yeah. I have to read, but my dad lets me do that before I go to sleep."

"Okay. Now what?"

My phone rang before Jude could answer.

"Can I take Dozer outside again?"

I nodded as I answered the call from an unknown local number. "Hello?"

"Chelsea. This is Ricky from Stone Auto Repair."

"Hey. Thanks for calling me back."

"Yeah, you're welcome. Listen. Derek is on his way to you right now. I let him know about Jude, and he had no idea all this was going on. He should be there soon."

"Thanks, Ricky. I really appreciate it. I'll have Jude ready."

"Sounds good, Chelsea. Thanks again."

"Thank you." I hung up and drew a breath. I wasn't sure if it was good or bad that my next-door neighbor was on his way to my house. But I was finally going to meet the man.

"Hey, Jude! Your dad's on the way. Why don't you come in and get your stuff together? We can wait in here for him so we hear when he arrives."

"Okay!" Jude said brightly.

I breathed easier as he raced toward me with Dozer on his heels. An absent dad made me a little worried that there was more going on than I realized. It made me think maybe Derek wasn't as devoted of a dad as I thought he was before he left his kid alone on his doorstep and with a stranger for the better part of the day.

I grew up with two parents who always worked. There were a lot of afternoons I was home alone. I learned as a young kid to rely on myself, but I always knew my parents loved me. I never thought they regretted having me. After a day with Jude, I worried he didn't have the same assurance with his dad, but his excitement said that wasn't the case.

Jude packed his backpack, then asked if I had a piece of paper so he could draw a picture of Dozer.

"Of course. I can send you some pictures, too."

"I don't have a phone," he said.

"I can send them to your dad. And you can put them with the drawing you do."

"That would be cool."

I smiled. Man, this kid. I loved his innocence. The way he was so open and caring with Dozer. The way he was more interested in drawing his own picture than one I took.

I handed him some sheets of printer paper since they didn't have lines and pulled out the pencils, pens, markers, and colored pencils I'd shoved in the junk drawer in the kitchen. I didn't have a lot of options, but Jude didn't seem to mind.

He stared at Dozer, tilting his head to the side. He chewed on the inside of his lip. He was focused on the best drawing ever of my dog.

I settled next to him and started my own drawing of Dozer. I glanced at Jude's paper every few minutes. He was a truly talented artist. Miles better than I was. My drawing barely looked like a dog, but Jude's actually looked like Dozer.

The knock on the door brought my head up from where I was focused on my paper. "I'll be right back," I told Jude. "That's really good." I tapped on his picture of my crazy dog.

"Thanks," Jude said absently.

The knocking grew more insistent as I walked from the kitchen through the living room and out to the porch-turned-mudroom. The big window next to the door opened to the living room so I couldn't see who was pounding on my door, but it had to be Jude's father.

My oh-so-friendly neighbor. Goody.

I opened the door and had to duck before he punched me in the face when his next knock didn't hit the door.

"My son. Jude. Where's Jude?" Derek breathed. He

pushed past me in a less-than-kind way, streaking through my home without waiting for an invitation.

"Jerk," I muttered as I closed the door.

"Dad!" Jude exclaimed, almost erasing his father's rude behavior. Spending a few hours with the kid and knowing how sweet he was made me soften my dislike of the father. A little. He was still a self-righteous jerk who thought he had a right to tell me how to live my life. But Jude was a great kid, so there was something Derek and his ex-wife were doing right.

"Jude," Derek exhaled, dropping to his knees next to the chair Jude was sitting in. Derek ran his hands over his son's head and hugged him close, his entire body sagging with relief when he accepted his son was okay. "Are you okay? Are you safe? I'm so sorry no one was there to get you. Why did the school let you off the bus? I'm going to call them and find out what happened. This never should have happened."

I stood in the entryway to my own kitchen feeling like I didn't belong. My heart warmed at the fear in his voice. A person couldn't fake that. And a parent shouldn't ever have to.

"Ms. Chelsea made me a snack. And lunch. And we played with Dozer. He's so funny, Daddy! He's not a pain in the patootie like you say he is. He likes to play catch and he licked me a lot and he runs around the room when he gets really excited, but he listens to Ms. Chelsea. She's really nice, too. Not a pain in the patootie either."

As if remembering I was there, Jude's dad glanced over his shoulder at me.

Holy hotness. I knew he was attractive, but with those dark brown eyes focused on me, my pulse shot straight to the stratosphere. Then he showed humility and hung his head like he truly regretted his words.

Or maybe he just regretted them being repeated in my presence.

Either way, he stood and turned to face me. He was taller than me, with wide shoulders and grease stained clothes. His jeans molded to his thighs and outlined the phone in his pocket, among other things. His black tee clung to his chest and hinted at a tattoo on his left arm. He took a step forward and reached his hand out.

"Thank you for taking care of my boy." He left his hand between us, waiting for me to shake it.

My manners forced me to meet him in the middle and slide my palm over his. The shiver that raced down my spine at the feel of his work-hewn hands was less than desired. He was my jerk of a neighbor who'd left notes on my door and made me feel like I was not welcome in the neighborhood. I could not be attracted to him.

Absolutely not.

"You're welcome," I stammered, pulling my hand back. I wiped it down my leg as soon as he turned to Jude again. It didn't stop the tingles left behind by touching him.

I was so screwed.

"Mrs. Walsh was supposed to be here. What happened? And why did you have a half day?"

"I called Mrs. Walsh," I interrupted, not willing to let the woman take the fall. "She had an appointment. She didn't know it was a half day today."

"Thank you," Derek growled, less than pleasantly. He kept his gaze locked on Jude instead of looking at me.

I clamped my lips shut, refraining from adding anything else.

"I really don't like that they let you off the bus without anyone there," Derek said. "It's not safe."

Jude shrugged, but he didn't say anything.

Derek stood. He smoothed his hands over his jeans. "We should go. Let Ms. Chelsea get back to her day. I need to go back to work, but you can come with me."

"Why? I don't want to go to your work. Can't I just stay here?" Jude asked.

"No. It's not fair to Ms. Chelsea. I shouldn't have agreed to let you leave afterschool care. I need to call."

"No! Dad, I don't want to go back to that! I hate it there."

"Jude..."

"Dad, please. I'll go with you today, but don't make me go back to that program. Please."

Derek hung his head. I watched the interaction. I wanted to say it was okay for Jude to stay with me, but I knew that would not go over well. Even though I didn't mind.

"Jude..."

"Please, Dad. I'm the only sixth grader who goes there. The rest of them are elementary school. I don't want to go back there. I don't want everyone to say I'm a baby."

My heart broke for Jude. He was just a kid who wanted to be like his friends. Who wanted to be the same as everyone else.

If anyone knew how that felt, it was me. Growing up overweight, I thrived on being invisible. I ached for it. I wore dark colors and stayed out of the spotlight.

Middle school was torture for almost everyone, but being a plus-size girl in sixth grade was worse. Bullying was everywhere, even at schools that shouted how strict they were against it. Even in small towns.

"Who would say you're a baby?" Derek asked.

Jude looked at his father with so much pain in his eyes that I knew it wasn't a threat. Someone actually said it. Someone called him a baby. And for a kid in middle school, a kid who wanted to be grown, that was the worst thing in the world.

"Never mind," Jude said, his voice dropping so low I almost didn't hear him. He slid to the floor in front of Dozer and wrapped his arms around the dog.

Derek looked up and met my gaze. He yanked his away as quickly as it collided with mine.

I cleared my throat. He looked at me again. I mouthed, "He can stay here," pointing to the floor so he understood what I was saying.

Derek shook his head slowly, his eyes falling closed as he did so. When he opened them again, he jerked his head toward the living room.

I led the way, stopping near the front door, close enough for us to keep an eye on Jude but far enough so he couldn't hear our conversation.

Derek looked back at Jude, then turned his entire focus to me. "I can't ask you to keep him."

"I know you don't know me, and I know you don't like me—"

"Whoa, wait. I never said that."

"Your notes made it clear." We glared at each other for a long minute. I finally gave in and sighed. "Listen, you and me don't have to be friends or talk. But I'm available today. I'm not working, and I'm home all day. Jude can stay here. He already finished his homework, and—"

"He did his homework?" Derek blurted.

I nodded. "Yeah. Why? Was that wrong?"

Derek shook his head. He ran a hand over his shaved head and down across his beard. He stared at Jude for a long minute. "He fights me on doing his homework. He fights me on everything these days. I... Thank you for being there for him today."

"You're welcome. He's a great kid."

Derek nodded. "He is." His gaze lingered on his son. "Are you sure you can keep him today?"

"Yes, absolutely."

"It'll just be until Mrs. Walsh can come get him. She usually gets him at three, so it won't be much longer."

"It's fine. I promise."

Derek swallowed roughly. "Thank you. I appreciate it."

"You're welcome."

Derek went back to the kitchen and gave Jude the good news. Jude whooped and told Dozer he was going to stay longer.

Dozer jumped up and barked, joining in the excitement.

Derek hugged Jude close, then walked back toward me. He nodded once, then slipped past me and out the door.

Only then did I remember I was mad at him for the note that morning.

5

DEREK

I WAS LEAVING MY CHILD WITH A WOMAN I COULDN'T STAND. The neighbor who drove me crazy.

In more ways than one.

I drove back to work with the look on her face in my mind. When she looked at Jude, I saw what everyone else said about her. Kindness. Generosity. Care. I'd never seen that from her. Not that I'd given her a chance to show it to me. I judged her from day one.

I parked in my normal spot behind the shop and climbed out of my truck. Ricky was on his way to me before I made it halfway to the shop.

"Where's Jude?"

"With my neighbor."

"You left him with Chelsea?"

"Do you know her?"

"Nah, never met, but Emily goes to her."

"Goes to her?"

"She's a stylist. Owns that Serenity Salon place."

I nodded. I had driven by it hundreds of times but never been in. "Used to be Teased By Debby, right?"

"Yeah, Debby retired, and Knox's girlfriend, Haley, and Chelsea took over. Emily loves going there. She's a big fan of Chelsea. I didn't realize until today that she was your neighbor."

"She moved in over the summer. Drives me crazy, if I'm honest."

"Really? Doesn't seem the type. Emily says she's great."

"Yeah, I get it."

Ricky's brows jumped at my less than thrilled tone. "Uh, boss?"

I shook my head. "The people she bought from were quiet. Kept to themselves. Didn't have a dog."

"Dozer," Ricky said, chuckling. "Chelsea always has stories about that crazy dog." Ricky looked at me closely. "Although I can see how being their neighbor might not be as much fun."

"It's not."

"But you left Jude there. You must trust her at least a little."

"Mrs. Walsh will be there soon. She didn't know it was a half day. Hell, neither did I. Jude's only with Chelsea a little longer."

"But he's still with her."

"Yeah."

Ricky laughed. "You sound like it's complicated, as the kids say these days."

I shook my head. "It's better if I just get back to work." I let Ricky lead the way inside. "Did you ever find out who took her first message?"

Ricky held the door and looked over his shoulder at me. "Yeah. Jason did. He wrote it down, but got pulled into a job and it ended up covered up on the desk and the note slid to the floor. He feels real bad, boss."

I exhaled a long breath. "I'm glad there was a reason."

"I told him, and everyone, if anyone ever calls for you, immediately take you the message. No writing it down and leaving it there."

"Thanks, Ricky. Hopefully this isn't something that becomes a trend."

Ricky chuckled and nodded with me.

The shop was running like it always did. I had great employees who didn't hesitate to not only get their work done but help each other when something was going on that needed extra hands. I walked through their work, checking in with each of them to make sure all was good.

When I made it to Jason, he looked up and all the color drained from his pink cheeks.

"Boss, I'm so sorry. I understand if you need to fire me, but—"

"Did you do it on purpose?"

"No. Of course not, boss. But I know your kid is the most important person in the world to you. I was about to take you the message when—"

"Ricky told me. It's all good, Jason. I know it won't happen again, and I know you feel bad. And I'd never fire you over something like that. It wouldn't be fair, and you don't deserve it."

"Thank you, but I would deserve it."

"Nope. Not at all. How's the project going? That's why I came over here. Not to say anything about the message."

Jason hesitated a beat, then told me about the work he was doing on the SUV. "It's a nice vehicle, boss. For the age, it's in great shape."

"Good. I'm sure the owner will be happy to hear that."

Jason nodded. I clapped him on the shoulder and moved on, hoping he let go of his guilt. He didn't need to carry that.

I helped Mick find a tool on the shelf that wasn't put back in the same place, then lifted a tire into place for Connor. It was always good to get my hands dirty and do some of the work. I didn't have time to do that much since I took over.

But I wasn't going to complain. The money was better, a lot better. The time and the stress offset that some, but it was part of it.

Back in my office, I returned a few calls from reps and customers who had my direct line, then went through messages and the schedule for the next few days to make sure we had all the parts we would need.

Before I knew it, the guys were heading out the door and the sun was sinking. It was past time for me to get the hell out of there.

I locked up the shop and walked around it to make sure nothing was left outside and none of the vehicles were unlocked. All was good, so I jumped in my truck and headed for home.

Jude was in the living room when I got inside. Mrs. Walsh was sitting next to him on the couch, listening to his stories about his morning with our next-door neighbor and her dog.

"Ms. Chelsea is a wonderful person," Mrs. Walsh told Jude. "And Dozer is a sweet dog. Best behaved dog I've seen."

"Have you seen the fence?" I asked her, feeling the familiar irritation mixed with the unwanted desire I felt for my neighbor. It was easy not to like her, but far too easy to want her.

"What's wrong with your fence?" Ms. Walsh asked.

"The dog has been trying to knock it over since they moved in. He snapped a few boards. I keep reinforcing them, but I'm going to have to do something more permanent, eventually. Especially since Ms. Chelsea doesn't seem too worried about repairing the fence. It's driving me crazy."

"Dozer is still young. And shelter dogs have a tendency to be a little more wild since they didn't get the attention they needed before they were adopted."

"He's not my dog," I said.

"He's awesome, Dad. You'd really like him," Jude declared.

I wasn't sure I agreed with my son, but I wasn't going to argue with him. Not when he was focused on yet another drawing of the dog that had been plaguing me.

"What do you want for dinner? Mrs. Walsh, want to join us?"

"Oh, no," Mrs. Walsh said, pushing herself up from the couch. "It's been a long day for me with the appointment earlier. I'm ready to sit and relax."

"If this is too much—"

She waved her hand. "Nonsense. I'm sorry I wasn't here this morning. I told Jude I'll have to check the school calendar more carefully and make a note of these weird days so I don't miss him again in the future."

"I didn't know about it either. It's my fault, not yours."

"I had fun with Ms. Chelsea and Dozer. Maybe I could go over there sometimes?" Jude suggested, avoiding my gaze.

I didn't reply, and I knew he expected it when he didn't push for an answer.

"I'm going to head out. I'll see you tomorrow, Jude. Have a good night."

"Good night," Jude said, looking up from his picture to smile at Mrs. Walsh.

"Thanks again," I told her. "Jude, I'll be right back."

"Okay."

I walked Mrs. Walsh outside and stayed with her across the street to make sure she made it home. "Is everything okay?" I asked her.

"Of course. Why would you ask?"

"You had an appointment."

"People have appointments all the time. Just a checkup."

"Are you sure?"

She nodded and patted my cheek. "You're kind for worrying, but yes, all good. Have a good night. And give Ms. Chelsea a break. She's a good person. Only wants to make a home in this neighborhood. Same as the rest of us."

I nodded, knowing it wasn't likely, but I wasn't going to tell her that.

Mrs. Walsh went inside, and I went home, catching sight of my neighbor through one of her side windows. I stared for a few seconds, then pulled my gaze away and went into my own house. Getting too close to the neighbor was a bad idea. A very bad idea.

I REACHED out to the middle school principal first thing the next morning. Jude hated going to afterschool care, but I didn't love him ending up stranded outside. What if it was winter? What if Chelsea hadn't found him?

How did she find him?

That question rattled around in my mind while I waited for the principal to answer my call. The woman who answered the phone said it would be a minute and put me on hold. I was willing to wait. My kid was too important not to.

"Good morning, Mr. Bailey. What can I do for you today?"

"My son was left on my porch yesterday, and I'm wondering why the school let him off the bus on a half day without making sure someone was home."

"I'm so sorry, Mr. Bailey. Is your son okay?"

"He's fine, but he shouldn't have been left there."

"Well, actually, sir, in the middle school, we don't have rules about an adult being present when students get off the bus. This was mentioned during orientation for the students. I see Jude had been going to the community center after school for the first week, but he's been going home since then."

"Yes. A neighbor has been meeting him, but the half day yesterday—"

"Was on the school calendar since it was approved by the school board last spring."

I sighed. The man had an answer for everything. And all of his answers added up to it wasn't his fault that my kid was left alone. Even though I knew he was right and I knew they would let him off the bus and leave. I guess I hoped it wasn't quite like that.

"Mr. Bailey, I understand the transition to middle school isn't always easy. There are lots of parents who struggle with letting go. We communicate all the changes many times, but we know it's still not easy."

"So, what am I supposed to do?"

"Unfortunately, sir, your options are what you've already done. Jude can go back into the afterschool care program or he can continue to ride the bus home."

"Where the bus driver lets him off the bus whether someone is there or not."

"A lot of our students have keys so they don't end up locked out of their homes."

I let out a heavy sigh. Jude mentioned having a key

before. He'd never had to keep up with something, and I worried he'd lose a key. I didn't like it. It would have meant he wasn't outside, but he would have been home alone for hours. "Basically, the school's policy is the students are old enough to be on their own."

"Yes, sir. It's been the policy for decades. I understand not all sixth graders are the same, and as a parent, I do sympathize with your concerns. I had a hard time when my kids went through this."

"Can I ask how you handled it?"

He chuckled. "My wife made all the decisions. But what she decided was to give my oldest a key when he started sixth grade. Even when she was home, she let him use his key so he got used to paying attention to where it was and being responsible."

"That's not a bad idea. I was thinking Jude would end up losing a key."

"You could also leave one with a neighbor or hide a key somewhere he can get to instead of counting on him to keep up with it."

I nodded. "Yeah. All good ideas. Thank you, Mr. Laurel."

"You're welcome, Mr. Bailey. I hope it gives you some comfort to know you're not alone."

I chuckled. "Yes, it does. I'll also feel better when we go through another unexpected day, and it's a little smoother than yesterday."

"The school calendar is posted online, and we send out reminders by email whenever there is something different, even if it's not new. You should have gotten a reminder email last week about the half day."

My inbox resembled the fallout from a nuclear reaction. Chaos would have been an improvement. "I'll probably find it in a year or two."

Mr. Laurel laughed. "The district also has an app and is on social media, if either of those would help."

I snorted. "Probably not, but thank you. I have a few options to make things easier in the future. And Jude is going to love the freedom."

"The kids always do. Good luck, Mr. Bailey. And please reach out if you have any other concerns."

"Thank you. I will." I hung up, not feeling much better but knowing I wasn't the only parent struggling.

As always, I knew everything would have been easier if I had a partner.

I couldn't remember the last time I heard from Jude's mom. I fell hard for Sasha when we met. She was exciting and fun and gorgeous. I'd never known anyone like her, and when she set her sights on me, I felt like I'd won the lottery.

We went from strangers to inseparable in weeks. I never told her no. I was so in love with her that I never considered telling her no. Not when she decided we should move in together during college. Not when she asked me to stay in the area when I graduated two years before her. Not when she wanted a kid.

Sasha was a whirlwind. After she graduated, she convinced me to move to the area where she grew up. My parents were gone, and my sister was married, and Sasha was my family. We got married and settled down. Her friends became our friends. I met the husbands and wives and we built a life.

Then they all started having kids. Sasha didn't want to be left out, but she was. The others grew closer because of their shared experiences, and Sasha felt like she was missing something.

She was almost thirty when she decided she was ready, and within months, she got pregnant. But from the day she found out she was pregnant, Sasha retreated. She lost her light, her spark. She stopped being the woman I loved and became someone I didn't recognize.

During her pregnancy, everyone said it was hormones. Afterward, her doctors said it was postpartum depression. It was more than that. Her spirit died. She was trying to be someone she was never meant to be. She tried to be who everyone around her was, but it was never her dream.

When she told me she wanted to move, I said no to her for the first time. And the last because she left. She couldn't stay in MacKellar Cove. She couldn't be a mom. She couldn't do any of it.

Jude wasn't even two when Sasha left, and she'd only seen him a handful of times since. The last time she visited was when her mom died, and she came up for the funeral. That was almost three years ago.

But even knowing how much she hated being in MacKellar Cove, I wished she'd stayed. I wished I had another person to count on for the years ahead. The years where my son would be growing up and becoming his own man.

I hadn't felt so alone since Sasha left. Facing being the single parent to a teenager, one who was being given freedoms I wasn't ready for, was terrifying.

"Hey, boss?" Mick said, knocking on the door as he walked into my office.

"Yeah?" I pulled myself away from the turn my mind had taken and focused on work.

"Can I get an extra set of eyes on this vehicle? It's for the mayor."

I chuckled and stood. "Yeah, we don't want to screw up something for Mayor Knight. Omar might not be too happy."

Mick nodded and led the way, distracting me and pulling me out of my funk.

I spent the rest of the day in the shop, fighting off thoughts about Sasha and what life would have been like if I had someone to share the daily chores of raising a kid with.

It wasn't in the cards. Not anymore. I missed my chance at forever, and I wasn't looking for a second one.

6

CHELSEA

I PUT THE FINISHING TOUCHES ON EMILY'S CUT AND SPUN HER around to face the mirror. I loved the look on client's faces when they saw the results I produced for them. The joy and surprise that the idea that was only in their mind an hour ago became reality and looked *that good* on them with my touch.

"Wow," Emily breathed. She scooted forward to get closer to the mirror and reached up to finger the edges of her new cut. It was a good look on her. Just enough off the ends to be different, but not so different that she looked like she was trying to be someone she wasn't. She was very aware of her age and always extremely cautious about not trying to look *too young*, her words.

I thought she was stunning and people should dress and style themselves however the hell they wanted to feel like their best selves.

Emily definitely felt like that.

"Do you like it?" I asked.

"I love it. Holy shit, Chelsea, you're a magician. Thank you."

"You're welcome. I'm glad I was able to bring your vision to life."

"You always do." She stood and winked at me. "Ricky is going to be very appreciative. We're going out tonight."

"Good for you. Did he tell you we spoke on the phone last week?"

"He did. He said you were there for Jude when no one else was. He adores that kid."

I smiled. "He's a great kid. Very sweet." *Unlike his father.*

"He really is. Jude comes to the shop most weekends with his dad. Ricky has Jude help him out. Keeps him busy while Derek gets work done. I think Ricky's biological grandfather clock is ticking louder than my grandmother clock."

I laughed with her and led her to the front to pay. "No takers yet?"

Emily shook her head. Her wry smile said she wasn't terribly upset by that. "I loved raising my kids, but I'm not really looking forward to raising another generation."

"Do you think they're going to ask you to help?"

"Absolutely. And with Ricky still working full time, I know I'll be the one taking on the majority of the work. I love my kids, and I will love being a grandmother, but there's still time. Ricky wants to be the fun grandpa like he was the fun dad."

"And he's practicing with Jude?" I asked.

Emily nodded. "Yep. But the kid doesn't have anyone besides his dad, so Ricky happily fills in."

"No mom?" I asked.

Emily smirked at me, her eyes twinkling with delight. "Mom hasn't been around for years. Why? Are you interested in the position? Derek is a very attractive man."

I groaned. "No. Definitely not."

Emily's brows pinched together. She looked at me carefully. "What's the story there?"

I shook my head and pasted on a smile. Derek was someone she thought highly of. It didn't matter that I adored Emily, I could not speak poorly about someone she liked. He was her husband's boss. I was just the woman who cut her hair. "No story at all." I told her the total and hoped she would move on.

Emily dug out a handful of cash. Far too much for her fee. "Ricky said to tip you double, so this is for you. And next time, you're going to tell me why you don't like Derek."

"Derek, the neighbor?" Haley asked, joining us and looking between Emily and me.

"Oh!" Emily gasped. "That's right. Dozer! How did I not put it all together before? Ricky said you're their neighbor, but I didn't connect it. I feel so dumb."

"Wait, what are you talking about?" I asked.

"Derek has been coming in to the shop with stories about his neighbor for weeks, about the dog destroying the fence and the parties. When Ricky said you were with Jude, I didn't process that you were the same neighbor."

"Chelsea's parties are not that loud. The first one was because a bunch of us were there after moving her in. After that, she's been afraid to do anything because he leaves notes on her door," Haley provided.

"No! Are you kidding me?" Emily asked with a laugh. "That's so Derek. He doesn't really like confrontation. And he probably thinks you're hot."

I rolled my eyes. "Not likely."

Emily shook her head. "You are gorgeous, Chelsea. Derek would be a fool not to think you're stunning."

"Unless this is elementary school, he's going about it all

wrong. Is he going to knock on my door and pull my hair, too?" I asked with a scowl.

"Now you're making me think you like him," Emily said.

"She can't stand him," Haley answered for me. "She just wants to enjoy her house and get to know her neighbors. She hosted a party for the neighborhood a few weeks ago. He left a note on her door the next morning about it being too loud."

Emily laughed. "That's ridiculous. Wow. This is a whole new side of Derek. Nothing like the man Ricky talks about. He seems very structured. I can't see him at a party, or doing much of anything fun. He's a great boss and a really nice guy, but he doesn't leave a lot of room for entertainment."

"He got home during the party and instead of walking over, he glared at me and went inside," I confessed.

"You didn't tell me that," Haley said.

I shrugged. I didn't want to admit it to her because it hurt. I didn't want it to, but it did.

"What a jerk," Haley whispered. Her next client walked in, so she excused herself.

"That is crappy," Emily agreed. "I never would have expected to hear anyone talk about him like you are. I'm sorry you don't know the same man I do."

Same story I heard from everyone else who knew Derek.

"I'll see what Ricky knows. Maybe there's something else going on."

"No, Emily, you don't have to get involved with this. It's fine."

She shook her head. "Don't even think about it. I'll find out why he's not his best with you. Before Christmas, you two will be the best of friends."

"You don't—"

"Consider it done. I'll see you in a couple of months. Or sooner around town. Bye, hun. And thanks!"

I waved to Emily, cringing at the thought of what she was going to do. The last thing I needed was another reason for my neighbor to dislike me.

I didn't have time to think about it long. My last client of the day walked in for her appointment, and I jumped in to creating another new style that would make someone feel amazing.

"SHIT, SHIT, SHIT," I whispered to myself ninety minutes later as I cleaned up my work station.

"Are you okay, Chelsea?" Rose asked. Rose was six years older than me and one of the sweetest people I'd ever met. Her blue eyes were tired and the hand on her back said she was worn out from standing, but she was still checking on me and smiling.

I nodded, pushing the broom around my chair. "My last client wanted to go shorter once I was done, and now I'm running late for dinner with my parents. My mom doesn't like when I'm late."

"Ugh. Mine is the same," Rose said. "My parents got on me one day when I was five minutes late for a movie. The previews hadn't even started. I was eight months pregnant and had to pee again."

I laughed with her. "Last week?"

She tossed a hand towel at me. "Not funny. And not true. Last pregnancy." Rose was due in a month with her third baby. She worked part-time for us, and had been at the salon before I started at Teased By Debby. Rose had no interest in working more hours than she did. She liked having some extra cash coming in, but she wanted to spend most of her time with her family.

"I don't have an excuse like growing a human. Although if I did, I'm sure everything would be forgiven."

"Yeah?" Rose rubbed her enlarged belly. "They want to be grandparents?"

I snorted. "I'm an only child, so all their eggs are in one basket. Me. I don't know if my dad cares, but my mom seems to be interested in having grandkids." I looked at my station and knew it was close enough to clean. I would have time to tidy up in the morning before my first client.

"You should go," Rose said. "Haley's still here to lock up."

"Don't you have keys?" I asked her. Haley and I were adamant that all our employees needed keys. If something happened and one of us wasn't there, we wanted them to all know they could get in and work.

It reminded me of Jude getting locked out. It was a shitty feeling, and avoidable.

Rose nodded. "I do, but they're buried in my handbag. It might take me half an hour to find them."

I shook my head. "You're as much of a mess as I am."

"It's the creative genius," Rose shouted as I headed for the door. "See you tomorrow!"

I waved as I burst through the curtain into the back. Haley was at the table, double checking the receipts from the day. We took turns keeping track of things and went through all of it together at the end of the month. Not just keeping each other honest, but reminding us that we were in it together. Neither of us was alone.

"You leaving?" she asked.

I nodded. "I'm already late. I have to wipe down my station again in the morning, but I swept the floor and put all my tools in to soak overnight."

"We've got it. You go. Dinner this week?"

"Yes. Sounds good to me."

"Excellent. Bye, hun!"

"Bye!" I waved as I hurried out the door. I started my car just as my phone dinged. Another ding followed the first, and I realized I hadn't checked my phone in hours. Just one peek.

I had a message from StoneColdDad. After nearly a month of talking almost every day, it had been a week since I'd heard from him.

STONECOLDDAD

Sorry I've been absent. Last week was weird. How are you?

CUTHAIRDONTCARE

I'm good. Going to dinner with my parents tonight.

STONECOLDDAD

Is that really where you're going or are you trying to spare my feelings and not telling me you have a date with someone else?

CUTHAIRDONTCARE

I really am going to dinner at my parents' house. No need for you to be jealous.

STONECOLDDAD

I guess that's one thing in my favor these days.

CUTHAIRDONTCARE

What's going on that's so bad?

STONECOLDDAD

I had a problem with my kid. Ended up arguing with him.

CUTHAIRDONTCARE

Sorry to hear that. It can't be easy being a single dad.

STONECOLDDAD

No, it isn't. But I wouldn't change it. I love being a father.

CUTHAIRDONTCARE

That's good. Not everyone feels that way.

STONECOLDDAD

You sound like you're speaking from experience. Do you have kids?

CUTHAIRDONTCARE

No. Always wanted them, though. Maybe one day.

STONECOLDDAD

I didn't mean to bring you down. I've definitely been doing that lately. Pouring out my mood and ruining everyone else's.

CUTHAIRDONTCARE

Nothing ruined. I promise. But I should go so I can get to dinner. I'm already late.

STONECOLDDAD

Sorry I made you later. I'm glad I don't have to be jealous tonight. Although I have no doubt I'll have lots of reasons to be jealous soon. A woman like you doesn't stay single for long.

CUTHAIRDONTCARE

Then maybe you should do something about it.

Three dots danced on the screen, then disappeared. I took a breath. Too far. But at least I knew the truth. He wasn't that interested in me. Flirting? Sure. But actually meeting? His silence said it all.

I turned the sound off and put my phone away. I didn't like using it when I was with my parents, anyway. Minutes later, I parked in the driveway behind Mom's side of the garage and hurried to the door. I was fifteen minutes late. I was always late, but not usually fifteen minutes.

I hurried inside my childhood home, making noise so they knew I was there.

"Chelsea? Is that you?" Mom called out.

"Yeah, Mom. I got caught up at work. Sorry I'm late." It was mostly true.

"Work is important," Dad said, his voice joining Mom's when I made my way through the house toward the kitchen. He was standing next to the island, watching for me to come in. "Clients should be respectful of your time, too. If they aren't, you should tell them it's not okay."

"I'll do that, Dad," I lied. There was no way in hell I was telling a client my time was more important than theirs. Not when I worked for tips and owned the shop.

"People don't have any respect for each other." Dad spent his entire career delivering mail and not interacting with people. If someone complained or had any issues, he never had to face them. And people had few options to go elsewhere.

"How are things going with the salon? Have you hired a new stylist yet?" Mom asked.

I nodded and picked up a plate. Mom had everything set up as a buffet in the kitchen with the dining room table set for us to eat in there. Even though I was late, I didn't want to delay eating any longer. "We did. She starts next week. Alexis has three kids. Her youngest just started kindergarten, and she's looking for something part time."

Mom shook her head. "That sounds like someone who's going to be a problem getting to come in every day. If school is closed or a kid is sick, she won't be reliable. Maybe you should think about someone else."

"She was the best candidate. Haley and I agreed she's talented and we get along with her. Plus, she's renting the chair, so it's on her if she doesn't show up."

"But it looks bad on you if she's unreliable."

"I think it'll be fine." I hoped that would end the conversation.

I carried my plate to the dining room and took a seat. It wasn't long before they joined me. I loved my parents, but I loved them more when they weren't trying to tell me how to do everything.

It was a constant struggle for me.

"How's Dozer?" Mom asked.

I smiled. I loved my dog, and I was so happy my parents got him for me. "He's good. You should come see him sometime."

"I need to. Dr. Harris said everything is okay, right?"

I nodded. "Clean bill of health."

"We picked a good dog," Mom said.

"Yeah, I just need a new doggy door. He won't use it since he got stuck."

"You're going to freeze when you get that door replaced. You should have done it right when you moved in," Dad said.

"I didn't plan on getting a dog, and I adore him, but I also didn't know he'd be too big for the doggy door. Even you guys said you thought he'd be okay when you got him."

"We thought so. I still don't know how he got himself wedged in there. You're lucky he didn't rip the door off the hinges," Dad said.

"I am."

"Maybe there's a door in stock that you can just swap out. Have you asked Knox?" Dad asked.

I shook my head. "No. I need to do it, but I spent a lot of money buying the house and getting things I needed for it, not to mention taking over the salon. I don't know if I have the money for a new door."

"It might not be as bad as you think. And..." Dad and Mom exchanged a glance before Dad continued, "maybe we could help. Since we got Dozer for you."

"No, I would never ask you to do that."

"We know you wouldn't, but you wouldn't be worried about the door at all if we hadn't gotten Dozer for you," Mom said.

"I adore him. I'm thrilled you guys got him for me."

"Good. But we still feel bad that we put an expense on you that you weren't counting on. We knew you always wanted a dog, and we thought maybe he would warm you up to having grandkids one day. When you're ready, of course. But until then, we want to make sure our grand-dog has everything he needs." Mom smiled like she hadn't just slid in something about kids. Innocent.

Not even close.

"Really, Mom?"

"What?" She feigned innocence that didn't fool me at all.

I laughed and shook my head. "Let's see how much a door is and we'll go from there," I told them.

"That's all we're asking," Dad said.

"For now," Mom said.

Oh, boy. Or girl. At least I knew they wouldn't be mad if I ended up pregnant by accident. Of course, I had to be having sex for that, but minor details.

7

———

My parents laid off the baby talk for the rest of dinner and we enjoyed our time together. I knew how lucky I was that I got along with my parents so well. They supported my choices, and they were always there for me to help when I needed it.

Not that I wanted them to do things for me. I was working hard on being a fully independent adult. I wasn't always good at it, but I was trying. And paying for my home was important to me. My parents were close to retiring, and they needed to save their money for their expenses. Just because they were healthy now didn't mean they always would be.

But if they were pushing me about the door, it was only a matter of time before my dad bought a door and installed it without my permission.

I was off the next day and went to Al's Hardware to talk to Knox. I was not a regular in the hardware store, but Knox had become a friend since he and Haley were dating. He was a nice guy, and he offered to help me whenever I needed something for the house. Sofia was the maintenance manager for the apartment building she and Haley lived in and offered to help, too, but I'd never taken either of them up on their offers. Again, being an adult and shit.

The store was busy when I arrived with customers lined up to checkout, and three men sitting at the counter and talking to each other and whoever else walked by and engaged with them. I skirted past the activity and tried to be invisible as I searched the store for outdoor doors with dog access built in.

After wandering for ten minutes, and not finding what I wanted, I was about to give up and go home. I was getting frustrated. I didn't like feeling so out of place and... dumb. I didn't know anything about home improvement, and walking around a store that was all about construction and DIY was making me tear up in frustration.

"Hey, Chelsea," Knox said, coming around the end of the aisle just as I was wiping the tears clinging to my lashes. "Whoa. Are you okay?"

I laughed and shook my head. "Just frustrated and being silly about it."

"Is there something I can help you with? Do you want me to call Haley?"

I smiled and sniffed and straightened my spine. I refused to fall apart in public, and definitely not in front of a guy who did not know how to handle my breakdown. "I'm good, Knox. I promise. I don't like not knowing what I'm doing."

"None of us know what we're doing all the time, Chelsea. Can you imagine me trying to cut hair?" Knox lifted a hunk of my hair and pretended to cut it with his fingers.

I laughed, as I'm sure he hoped I would, and felt better. "You're right. Okay. Thank you."

He smiled, his eyes crinkling around the edges. "You're

welcome. Now, what did you come in here for? Because I know it's not to hear those old farts at the counter drone on and on about the good ol' days."

"We heard that!" the old men up front shouted.

"What'd he say?" one of them asked.

"Turn up your hearing aid, Tony," another one said. "He's making fun of us."

Knox winked at me and laughed. "Ignore them."

I chuckled, feeling more comfortable in the store than a few minutes earlier. "I need a new door. For the back. One Dozer can fit through."

"Are you looking for a whole new door or just a new dog door?"

I sighed. "I think I need a new door. He got stuck and almost ripped the hinges off my current door."

"That's a strong dog."

I snorted. "Yeah. And he's a wimp, so he freaked out when he got stuck and whipped around like that would help. Thankfully, he didn't hurt himself."

"That definitely would have been worse." Knox started down the aisle in the direction he'd come from, toward the back of the store. "I don't have any doors that come with a dog door built in, but we have doors and we have dog doors, so we can make anything you want work."

I followed behind him and nodded. "That's what I figured."

He turned the corner, then walked a few aisles and turned again. He stopped in front of a display of doors that I hadn't made it to yet. "These are the ones I have in stock. There's a catalog I can order from, too, if there's nothing here you like. Do you know what you're looking for?"

I flipped through the doors and shook my head. "Not really. The house is brown with white trim, so something that doesn't clash with that. Obviously glass isn't going to work."

"You could do glass on top, though. Lets in some light, and you can watch Dozer without needing to go outside or leave the door open. Not everyone likes glass, though."

I nodded. I hadn't thought about that option, but since the backdoor was in the kitchen, it would be nice to have more light in there, and be able to keep an eye on Dozer. "I think I like that. But something big enough for Dozer is number one. If I have to lose the glass, I'm okay with that. The cost will determine a lot for me."

"We can find something in your budget, whatever it is. Let's look through choices and make a plan. Do you have someone to install the door?"

"My dad is threatening to do it, but I don't want them to spend their time or money."

"That's really nice of him, though."

"Yeah, it is." Knox wasn't wrong. Even though I didn't want my parents to spend their money on my house, it was pretty awesome they wanted to help me out.

I spent the next hour with Knox, going through all the options and picking out a door I could afford easily. It was more affordable than I expected, and I regretted not going in there sooner.

Dozer was going to be a happy dog. And I was going to get to sleep in again.

Knox offered to install the dog door into the backdoor for me before he delivered it. He said it would be easier to do ahead of time, and that he'd stop by my house to take measurements first, then he'd get the whole project rolling.

I felt accomplished. Even though I wasn't doing anything, I made decisions and was going to make my life easier.

When I got home, I took Dozer for a walk, then settled onto my couch to relax, pay my bills, and tell Dozer about his new door. I knew he didn't understand me, but I wanted to believe there was a little bit of it he would get.

After lunch, we dozed off together, then Dozer woke me up to go outside. We went to the backyard and Dozer was running around and chasing his ball when Jude peeked over the fence.

"Hi, Dozer!" Jude called out.

Dozer ran toward the fence, stopping just before it so he could bark at Jude.

"Can I come play with him, Ms. Chelsea?" Jude asked.

"As long as it's okay with your dad," I told him. "Do you want to go ask him?"

Jude shrugged, keeping his gaze focused on Dozer instead of me. "He's not here."

"Are you home alone?"

"No. Mrs. Walsh is here. But Dad doesn't want me going into anyone else's backyard."

I started to ask why not but knew that wasn't a fair question. Derek didn't have to have a reason to keep his son from coming to my yard to play with my dog. He was Jude's father, and that meant he had final say on everything concerning Jude. Period.

"What if we come out to the front yard? Do you think that would be okay?"

"Can you?" Jude asked, his eyes brightening and his face transforming with the smile that lit his entire face.

"Of course. I need to get his leash, though. It's not safe if he's just running around. But we'll go through the house and meet you out front. Why don't you let Mrs. Walsh know where you're going to be?"

"Okay. See you in a minute, Dozer!"

Jude took off, hurrying toward his house and calling out to Mrs. Walsh before he made it inside.

Dozer looked at me and barked.

"Let's go," I told him, opening the door for him to go inside.

Dozer ran in and went to the front door, as though he actually understood what was going on. I followed him, clipped on his leash, then opened the front door.

Dozer raced outside, tugging me toward the side of the house, where Jude was waiting for us. Dozer skidded to a stop right in front of Jude, licking the kid's arm before Jude dropped to his knees and wrapped his arms around Dozer's neck.

"Hey, buddy," Jude whispered against Dozer's collar. "How are ya?"

Dozer barked softly, his version of an answer.

Jude chuckled and sat back. He looked up at me. "Can I hold his leash?"

I nodded and handed it over. "Absolutely. He's pretty good, but if he takes off, let go. I don't want you getting hurt."

"I don't want him getting hurt either."

"He's almost indestructible. I'm not sure anything could hurt him."

Jude laughed. "Come on, Dozer. Let's play in the front yard."

Dozer looked up at me. I nodded, following behind them as we walked into the yard. There wasn't nearly as much space as there was in the back, but it was open and it meant the two of them could play.

I smiled as they played. Jude was careful to keep the leash in his hand while still jumping around with Dozer. A minute later, the door to Derek's house closed.

I turned to see Mrs. Walsh walking toward me. She wore a thick sweater with a jacket over it. She smiled when she saw Jude and Dozer playing, then approached me. "I should have known this was why Jude wanted to play in the front. I was a little worried about it, but if I'd known he was coming to see you, I wouldn't have thought twice."

"That's sweet of you. I asked if he wanted to come into the backyard, but he said his dad doesn't want him going into people's backyards. I figured this was easier."

"You're a good person, Ms. Chelsea. Derek needs to pay attention to that."

"I am trying to be a good neighbor."

"I know you are. Are you going to the party at the Davidson's this weekend?"

"I am. It should be fun. I'm happy you talked me into the party here a few weeks ago. It was great to meet so many neighbors. When Dozer and I walk, it takes twice as long now, but it's loads more fun to stop and talk to people."

"That's how a neighborhood should be," Mrs. Walsh said.

"I couldn't agree more. It's what I was hoping for when I bought this house."

"You make a great addition to the neighborhood."

We were both quiet for a minute, watching Dozer and Jude.

"So, Ms. Chelsea, is there anyone special in your life?"

I laughed. "Just my crazy dog."

"Haven't met the right one or aren't interested?"

"I'm interested. I always wanted to get married and have kids. Just haven't found anyone who fits."

"The Davidsons have a son, you know. He's about your age. Single and looking for someone. Maybe I could introduce you at the party this weekend."

My first instinct was to say no, but what did I have to lose? I wanted to meet someone. If he was someone my neighbor introduced me to, what was the downside to that? "Sure. I think that's a great idea."

"Good. I think you might like him. Andre is a very nice man."

I smiled. "Thank you, Mrs. Walsh. I'm looking forward to meeting him. Is he local?"

"He still lives at home with his parents."

My stomach dropped. "How old is he?"

"I think around thirty. Mr. Davidson had a stroke a few years ago, and Andre moved back home to help."

"I didn't realize that. He looked healthy when he was here for the party."

"He's recovered well. The first few months were tough, but he's made almost a full recovery."

"But Andre still lives there?"

"They've had little things come up every time Andre is ready to move out. I think they're doing everything possible to keep him home."

I laughed. "My parents would have done the same if I lived with them."

Mrs. Walsh laughed, her laughter turning into a cough. "Oh, I hope I'm not getting a fall cold. But yes, I would have done the same with my kids. It's hard to let go and accept that they have their own lives and can take care of themselves."

"Are you okay?"

She waved a hand. "I'm good. Just a tickle, I think. The cold gets to me sometimes, but I can't imagine living anywhere else. This town is just too special."

"I agree," I said, watching Dozer and Jude. A couple walked by and waved to us. Kids played in the street a few houses away, their laughter reaching us. It was peaceful and perfect.

I grabbed two chairs from my backyard and dragged them out to the driveway for Mrs. Walsh and I to sit and watch Dozer and Jude. She wrapped up in a blanket and told me about her family and life in MacKellar Cove when she was growing up.

When Derek's truck pulled in, he looked less than pleased to see us sitting outside.

"Hello, Derek," Mrs. Walsh said.

"Hi, Mrs. Walsh." He pocketed his keys and approached us. "How is everything today?"

"Good. We're having a fun afternoon. Jude wanted to play with Dozer, but he knew you wouldn't approve of being in Ms. Chelsea's backyard, so we're out here."

Derek spared me a glance. Brief.

I hadn't seen him in a week, since the day he came to my house when Jude was left on the porch. The day I realized I was attracted to my jerk of a neighbor.

And the shit part was, I was craving something from him. A smile. An acknowledgement. Something that said I wasn't the only one affected that day.

Nope. I wasn't going there. I didn't want to go there. I wanted a man who didn't make me question everything.

Although when I thought about it, I hadn't gotten any notes from Derek since Jude stayed with me for the afternoon. Not one word. Was that better or worse?

"Chelsea," Derek finally said.

The way my name grated out of his mouth and vibrated over my spine was enough for me to wish for extra batteries in my vibrator. Good Lord, the man was potent, when he wanted to be.

And I was in so much damn trouble.

"Derek," I said. I was not going to give him anything more than he gave me.

"Dad, watch! I taught Dozer a trick."

All three adults turned to focus on Dozer and Jude.

Jude looked at us again, making sure he had everyone's attention, then stood tall in front of Dozer. "Okay, Dozer, sit."

His butt dropped instantly. Not a shock since it was the first thing I taught him.

"Down."

Dozer laid on the ground, his head on his front paws.

"Now shake!" Jude yelled.

Dozer jumped up and wiggled his entire body like he was shaking water off himself after a bath.

Jude cackled with glee and shook with Dozer, the two of them gyrating and twitching.

Mrs. Walsh, Derek, and I laughed at the boys.

The deep rumble of Derek's laugh sent another bolt through me. It was not fair. At all. The man was not supposed to be a temptation. He was supposed to be my enemy. He made himself my enemy.

"I don't think that's how shake is supposed to go," Derek said. "But it's pretty cool you taught him that."

"He's a good dog. Can I stay out here a little longer?"

I could see Derek getting ready to say no. I looked at him, not hiding from his gaze, and was shocked when he opened his mouth.

"Sure. If it's okay with Ms. Chelsea."

Jude swung his gaze to me and clasped his hands together. "Please, Ms. Chelsea?"

"Of course," I said. "Dozer is having a great time."

"Thank you, thank you, thank you!" Jude shouted, circling around Dozer, who barked happily and jumped with Jude.

"I should head home," Mrs. Walsh said. "Derek, why don't you take my seat?"

"I'll walk you across the street," Derek told her, offering her his arm once she stood. "Jude, listen to Ms. Chelsea and stay here."

"Okay, Dad!" Jude said.

I watched Derek and Mrs. Walsh walk to her house. He walked her right to the door and laughed at something she said before she let herself inside. He shook his head at something she said, then smiled as she closed the door.

He jogged back across the street, but instead of taking a seat in the chair Mrs. Walsh had been in all day, he reached into his truck. "Do you mind if I go inside and put this stuff up?"

I shook my head. "Not at all. I'll keep an eye on them."

"Thanks."

I absolutely did not watch Derek walk away. And I absolutely did not wish he sat in the seat next to me and started talking. We didn't have to be friends. We were just neighbors.

8

DEREK

FUCKING HELL, I WAS IN TROUBLE. KEEPING MY DISTANCE WAS the better option, but my neighbor was sitting in her driveway watching my son play with her dog. I had no choice but to sit with her and talk.

Talk.

To a woman I'd jerked off to more times than I could count. Fuck.

I took the chance to run inside and get rid of my bag, but I couldn't delay for long. If I did, it would be obvious I was trying to get away from her. I ached to shower, but that would lead to way too many thoughts. And would be far too tempting to invite her to dinner. And other things.

Nope. Not going there. Not at all.

I chugged a glass of water and slammed it down on the counter too roughly. I blew out a breath and shook my head. She was just a woman. A woman with a dog who drove me crazy and a smile that made me ache.

"Gah!" I shouted. She was not an option. I didn't want her to be an option. She was disrespectful and frustrating. She made my neighborhood too loud and busy. Jude was paying the price with too many nights up later than usual. I wasn't going to overlook it and get to know her.

I went outside again, smiling at Jude and his antics with the dog. The leash was wrapped in his fist, keeping a hold of the dog. I approached the chair Mrs. Walsh vacated, trying to keep the pep talk I gave myself on the top of my mind.

Chelsea shifted in her seat when she saw me approach, sitting up straighter and positioning herself farther away from the empty chair. She wiped the smile off her face and flashed me a polite but distant one that made me want to push her.

She was the unwanted one, not me. She didn't get to treat me like I was the problem.

"He's better behaved than he seems at other times," I said, knowing a dig on her dog would piss her off.

The small gasp had the opposite effect I'd hoped for. Sure, she was enraged, but that tiny sound send a bolt of lust to my dick that made me wonder if she'd make the same noise when I filled her up.

"He's very gentle with Jude," she said, not rising to the occasion the same way my cock was.

"Dogs have a sense of people."

"Yeah, they do," she growled.

"Are you saying I don't?"

"Are you a dog?" she asked.

I scowled. "I'd assume most single women would say all men are."

"You know nothing about me. Don't pretend you do."

"That's not true. I know you let your dog run wild in your yard. I know you don't care about being considerate of your neighbors. I know you took a quiet, family-friendly neighborhood and turned it into something else. Something I don't like."

"Then maybe you should think about moving, because I'm not going anywhere." She stood, unwrapping the blanket Mrs. Walsh had been using from her body. She wore yoga pants that hugged every single one of her luscious curves.

I nearly choked on my saliva. She was mouthwatering. My fingers itched to touch her. To smooth over those curves and find out if they were as soft as they looked.

"Please get up," she said, her voice cold as ice and directed at me.

I looked up at her, taking my time enjoying her curvy figure. I loved a woman who looked like she could handle me. Who wasn't so thin she disappeared if she turned sideways. Chelsea could be seen from a mile away with her thick thighs and full breasts. Her long hair was blowing around her shoulders. Her face twisted into a sneer.

"Excuse me?" I asked, having missed the last few seconds from staring at her.

"Please. Get. Up. I'm taking Dozer inside so I don't have to sit here and listen to you," she hissed.

I stood, her words registering a few seconds too late. She grabbed the chair I'd been sitting in, stacking it with the other one and walking away with them before I could argue with her.

When she came back, she called out to her dog. "Time to go in, Dozer. Sorry, Jude. He needs dinner. I'm guessing you do, too."

"Just a few more minutes. Please?" Jude begged.

Jude knew better than to argue when an adult told him something, but before I could chastise him for his behavior, Chelsea spoke up.

"How about you two can play again on Thursday? I'm

only working in the morning, so I'll be home by the time you get off the bus. I can visit with Mrs. Walsh again."

"Really? That's so awesome. Thanks, Ms. Chelsea! You're the best." Jude rushed over to her and threw his arms around her waist. His head rested against the soft pillows of her breasts for half a second, long enough to hug her tight and let go.

She hugged him back, her eyes falling closed just long enough to hide her emotion, but not so long that I didn't see it. "Dozer loves getting together with you. He doesn't get anywhere near as much exercise with me."

The subtle dig at her weight pissed me off. Jude wouldn't have noticed it, but I heard it.

"I'll play with him any time. Thanks, Ms. Chelsea. See you Thursday, Dozer!" Jude called as Chelsea tugged her dog toward her house.

"Dad, wasn't he awesome?" Jude asked, pulling my attention from Chelsea's retreat to my son. The one who mattered.

"Yeah, he was great. I'm glad you're having fun."

"So much fun. I finished my homework so Mrs. Walsh said I could play outside as long as I wanted. When I saw Dozer, I knew it was worth it to do my homework early. Man, it would be so awesome if we had a dog."

Jude led the way inside, talking animatedly about Dozer and all the things they did. They spent more time together than I realized, but he was happy and he was good, even if it was a bit cold to be outside for so long.

"I'm going to shower, then fix dinner. Okay?"

"Yeah. I'm going to watch TV."

"Sounds good. Love you, Jude."

"Love you."

Those words were the ones that meant everything.

I rushed upstairs and jumped in the shower, turning the water as hot as it would go to fight off the chill from being outside. The shop was getting cold overnight, and the cold was lingering in the morning. Fall had arrived.

I soaped up and forced thoughts of Chelsea from my mind. It didn't matter that I upset her. Or that she didn't think she was gorgeous. She wasn't my wife or girlfriend or anyone I cared about. She was just my neighbor. And she and her destructive dog could stay on their side of the rickety fence.

THE NEXT AFTERNOON was quieter with Jude and Mrs. Walsh inside when I got home. Chelsea's car wasn't there, telling me she was at work before I remembered her offering to let Jude and Dozer play again on Thursday. I was dreading it every minute before I pulled into my driveway Thursday afternoon and found Mrs. Walsh and Chelsea sitting outside with Jude and Dozer. If that was how every day was going to go, I was going to lose my damn mind.

On Friday, Jude and Mrs. Walsh were back inside. Thank God. But Mrs. Walsh had another surprise up her sleeve.

"There's a get together at the Davidsons' tomorrow evening. You and Jude should come," she said, with Jude right there so of course he heard the conversation.

"I have to work tomorrow," I said before Jude could beg me to take him.

"A lot of the local families will be there. Maybe Jude can come with Chelsea and me. We were going to go together."

"No," I said before she finished her sentence.

Mrs. Walsh's gray brows jumped up. And she waited me out.

"I don't like how much we're leaning on you. It's not fair to you."

"Chelsea is the one who offered. Not in front of Jude, of course. She's kinder than that. I've forgotten to do those things in my old age."

I snorted. There was nothing forgetful about the conversation. It was full of underhanded intention. And we both knew it. "I'm sure that's it."

"Jude mentioned he doesn't get to see a lot of his classmates on the weekend because of your work. I thought it would be nice for him to have a day off and have some fun."

"It's a very long day for you to be with him."

"It is, but we have a plan. We're going to walk Dozer for Ms. Chelsea because she's working. And we're going to go out for lunch. And we might try to catch a movie. Jude said he's friends with Sebastian and Zoey Parks' oldest. Cameron?"

I nodded, knowing where things were going before Mrs. Walsh could continue.

"Sebastian went to school with my oldest. He's a good man. I was going to reach out to them and see if we can meet at the movies or do something together."

"Mrs. Walsh."

"This is what neighbors do, Derek. They help each other. I gave you a pass when the party was in Chelsea's yard because I was only just wearing you down, but it's been weeks. Let me take Jude. It's one day out of the month."

"You have him five days a week."

"I do. Which means we know each other well."

I was losing the fight, and I knew it. I didn't want to put her out, but Jude would love it. A full Saturday with his friends, Dozer, and no time at the shop?

"Okay, but you call me if it gets to be too much."

"I will, but it won't be. The party? Will you meet us there after your day?"

"I'll try," I agreed, knowing I wouldn't be able to resist as much as I didn't want to go.

Jude was in a good mood the rest of the night, and when I woke him up early the next morning when I was leaving for work, he jumped out of bed and got dressed without one word of argument.

"Eat some breakfast before you go to Mrs. Walsh's. I need to grab the fruit tray for the party, and I'm going to give her some money, too. I don't want her paying for everything."

"Okay," Jude said, still half-asleep but definitely happier than any other Saturday morning.

I drank my coffee and ate a piece of toast. I wasn't a breakfast person, and we usually ordered food on Saturday for the shop, so I was looking forward to that more than breakfast.

When Jude was ready, we walked outside, only to come face-to-face with Chelsea.

"Hi, Ms. Chelsea!" Jude said brightly.

She smiled at him. "Good morning, Jude. How are you?"

"I'm good. Going to Mrs. Walsh's today."

"I heard. And you're coming with us to the party this afternoon?"

"Yeah. I'm excited. Is Dozer going?"

Chelsea laughed, the sound kind and humorous, not mocking. "He would love that, but I wouldn't take him to someone else's house."

"Oh."

"You're going to walk him for me today, and you can say hello before we go."

"Yeah?"

"Of course."

"That would be awesome. Thanks, Ms. Chelsea!"

"You're welcome."

The smiles she gave my son were enough to make me a jealous asshole. Of my kid. Because she liked him and not me.

"We should get to Mrs. Walsh's house," I said a little too roughly.

"Okay. See you later, Ms. Chelsea!" Jude called, hurrying down the driveway and stopping at the end, waiting for me before he crossed the street.

I waved to Chelsea, pressing my lips into what I tried to believe was a smile.

She barely returned the expression, an eye-roll she probably thought I didn't see tacked on at the end.

I caught up to Jude and walked him across the street. Mrs. Walsh was waiting for us, opening the door before we made it up the driveway to her porch.

"I guess I should have offered to come to your house. I didn't think about that," she said. She was dressed for the day with her hair twisted into her signature bun at the nape of her neck and a warm sweater to fight off the cold morning.

"You are welcome to go over there if you want. You have a key. It's up to you guys what you do with your day," I told her, making sure she knew I didn't have a problem with her being in my house.

"We might do that. We'll see. Did you have breakfast, Jude?"

"Yeah," he said.

"Well, maybe you'll be hungry again in a little while. I made too many pancakes this morning."

"Pancakes?" Jude's eyes were huge. "I love pancakes."

She eyed him thoughtfully. "Do you like them with chocolate chips?"

"That's my favorite."

"Go tell me if they're any good. If you can fit one in that tummy."

"Okay! Bye, Dad!" Jude called before he disappeared into the house.

"You didn't have to do that."

She shook her head. "You keep acting like you're putting me out. It's nice to have some life around here. You and Ms. Chelsea and some of the other young neighbors. It's good to have young people here again."

"I really appreciate you taking him today. I should be done around six. Is that too late?"

"Not at all. We'll be at the party. Come over when you're ready. Chelsea is going to drive us. If that's okay?"

I nodded, knowing I didn't have much of a choice. I handed over the fruit tray. "Of course. Thanks again, Mrs. Walsh."

"You're welcome. See you later. I'm going to see how many pancakes are left." She winked and grinned, looking perfectly delighted with her scheme.

She clearly knew my kid well enough to know chocolate was basically an entire food group for him. Probably her plan all along.

Chelsea was locking her front door when I crossed the street. We both made it to our vehicles around the same time. I wasn't sure if she was going to say anything or not, but I wanted to thank her for all the time she'd been spending with Jude.

"Jude really adores Dozer," I said.

She smiled at me. "He's a really good kid."

"Thank you. I'm not sure I can take a lot of credit for him."

"I wasn't exactly giving you credit. I'm thinking he takes after his mom, maybe?"

A spark of rage fired inside me. "The woman who had kids because her friends were and decided she never really wanted to be a mom and left when he wasn't even two? Yeah, she's someone to model your life after."

For once, she looked like she was sorry for what she said. "I didn't know."

"Why would you? We aren't friends."

"You've made that very clear."

I sighed. "I didn't mean to start a fight with you."

"Now or every time you left a note on my door?"

"Both? The notes were just... Jude's room faces your yard. When you're up late, he doesn't sleep. When he doesn't sleep, he's a nightmare."

"And knocking on my door and asking me to be quiet never occurred to you? You just wanted to threaten to call the police on me?"

"I never intended to actually call the police. I just..."

"It's fine," she said. "I will make sure I don't violate any ordinances, which I haven't so far, and I will keep my distance from you."

"I..." I stopped when she opened her car door.

She sighed, her entire body rising before her shoulders sank. She was still for a second before she turned to face me. She raised one eyebrow. She was different when she was ready for work. The endless waves that cascaded over her shoulders were tied up in a braid that pulled everything tight and showed off the curve of her neck. Her clothes were fashionable but comfortable, with sneakers on her feet and jeans that molded to her legs. Her jacket covered her top, but the pink fabric peeking out below the edge of her coat made me want to unwrap her and find out what other pink she was hiding beneath the clothes.

She cleared her throat, drawing my gaze to her face. She was waiting for me to speak. Waiting and watching me.

"I appreciate you taking Jude to the party tonight. Mrs. Walsh said you were going to drive."

"She doesn't see well after dark. I was hoping it's okay. If it's not—"

"It's fine. Thank you."

She nodded.

"You know—"

I stopped again when she made another move to get into her car. She turned once more and looked at me.

"Sorry. I was just going to say I'm not as horrible as you think I am."

She raised a brow and laughed mirthlessly. "That goes both ways. Just like respect and consideration. But I'm not sure you understand any of that."

"I—"

This time, she didn't stop when I spoke. She just got in her car and backed down her driveway, driving away before I could make a fool of myself.

Probably a good thing.

9

I HAD A SHIT DAY AT WORK. I KEPT REPLAYING THE SHORT interaction with Chelsea that morning. I didn't want to want her, but it was a lot more than that.

She wasn't wrong. I judged her based on one day. Because I was envious of her community. The same community I wanted to be a part of but did nothing to join.

I was a hypocrite and an asshole.

"Hey, boss?" Connor asked, knocking on my door as he opened it.

"Yeah? What's up?" I waved him in.

"Ramsey Holland is here. He asked if you're available."

I stood, moving toward the door before I spoke. "Of course. Does he have a vehicle here? Right now?"

Connor nodded. "Jason's working on Mrs. Holland's vehicle."

"Make sure everything is good before he turns it over. They have a kid."

"We know," Connor said.

I released a slow breath. "Sorry. I know you do. I'm just off today."

"We all have those days, Derek. But we're all in this together. Just because you're the boss doesn't mean we don't still like you."

I chuckled at his phrasing. "I guess that's good."

Connor clapped me on the back. "All good, boss. But you need to take it easy sometimes. You've been working too many hours. The rest of us get days off. You should, too."

"I don't feel right having you guys here and not being here myself."

"That's not how things work. You have different responsibilities than we do. And you know we can do what needs to be done."

"I never doubted that," I assured him.

"I never thought you did. But you need a break. Time goes by fast. It won't be long before Jude's going to parties on his own because he can drive and off to college and bringing his own vehicles here. Trust me when I tell you working every day when he's little is exactly how you cut off any chance at a good relationship with your kid."

"Still having trouble with Lexi?"

"She talks to her mother all the time, just not me. At least I know she's safe."

I nodded, hating for Connor that his oldest daughter cut him out of her life. She told him he was never there for her and she didn't want him around her kids, teaching them to be the same. Connor admitted he wasn't the best husband or father for years, but he was working hard to change that. Too little, too late, he said. With Lexi, at least. His wife, Rebecca, never gave up on him.

"I'm sorry she's still keeping you away. Maybe one day she'll come around."

Connor crossed his fingers as he pushed open the door to the waiting room. "Hope so."

I slapped his shoulder, offering thanks and encouragement at the same time. He was right. But it was another thing that worried me.

Did it ever stop?

Connor went through the door into the shop, and I walked over to Ramsey. He leaned against a window on the far side of the waiting room and stared at his phone.

"Ramsey Holland," I said as I approached.

He slid his phone away as he looked up. "Derek Bailey. I thought for sure you wouldn't be here on a Saturday. How are you?"

I shook his hand, resisting the urge to pull him in for a hug. Ramsey and his wife, Melody, were neighbors and friends, but I hadn't been good about staying in touch. I couldn't remember the last time we saw each other that wasn't a coincidence or for work.

"I'm good. Good. Busy with Jude. How are you? How are Melody and Amber?"

Ramsey's lips lifted into a smile. "They're both good. Amber is turning ten this winter and every day comes up with a new idea for her party."

"I bet Melody is loving that," I said.

Melody was a party planner. She created party packs with coordinated decorations and games for kids, but as Amber got older, she'd added other party supplies to her list of products. She not only sold party packs online, but she worked with local families to set up and run their parties in person for an additional fee. Jude asked a few times if we could hire Melody, but parties were not my thing.

One more failure as a single parent.

"Mel is using it to collect new ideas, but I know she's thrilled that Amber is still interested in parties. She's definitely like her mom that way."

I laughed. Ramsey and Melody almost ended up divorced a few years ago. Ramsey shared with me that he missed a lot of things about Melody and almost lost her because of his inability to see his wife entirely. It sounded like he was not only seeing her, but seeing Amber more clearly lately.

"Jude always wants a party. I should do something for him one of these days."

"He's never had a party for his birthday?"

I shook my head, knowing Ramsey wouldn't judge me for my failure as a father. "I didn't have it in me to do it all."

"I'm lucky that Melody handles all of that for Amber. I wouldn't know what to do. Melody would take care of it for you if you wanted."

"I should. The things I'm lacking have been adding up lately."

"I find that hard to believe."

"We started the school year with him going to the community center and hating it. Now he stays with Mrs. Walsh and ends up playing with the neighbor's dog every afternoon because I won't get him one."

"Dozer?" Ramsey asked, chuckling.

I'd forgotten Melody was friends with Chelsea. I nodded. "He loves that thing."

"Chelsea's great, too. Smart as hell and one of the nicest people ever."

"I didn't know you were friends with her, too. Just Melody."

"I worked with Chelsea and Haley when they took over the salon. Got to know both of them pretty well. Chelsea is creative and talented, and Haley is a little more reserved, but they make a great team. You haven't gotten to know Chelsea much?"

I shook my head, thankful my dark skin didn't reveal the way my cheeks heated thinking about my too young and tempting neighbor. "I'm here a lot."

"If you have a chance to get to know her, you should."

"Why?" I blurted, wondering what he was getting at.

Ramsey, never one to miss something, paused. He looked at me closely, his gaze falling to my clenched fists, then lifting to take in my tight jaw. "Is there a reason you shouldn't get to know your next-door neighbor?"

I shook my head. "It seems as though everyone loves her."

"You don't agree?"

"I don't know her," I hedged. It was true, but it wasn't the full truth.

"Ramsey Holland," Jason called out, interrupting our conversation.

"You should get to know her. I think you'd get along. And it would be nice to have another person to count on where Jude is concerned. A village and all that."

I nodded and shook Ramsey's offered hand. "I'll think about it."

"Good. Hey, are you going to that gathering tonight? Davidson's?"

"Jude will be there with Mrs. Walsh and Chelsea. I said I'd stop by after work."

"Well, then we'll see you there. Melody helped them put it together."

I grinned. "Looking forward to seeing her work."

Ramsey slapped my shoulder and walked by. "See you tonight."

I waved, raising my brows at Jason.

Jason nodded, telling me he'd gone over the vehicle carefully to make sure everything was good. They did it with all the vehicles we saw, but definitely when it was someone with a kid.

Ramsey swiped his card and took his keys from Jason. He said bye to everyone in the shop on his way out, definitely a part of the community I was hovering on the outside of.

No more. Ramsey was right. Connor was right. I was holding back, not counting on anyone else. I'd spent most of Jude's life telling myself I couldn't count on others. But there were people who were showing me that wasn't the case. Mrs. Walsh, Connor and my other employees, and Ramsey and his friends.

I was going to go to the party after work, and then I was going to hire someone to manage the office for the auto shop.

And I was going to set up a date with the woman I'd been talking to. The one who left it open for me to do so, but I chickened out.

I went back to my office and closed the door. It was bad enough I was asking a stranger out. I couldn't do it if someone walked in.

The last message between CutHairDontCare and me was five days ago. I told her I was jealous she had plans, but when she confirmed it wasn't a date, I was relieved. She said I should do something about being jealous, and I never replied.

Because I was even more scared than I was jealous.

No more.

STONECOLDDAD

I should do something about it. I should ask you out. What do you think?

I hit send and read over the message, cringing when I

realized what an idiot I sounded like. Demanding and unclear. Was I asking her out or asking her if I should ask her out?

Ugh.

Too bad I couldn't take the text back before she saw it. It would pop up on her phone and tell her what a moron I was.

STONECOLDDAD

That was intended to be me asking you out. I'd like to meet you. In person. If you're willing and still interested. I know I haven't been around, and I'm sorry.

I hit send and stared at the screen. Again. Nothing. No reply, no indication she read the message.

She was blowing me off.

I shook my head. No. She could be busy. Not everyone sat around all weekend without anything to do.

A clang from the shop reminded me I wasn't sitting around either. I was working. And I needed to get back to it.

I shoved my phone in my top drawer so it wouldn't distract me and went out to the shop floor. Better to get things done and help everyone get out of there early than to sit around and wait for a woman to text me back.

THE LAST CAR DROVE AWAY, and everyone rushed to clean up and get home. We were a little early ending the day, which was a nice change. I was right behind the rest of them, heading home to shower and change before going to the party I was dreading and looking forward to at the same time.

I'd never been an overly outgoing person. I tended to be brought in instead of inserting myself when it came to groups of people. I had a few friends, but clearly not many if I struggled to remember the last time I saw Ramsey and his family.

The house was quiet. I couldn't remember the last time I was home alone. Jude didn't go to friends' houses often, another failure by me. I didn't want to raise my son to be a lonely, bitter man like I was becoming. I wanted better for him.

I was tempted to enjoy the shower a little too long, but I didn't want to let Jude or Mrs. Walsh down, so I hurried through it and got dressed. Chelsea drove, and I decided to do the same. The first weekend in October was too cold for a walk around the block, especially after dark. Even though it wasn't far, it would be better coming home in the truck instead of walking.

The street in front of the Davidsons' house was busy. I lucked out and found a spot two houses down and parked along the curb. I locked my truck and headed toward the party.

I knocked on the door and smiled when Wendy Davidson opened the door for me.

"Derek! We were hoping you'd make it. Thank you for the fruit tray you sent. It was a big hit. Jude is having so much fun. And you're just in time for cake."

The rapid-fire commenting took me a minute to catch up to. "I wanted to make sure we contributed and since I knew I'd be late, I asked Mrs. Walsh to bring the fruit. I didn't know there would be cake."

"It's Chelsea's birthday on Monday. Faith brought a cake over yesterday so Chelsea wouldn't see it. Chelsea has no idea we're going to sing, though. Come on in so we can get started."

I nodded and hung my coat on one of the many hooks just inside the door. I followed Wendy into the house, nodding to some of the neighbors I recognized and smiling at others. Jude was talking to three boys who looked close to his age. Mrs. Walsh was in a chair near the dining room table. And Chelsea was laughing at something Andre Davidson said.

I had no right to get mad about that, but I wasn't happy.

"Ooh, Tom is bringing the cake out now," Wendy said. "Happy birthday to you."

She started the song, and everyone else joined in. When Chelsea started to sing and looked around for whose birthday it was, I found myself smiling at Mrs. Walsh for pulling off the surprise. Mrs. Walsh waved and winked at me.

When the crowd said Chelsea's name, her cheeks turned pink, and she pressed her hands to them. Tom nodded for Chelsea to go to the table, and Andre was right behind her, hands on her shoulders as they moved to the dining room.

I stayed at the back, letting the ones who'd been there all day squeeze to the front.

"Happy birthday, Chelsea," Wendy said. "Faith wanted to surprise you, and we all wanted to thank you for bringing us all together."

A hand on my shoulder startled me. I looked over and smiled at Ramsey with his arm around Melody.

"You made it," Ramsey said.

I nodded and bent to kiss Melody's cheek. "Keeping him in line?" I asked her.

Melody laughed and shook her head. "I'm not sure that's possible, but I'm trying."

"I hear you're the mastermind behind this party," I said.

Melody shook her head. "I can't take credit for all of this. I helped some, but Wendy is very good at throwing parties. As you probably could tell from the massive amount of hooks by the door. This isn't her first gathering."

I grinned. "I was wondering about that, but I wasn't going to ask."

"Wendy had more parties when her kids were younger. Andre is the youngest, and he's, what, five years younger than we are?" she asked Ramsey.

Ramsey nodded. "Probably. I graduated with Nate, who's the oldest. Then there's Nicole, right?"

Melody nodded. "Nicole was a year or two younger than me. I think we came to one of their July Fourth parties one year."

"Yeah, we did. I remember that now. We spent most of the time in the backyard. Great spot. They have a pool and had a ton of yard games. Wendy did it up right." Ramsey looked around the house as though seeing it new.

"Funny how we came here when we were the teenagers and now we're back with our daughter and a whole new generation of kids," Melody said.

Ramsey pulled her in and kissed her hairline. "We're getting old."

She slapped his stomach. "Speak for yourself. Derek and I are still young."

I laughed. "I'm older than both of you."

"Really?" Melody asked.

"I'm forty-three."

"I didn't know that," Ramsey said.

"My ex never really wanted kids, but all her friends had them so she decided she was ready. It was kind of a now or never thing, and she was getting pressured by everyone. I wanted kids younger, but people always think I'm a lot younger than I am because Jude's only eleven."

"That and you look young. No gray or anything," Melody said, rubbing her hand over Ramsey's gray temples.

"Hey, now," Ramsey said, pulling her hands away and kissing them. "Not nice."

Melody laughed.

"We can't change our genetics," I said. "My grandfather was never gray. Died in his eighties. Bald, though."

"Tell me you're at least going bald. Something to make me feel better about the gray," Ramsey said.

I smiled and shook my head. "Sorry, but not yet."

Ramsey groaned. "Not fair. Some men have all the luck."

I looked between him and Melody and raised an eyebrow. "From where I'm standing, I should be the one saying that."

Melody sucked in a surprised breath and smiled at me. "That might be the sweetest thing ever, Derek. Thank you."

I winked at her. "When you get sick of this one…"

"First my age, now my wife?" Ramsey said, his voice full of humor and aware I was teasing.

"I'd never come between a happy couple." My gaze landed on Chelsea and Andre again. I wished I had something to do to hide my unease at seeing her flirting with another man.

"I thought you didn't know each other well," Ramsey said.

I shook my head, yanking my gaze from Chelsea. "We don't. She brought Jude, though, so need to thank her for that."

"You should go now," Melody said. "Say hi to Andre, too."

I nodded. "I will. Thanks. Make sure to say bye before you go."

"We're not leaving for a while," Melody said. "Valentina made that cake, so I'm definitely getting a piece."

"As you wish, my love," Ramsey said, following me toward the cake.

And Chelsea.

10

CHELSEA

I was in a great mood. My match asked me out on a date, work was good, and my evening was fun. I loved a good party, and Wendy threw a great party. I didn't even mind that Andre was hanging a little too close to me or that Mrs. Walsh surprised me with a birthday cake. It was a good night.

Not even Derek could ruin it.

"Derek Bailey. You're Andre, right?" Derek offered his hand to Andre.

The good thing was it meant Andre stopped touching me to shake Derek's hand. "I am. I'm a customer of yours. Nice to meet you. Is your son the one who came with Chels?"

Derek spared me a glance and nodded. "He is. I was just coming to tell Chelsea thank you." He turned to me. "I really appreciate you bringing Jude and Mrs. Walsh tonight. It means a lot."

I waited for the punchline. The insult or backhanded compliment or whatever I'd come to expect from my interactions with Derek. "You're welcome?"

"I didn't know your birthday was coming up," he said.

What in the fresh hell was going on? "Um, yeah. I didn't know Mrs. Walsh knew my birthday was coming up either. I don't usually do a lot for my birthday, though."

"I'm the same," Derek admitted. "I was talking to Ramsey and Melody about something for Jude. He's never had a good party for his birthday. I think I'm going to throw him one this year."

"I'm sure he'll love that," I said. What else was I going to say? Jude would love a party because he was a sweet kid who probably had a bunch of friends, but I knew from experience telling anyone with kids what to do was a bad idea for a person without kids. Hell, even a parent shouldn't comment on another parent's decisions with their kids.

"I hope so."

"My mom's always thrown parties. She was thrilled to do this for Chels," Andre said.

I cringed. I'd almost forgotten Andre was there.

"How long have you two known each other?" Derek asked.

"Just met today. Mrs. Walsh and my mom set us up. I think it's going well, don't you, Chels?"

I smiled up at him, not wanting to tell him he was making me feel claustrophobic.

"Do you think I could borrow Chelsea for a minute?" Derek asked. "I promise I won't be long."

Andre nodded. "Of course. I'll be waiting."

Gag me. He was a nice guy, but he was definitely coming on too strong for me. Smothering me in a way that did not appeal to me.

I followed Derek a few feet away, not loving the idea of being up close and personal with him much better. We weren't exactly friends.

"Did I read that wrong?" he asked.

"Excuse me?"

Derek glanced back at Andre. "It just seemed like you needed a breath of air."

I snorted before I schooled my expression. "I... Yeah. I didn't realize I was being so obvious, though. He's a nice guy, but I don't like being stuck talking to only one person."

"You weren't being obvious. I'm being a jerk. And I wanted a second to tell you I'm sorry for not being the best neighbor."

I leaned back and looked closely at him. Same attractive man I'd always seen. Same endless brown eyes and rich brown skin. Same strong arms under cotton that looked ready to burst.

But something weird was going on. He didn't sound like the neighbor who made my life hell since I moved.

"Did I inhale too much smoke from those birthday candles and this is a hallucination?"

He chuckled, the skin next to his eyes wrinkling with the under-used action. "Am I really that bad?"

"To me? Yes. You've made it clear you don't like me."

"My son adores you, and I know it's not just because you have a dog and he wants one. He didn't stop talking about you for days after you found him on the porch that day. And I never properly thanked you for being there for him when I wasn't. Or for not ripping me a new one when I did show up."

"I'm not—"

"I know," he interrupted. "That's not you. I have been told that by so many people, but it took me a long time to really get it into my head. I've been a jerk, and I'm sorry for that."

"I'm not really sure what to say," I confessed.

Derek smiled again. At me.

My heart sped up too fast. It was not good. I was not looking to fall for him.

"Now you don't have to pretend to like Andre."

"Who said I was pretending? He's a nice guy. Maybe a little intense for me, but that doesn't mean he's not someone I am willing to get to know better."

"Do you really expect me to believe that? He's not your type."

I scoffed. "How would you know what my type is? This is the longest we've ever spoken."

"Well, I know your type is not puppy dogs. Although, maybe it is. Maybe that's why you have Dozer."

I inhaled sharply and let my breath out slowly. "And just when I was starting to think you were decent and not a complete jerk."

He scowled. "Guess you were wrong."

I shook my head and walked away. Why did I try? Why did I think he was being nice to me? No, he was just trying to be an asshole. Trying to mess with me. I wish I knew why.

"Happy birthday!" Melody said, stepping into my path a second later. "You sneak. You didn't tell anyone it was your birthday."

I forced a smile to my lips and hugged Melody. She and her sister, Willow, were good friends with my cousin, Elise, so Melody and I had known each other for a while. It was only in the last few months that I'd gotten to know her better. She was a client, and as a neighbor, she was becoming a friend.

"Elise knows. She and Colin are coming to dinner at my parents' house on Monday night."

Melody clucked. "She didn't tell me. Maybe she's planning something for tomorrow. Are you going to be at book club?"

"I think so," I said. I was trying to go more often. I loved the women who were there, and with Elise, Haley, and Sofia, I felt more comfortable than the first time I went.

"You need to. It'll be fun."

"I don't have any reason I won't be," I told her. "Did you get cake?"

"Of course. Valentina made it."

I groaned. "No wonder it was so good. I might have to see if there's more."

"I'll go with you," Melody said, looping her arm through mine and guiding me toward the cake. "One for each of us, please."

Tom Davidson was friendly and kind. He was the perfect helper for Wendy, jumping to do whatever she asked him to do without batting an eye. Like cutting the cake and dishing it out to guests.

"Thanks, Tom," I told him.

"You're welcome. Happy birthday."

"Thank you."

Melody took a bite of her cake and led me to two empty seats in the corner of the room. "It's a really good weekend when I get to eat cake twice."

I chuckled. "So true. I can get behind that. What else matters besides enjoying life?"

"Right? Life's too short to be unhappy."

"Yes, it is."

Melody took another bite of her cake, then looked at me. "What?"

"Andre Davidson?"

I rolled my eyes. "Mrs. Walsh and his mom set us up."

Melody lifted one brown eyebrow. "At your birthday party?"

"Well I didn't know they were going to have cake here, or sing, but yeah, I guess."

"No pressure at all."

I snorted. "Right?"

"What do you think of him?"

I shrugged. "He's nice."

"That sounds like a good review for a ride share driver, not so much for a potential date."

I laughed out loud, the sound far too loud and drawing the attention of more than a few people.

Melody smiled at me.

"True, but not what I meant."

"Then what did you mean?"

I shrugged again. "I don't know. I've been talking to this one guy."

"Derek?"

"What? No. Why would you say that?"

"I saw you two talking. I just thought... Never mind. Who else are you talking to?"

"On Book Boyfriends Wanted."

"Oh, boy."

"I know, I know. I've heard it all. But you've all been matched with people who weren't the one, so I'm just enjoying it. Anyway, this guy is funny and nice and he's a single dad, and we've been talking for a while."

"But?"

"But... He said something about being jealous one night. I said he should do something about it. Then it took him almost a week to ask me out."

"Isn't that a good thing?"

"I'm excited he wants to meet, but it took him a long

time to decide he wanted to meet me in person. Does that say he's unsure?"

"Or he's just not someone who dates a lot."

"Yeah, maybe."

"Do you know anything about him?"

"No. We've been careful not to share anything too personal."

"Except that he's a single dad."

"Yeah."

"When are you getting together?"

"I don't know yet. He probably has to find someone to watch his kid."

"Makes sense. But this is good, right?"

"Yeah, I think so. I'm looking forward to it because I do like talking to him. I just hope it happens."

"And you're not sure?"

"I'm not sure about anything. I don't have a ton of luck dating. Starting something new makes me more than a little anxious."

"This is why you need to come to book club tomorrow. We will boost you up so high you'll never doubt yourself."

I chuckled. "Sounds like I need that for sure."

"We all need friends. Something I didn't accept until I was dragged into their group by Blake. I have her to thank for the life I have right now. Including getting my husband back."

"That's a massive compliment."

"She deserves it. And you deserve to know you're great. Show that guy you're worth it to get a babysitter."

"Thanks, Melody."

MELODY'S ASSURANCES were still playing in my head the next afternoon when I got a message from StoneColdDad asking if I could meet him Tuesday or Wednesday for lunch.

"Lunch?" I said out loud. I knew what lunch meant. Lunch was for dates you didn't really want to go on.

I was working Tuesday but off Wednesday, so even though I wasn't sure I wanted to have lunch with StoneCold-Dad, I sent him a message agreeing to it.

I went back and forth the rest of the day, debating if I made the right choice. I decided to bring it up at book club and get the collective answer.

"Do you have a date yet?" Melody asked when I walked in.

All eyes turned to me.

"A date? With who?" Elise asked. My cousin threw her arm around my shoulders and nudged me with her hip.

"Chelsea has been talking to someone on Book Boyfriends Wanted," Melody answered for me.

"Duh, duh, duh, another one bites the dust," Willow sang.

I rolled my eyes as the others laughed. "Not even a little."

"He said he was jealous when she had plans, then asked her out days later," Melody told the others.

"Uh, I don't like that," Blake said.

"He's also a single dad," Melody said.

"Which means he might have needed to find a sitter," Anna said.

"I can understand that," Zoey added.

"I get it, but is it enough? Is he one of those guys who's just a jerk who thinks he can yank her around? Jealousy isn't a great first start," Elise said. My cousin was in an abusive relationship with her college boyfriend. She didn't tell anyone about his abuse until years later, after she got away from him. She was always the first one to pick up on things that might be a concern.

"I agree, but I get jealous when women hit on Hudson," Anna said. Her husband owned the best local bar, and he was hot. Women flirted with him all the time. "It doesn't mean I'm going to do anything about it, but I do get jealous."

"I understand. But this is a guy Chelsea's never met telling her he's jealous," Elise said.

"I told him I had plans, and he thought I was trying not to tell him I was going out on a date. When I said I was having dinner with my parents, he said he was glad he didn't have to be jealous. I said he should do something about that, and then I didn't hear from him for days, until he asked me out," I admitted.

They all looked at me with varying degrees of curiosity, all trying to figure out what they thought it all meant.

"This is why I came here. You're all supposed to help me figure this out!" I said.

They snorted their laughter.

"We're not magicians," Elise said.

"And we definitely can't understand the inner workings of the mind of a man," Finley said with a shudder. She owned Book Boyfriends Unlimited, the romance only bookstore we met at for book club. And she was happily married with a son. Understanding the mind of men was almost a part of her DNA.

We laughed at Finley's comment.

"When are you going out with this guy?" Elise asked.

"Wednesday for lunch," I said.

"Lunch?" Melody asked.

"That's what he offered," I told her.

"So his kid is in school," Anna said.

"Ah," Melody said, nodding. "That makes sense. He

doesn't need a babysitter if his kid is in school during the day."

"That's what I'm thinking. It makes sense for a single parent. If things go well, you don't want to bring someone home to your kid. Lunch gets a bad rap, but I think it's a great time for a date." Anna winked and smiled, telling all of us exactly how she spent her latest lunch break.

"Good for you," Elise said. "And good for Hudson."

Anna laughed loudly. "He is never disappointed, but yeah, when there are no kids in the house, we have a little more fun."

"I never thought of that," Karissa said. "How is it possible I never thought of that?" Her husband ran the local movie theater, and Karissa was the genius programmer who created Book Boyfriends Wanted.

"Why do you think my parents keep George even when I'm not working?" Finley asked.

Karissa snorted. "You all need to share more of these tips with me. But first, Chelsea, go have fun. If he's a dud, you know it and you can move on. If he's hot, screw his brains out. If you're undecided, that's okay, too. But you're young and you're gorgeous and any man who disagrees with that isn't worth your time or your sheets."

I chuckled while Elise hooted and high-fived Karissa.

"Hell, yes! That's a mic drop right there. Enough said," Willow agreed.

Best advice I'd ever gotten.

WEDNESDAY MORNING, I woke up with a smile on my face. It had been a good birthday week so far, and I was excited about my lunch date. I was going to meet StoneColdDad, and see if he was worth my sheets.

I let Dozer out, then started the coffeemaker and cooked eggs for my breakfast. My stomach was twisted with anxiety, but it always was before a date.

When my phone dinged as I was getting out of the shower, I smiled at the message that popped up.

STONECOLDDAD

I'm looking forward to finally meeting you. I can't wait to see the smile on your face instead of just picturing it.

CUTHAIRDONTCARE

Me, too. I'm glad this worked out.

STONECOLDDAD

I know lunch isn't always the best, but it's when my kid is in school. It's not me telling you I'm not that interested.

CUTHAIRDONTCARE

I did wonder, but I wasn't going to ask you.

STONECOLDDAD

Sorry. I should have said something before today. I guess I should be happy you agreed at all.

CUTHAIRDONTCARE

I'm looking forward to today, too.

STONECOLDDAD

Good. So am I.

I set my phone down and smiled into my mirror. It was going to be a good day. So far, being thirty-two was agreeing with me. Maybe it was my last birthday as a single woman.

Dozer watched me while I got ready for my date. I wore a pair of jeans that were soft and comfortable. I added a wrap top that hugged my breasts and hinted at my abundance of cleavage. The booties I treated myself to for my birthday were the perfect addition and gave me a tiny bit of height but not too much.

I grabbed my jacket and let Dozer out once more before I left.

The restaurant was a good pick. Nice enough for us to sit and talk, but not so fancy that it would be awkward if things didn't go well. I walked in and asked for a table for two, then sent StoneColdDad a message.

CUTHAIRDONTCARE

I have a table. I'm wearing a black top with pink and purple flowers all over it. I can see the door from where I am, so I'm sure you'll see me.

STONECOLDDAD

Pulling in now. I'll be inside in a few seconds.

I drew a breath to calm my racing heart. I liked this guy. I was nervous. He was almost here.

The outside door opened. The light blinded me so I couldn't see who was there until he opened the second door to come into the restaurant.

His eyes scanned the restaurant and stopped when they landed on me.

No. No way. It was not possible.

My asshole neighbor was StoneColdDad.

Fuck me.

11

———

Derek approached me slowly. His gaze slid over my outfit, taking in the clothes I wore. The clothes I told him I was wearing so he would recognize me when he arrived for our lunch date.

When he reached my table, he stopped. He gestured to the other side of the booth, waiting for me to nod before he sat down. "So, you're CutHairDontCare? Guess I should have figured that one out."

And there was the confirmation. For half a second, I hoped it was coincidence, and he only came over because he recognized me and not because we were supposed to be meeting. "And you're StoneColdDad."

He paused for a second, then nodded.

Fuck, fuck, double fuck.

"How did this happen?" I blurted.

He chuckled. "How did you get paired with someone you hate?"

I looked up at him. His words hit me. Hard. "I don't hate you, Derek. I am not the one who disliked you before we met. You're the one who left notes on my door. Who refused to get to know me. Who made things difficult between us."

"I—"

"Good afternoon, folks. Are we ready to order?" the server said with far too much cheer for the conversation she interrupted.

Derek looked at me and raised an eyebrow. A challenge or a question? I wasn't sure. But screw him. I was hungry, and this was my chance to get something to eat. Sure, I could go home and make something, but I'd been planning on eating at the restaurant, so I was going to.

"I'd like the turkey club with sweet potato fries and a side salad, please," I told the server with a fake smile.

"That's my favorite," she said, tapping the screen on her tablet to enter my order. "Drink?"

"Just water, please."

"Lemon?"

"Sure. Thank you."

She smiled, then turned to Derek. "For you?"

He glared at me, the war waging in his gaze. Finally, he lifted his eyes to the server and smiled.

Dammit, I was jealous that he smiled at her and not me.

"I'll have the cordon bleu sandwich with extra chips, please. And a water, no lemon."

"You got it. I'll get those right in for you two."

"Thank you," Derek said.

The server walked away, and Derek settled into the booth. His knee bumped mine, shooting a spark of awareness through me.

From the way he gasped, I wondered if it lit him up, too.

"I apologize for the way I've behaved toward you."

I eyed him. I wasn't buying it. What was his angle? Sure,

he apologized before, but then he turned around and insulted me again.

"I want a good life for my son. He's the most important person to me. Always has been."

"And how am I preventing that?"

"The people you bought the house from were quiet. They never had anyone over. We barely knew they were there. But you... The first night you had a party."

"And I'm sorry we were loud. But after that?"

"Jude's room faces your house. When you're up late, it keeps him up."

"I... I will do my best to keep the noise down."

"Thank you."

The server brought our drinks and said our lunches would be right out.

Derek nodded to her and sipped his water.

"Why did you ask me out?" I asked him.

"I didn't!"

I gestured to the table.

"Oh. Well, I like the person online. I enjoy talking to her."

"You just don't like me in person."

He opened his mouth to say something, then clamped it shut.

"What?"

"How old are you?"

"Excuse me?"

"How old are you?"

"Thirty-two, why?"

"I'm forty-three."

I shrugged, unsure where he was going with that comment. "And?"

"Doesn't that bother you?"

"Your age? Why would it bother me?"

"You would date a man my age?"

"I would date a man I was attracted to. A man who was good to me. A man who treated me the way I deserve to be treated. A man I enjoyed spending time with."

"Like Andre?" he spat.

"Andre... Why do you care?"

He exhaled a rough breath. He looked away and shook his head. The tick in his jaw said there was something else going on, something he was holding back from saying.

Oh. It finally dawned on me.

He wanted me to make this easier on him. He wanted me to be the one who walked away. So he could save himself from saying what he really thought about me. What he really wanted to say.

He didn't want me.

I bit down hard on my lower lip. Tears still welled in my eyes, so I bit harder. I was not going to let him see how much his opinion bothered me. He wasn't the first man to meet me in person and not be interested. He wouldn't be the last. But he was the only one I'd ever lived next door to and been forced to see on a regular basis.

I signaled the server. She approached our table. "Everything okay?"

"Can you pack my lunch to go instead? I have to get out of here."

"Of... of course." She glanced between Derek and me, her gaze uneasy.

I smiled in an attempt to tell her everything was fine.

She returned the look and walked toward the kitchen.

"Why are you leaving?"

I focused on pulling my wallet out of my handbag and retrieving cash. I didn't want to wait any longer than I absolutely had to. I knew how much my lunch was, close enough, and I pulled enough bills out to cover it and give the server a tip.

"You're not even going to tell me why you're ditching me?"

"You don't want to be here. You've made it clear you don't like me. And you've made it clear you have no interest in dating me."

"You have no idea what I want."

"Maybe." I nodded, giving myself a minute to shove the emotions back down to where they belonged. Buried in a place where he wouldn't see them. Deep below the surface. I could call them back up later, when I was alone and he'd never know how badly he hurt me.

"What does *maybe* mean?" he asked.

I swallowed roughly, choking back my tears. "You won't hear from me again. I will keep my distance from you and Jude. Since you find me so... appalling to be around, so unappetizing, I'll make sure you don't have to be reminded of my existence."

"What are you talking about?"

"I'm talking about you not being attracted to me. You finding me repulsive, Derek. I'm talking about you trying to make sure I don't get any ideas about this being more than a mistake. Don't worry. Message received. I know you don't want me. I'll stay away from you. And Jude so we don't accidentally bump into each other."

Thank God the server approached with our food as I finished speaking. I handed her the cash to cover mine and took the bag from her, sliding out of the booth before Derek could reply.

He called my name, but I wasn't sticking around. I had

nothing else to say, and I didn't want to hear whatever bull-shit he was going to try to come up with.

The first tear fell as I drove home. I hated that I'd put any hope in him. In the match I thought was a good one. I wanted to get to know the man I'd been speaking with, but he was just like so many others.

I'd dated all different kinds of men. Overweight men and thin men. Athletic men and scrawny men. I cared more about what was inside than outside, but a lot of people weren't that way.

Being reminded of it always hurt. I knew I was big. I knew not everyone found me attractive. I knew my hips were wide and my thighs were chunky and my boobs were too big. I knew I could stand to lose weight. But after high school, I quit trying. My body didn't need to be different. I could hold my own at the gym, and I could enjoy the things I wanted to enjoy. Whether that was food or activity.

But men like Derek didn't see me as a whole person. They saw me as a person who needed to change. Who needed to lose weight to be complete.

Fuck him.

I pulled into my driveway and grabbed my food. I was going to enjoy my lunch. I was going to sit on my couch and watch TV with my dog, who was happy to see me.

Dozer barked when I walked in, and I cooed at him.

"I don't need any man besides you," I told him. "You don't judge me."

I went to the kitchen and poured myself a large glass of water. I chugged it, then refilled the glass and carried it back to the living room.

I'd just sat down when there was a knock on my door. Not really a knock. Someone pounded on my door.

My heart jumped into my throat, fear wrapping around me. Who was pounding on my door like that? And why?

I reached for my phone to look at the video doorbell.

"Chelsea! Open up!" Derek shouted.

Anger replaced the fear, and fury drove me to the door. I yanked it open, again having to duck before he punched me in the face. "What the—"

I didn't get a chance to finish my question before his hands were cupping my jaw and his lips were crashing down on mine. He backed me up into my house and kicked the door closed behind us.

My hands rose to his shirt, grabbing at the fabric. Push or pull?

"Tell me to stop," he whispered against my lips. "Tell me to stop or I'm going to show you exactly how repulsive I find you."

"What?"

"Fuck, Chelsea, I've wanted you since the first morning you walked into your backyard in one of those tiny little tank tops and barely there shorts. I've been dreaming about you. Tell me to stop."

I looked into his eyes, seeing the truth I never saw before. "No."

He surged at me, his lips leading the way. He pulled me closer, my hands trapped between us.

My back hit the wall just inside the living room, and Derek covered my front. I felt the evidence of his arousal against my stomach. He didn't back up or give me a chance to catch up. He just kissed me until I stopped thinking. Until I stopped wondering if he was being serious.

He leaned back and yanked his shirt off, tossing it aside before he covered my body again.

My hands splayed across his chest, the tightly curled

hairs scratching my palms. His skin was warm, smooth. I wanted to feel it against my skin.

I pushed him away. His eyes were dark, tracking my movements. I tugged the string that kept my top on, letting the fabric fall from my breasts. His lids fell to half-mast, but that was the only part of him.

He shoved at his jeans, grabbing them before they hit the floor. He dug in his pocket, came out with his wallet.

I knew where things were going, and I was all on board. It wasn't how I planned, or even hoped, lunch would go, but I wasn't disappointed by it.

"Let me see all of you, Chelsea," he whispered.

I swallowed at the thick promise in his tone. My shirt fell from my shoulders, and I reached back to unhook my bra.

His gaze fell to my bare breasts and hung there. He licked his lips and clenched and unclenched his hands.

"Jesus, you're gorgeous."

I snorted. "You don't have to say that."

He exhaled. "You really have no idea, do you? You really think you were right. That I wasn't attracted to you. That I'm still not." He let his jeans fall and cupped his erection through the black boxer briefs he wore. "This is not because of some other woman. This is not because I don't want to fuck you. I've wanted to fuck you for months, Chelsea. If you want me to walk away, I will, but it's not going to be because I'm the one saying no. That choice is yours. I'll respect it, without a doubt, you can say no to me. You can tell me to get the fuck out, and I will. But trust me when I tell you that you're fucking beautiful."

I inhaled sharply, letting his words sink in. No man had ever told me that before. I'd had my share of partners and enjoyed sex, but usually it was a few quick rolls in the sheets and then we moved on. I'd never had a relationship last long enough that a man told me I was beautiful.

"What's it going to be, beautiful? Are you taking the rest of those clothes off, or am I walking out of here?"

I could ask why he wanted me, but I didn't care. Even if this was the one and only time we were together, I wanted him.

Instead of answering him with words, I hooked my thumbs in my jeans and panties and slid both to the floor.

His eyes widened. He stroked himself. He stepped away from his jeans, approaching me. "Let me feel you." He reached for me, setting the condom on the table by the door before his hand touched my skin. He brushed his knuckles over my belly.

I sucked in a breath, tightening the flabbiest part of me.

"Don't hide from me," he whispered. He ran his hand over my stomach, teasing between my thighs with his fingertips. "Open for me, Chelsea. Are you wet?"

I spread my legs and let him feel.

He groaned. "I'm glad I'm not the only one who wants this." He pressed one finger inside me, drawing it back out to spread the wetness over my clit.

One brush against my clit and my hips jerked.

"Damn," he hissed. He slapped his hand against the wall behind me, trapping me between his body and the wall. "Wrap your arms around me."

I did as he said, my body weakening as he stroked my clit. I was already close. Too close for a few seconds. But I couldn't stop the train once it left the station, and this one was rolling right along.

Derek kissed my neck, nudging my head back so he had access. He licked the column of my throat and thrust his fingers into me again.

I moaned, holding on tighter to him as my orgasm picked up speed.

"Come for me, Chelsea. Let me feel you."

My brain stopped the fight to hold on to control. My body took over, immediately handing command over to Derek. I gasped and moaned and let go, coming hard and loud. "Yes, yes. Oh, fuck, yes."

"Yes," he groaned with me. "Fuck yes."

The condom wrapper tearing was the only sound I heard above the roaring in my ears. I hung off Derek like a spider monkey, barely able to support myself after the freight train of an orgasm that just bowled me over.

"Couch," he said, moving his hand from the wall and encouraging me toward the couch.

I opened my eyes to move across the room and laughed when I saw Dozer sitting in his bed, watching us.

"What are you laughing at?" Derek asked.

"Dozer looks confused."

Derek looked over, chuckling when he saw the look on Dozer's face. Head tilted, eyes wide, a little bit of fear.

"It's like he's never seen people having sex before."

"He's definitely never seen me having sex before."

"What?" Derek asked.

"I've only had him a few months."

"Oh, I didn't realize."

We stopped next to the couch. Talking about my dog slowed down the rush I was feeling, but I didn't want to be done.

The look Derek gave me said he was feeling the same. He took a step toward me, blocking Dozer from my view. "Do you want me to leave?"

I shook my head slowly.

"Good." He kissed me hard, stealing my breath. His

hands explored my curves, reverent and tempting. Within seconds, I was right back in the moment, ready for more.

He took another step toward the couch. My legs hit the edge, and we broke the kiss. I sat down, coming face-to-face with Derek's crotch.

I licked my lips, and his dick jumped. He still wore his boxer briefs. I reached for them, pulling the fabric wide to accommodate his size.

"Wow," I whispered when he was free. I leaned forward, licking his dick.

He hissed, one hand going to my hair. He pulled it back, tightening his fist around the ponytail he created. "Chelsea."

I took him into my mouth, unable to fit most of him in, but groaning at the way he smelled and tasted. A hint of soap was there from his morning shower, but the musk of him had my core flooding. I wanted him. Bad.

I sucked and licked him enough to tease him, and when he pulled back, I didn't fight or argue. He rolled the condom on and kneeled on the couch, pushing me to lie down. He lined himself up and eased into me.

My body stretched to make room for him, the underutilized muscles needing steady encouragement to accommodate him. Every stroke brushed against my clit and provided more than enough encouragement.

"Derek," I whispered, an orgasm building.

He held himself up with one hand on the back of the couch. He reached the other between us and pressed down on my clit. He surged in deeper as I started to come and triggered another orgasm.

"Fuck! Derek!" I screamed, the suddenness and intensity shocking me and feeling so fucking good I wasn't sure I'd ever have another one that gave me so much pleasure.

"Oh, fuck," he groaned, slamming all the way into me.

His hips surged back, then pounded in deep, setting a rhythm that had my back arching and my body flooding, ready for him again.

I tried to keep up with his strokes, lifting to meet him for one out of every three or four. He didn't seem to mind, grunting his way closer until he slammed in deep and stilled.

"Chelsea," he groaned, a grunt and a sigh adding to the sounds before he lowered himself onto me.

I trembled with his body on mine, the weight of him a comfort to my previously battered heart. He definitely proved I was wrong about him not wanting me.

And that was almost as good of a feeling as the orgasms he gave me.

12

————

WE LAID ON THE COUCH FOR A FEW MINUTES, DEREK'S BREATH
soft on my neck and his weight pressing me into the
cushions.

I didn't want him to leave. I didn't want our lunch date to
be over. But I knew it was temporary. He had to go back to
work, and us having sex didn't mean everything was fine
between us.

Hell, I didn't even know if there was anything between
us. Did he want to see me again? Did I want to see him? Was
this a secret fling? Were we going to date?

"I can hear you thinking," he whispered, pushing his
weight from me to look into my eyes. After a second, he
avoided my gaze. "I should go."

"Okay," I said.

He crawled off me, his head down as he returned to his
clothes. "Um, do you mind if I use your bathroom?"

"Yeah, of course. It's off the kitchen."

He nodded and carried his clothes toward the kitchen.
Dozer watched him go, only looking at me when Derek
disappeared from view.

"I know," I hissed at my dog. I sucked in a breath and rolled off the couch. Naked. I was naked in my living room in the middle of the day because I just had sex on my couch with my next-door neighbor who I was at war with since the day I moved in.

What the hell was wrong with me?

I scrambled to grab my clothes and get dressed before Derek came back. The bathroom door opened just as I was pulling my shirt on. I fumbled with the tie, racing to secure it before he was back.

"I... I have no idea what I'm supposed to say right now," he said.

I forced a smile and turned to look at him. "You don't have to say anything."

He narrowed his eyes as he studied me. When he closed his eyes and sighed, I knew it meant he was relieved I wasn't pushing him for more. "This isn't me brushing you off, Chelsea."

Well, that wasn't what I thought. "Okay?"

"I meant what I said. I've wanted you for months. I'm... Shit. I knew I shouldn't have barged in here like I did."

"Why? Because now you think I'm going to create problems for you?"

"Jesus. Fuck. I liked the woman I talked to. The woman on that dumb app. The one who was honest and kind and funny. And I wanted my neighbor with all her curves and sexiness and temptation. Finding out you're the same person is like someone is gifting me a sports car. It's the best of both worlds."

"I'm not... I don't want you to feel like you have to say things like that."

He stomped across the room so fast I didn't have time to back up and get out of his reach. His lips covered mine, his tongue prying my lips apart with far more ease than I should have given in to. He stole my breath, and he righted my sanity as his tongue swept through my mouth and told me he wasn't done.

"I want you, Chelsea. I want the woman who loves her job and cares about her friends, and I want the woman who adopted a pain in the ass dog who is going to destroy my quiet and disrupt my sanity. I want the woman who has me wanting to say fuck it and tell my employees I'm not coming back to work. I want the woman who takes in my son when he's alone and scared and does everything possible to make sure he's okay. I want all the different sides of you. If you are okay with finding out where this could go."

"No one's ever said things like that to me."

"They're all idiots. And I'm lucky to be the first one smart enough to see who you are. Even if it took me far too long to figure it out."

"Is all of this real? You're not just messing with me?"

He shook his head slowly. "Definitely not messing with you. I'm sorry I gave you that impression."

I inhaled deeply, nodding. "Okay."

"Okay, what?"

"Okay, let's find out where this can go."

"Yeah?"

I nodded again.

He leaned in again, then stopped and pulled back. "I... I hate to ask this, but can we keep this between us?"

"Why?" All those fears I was trying to ignore, the doubts that were ringing in my mind, got louder with his request.

"Because of Jude. No other reason. His mom... I've never introduced him to a woman I've dated. I don't want him getting attached to someone and then having her walk away like his mother did."

I didn't like it, but I did understand it. It sounded reasonable. There was only one problem. "Jude already knows me. He loves Dozer. How...?"

"I know. And I don't know. But... Can we try? For his sake. That's the only reason."

"Okay."

"Are you sure?"

"If that's what's best for Jude, then yes. I get it."

"Thank you. I know it's a lot to ask, but it means a lot."

I nodded, uneasy about the request, but unable to find an argument that didn't make me a bitch. Maybe he was being honest. And maybe he didn't want anyone to know he was dating me. Either way, I was going to play by his rules.

For now.

I HEARD from Derek sporadically over the next few days. I was unsure about the whole thing, but he reached out a few times to see how I was doing. Nothing earth-shattering or personal, but more than zero contact, so I was cautiously optimistic.

Haley talked me into going to book club Sunday evening, not that it took too much convincing, and she offered to pick me up. I had a feeling there was something she wanted to talk to me about.

I was right.

"I found a ring," she breathed when I got into her car.

"You what?" I gasped.

Haley backed out of my driveway and started down the street. Her hands were tight on the steering wheel, her knuckles white. "Knox has a ring. A suspiciously engagement looking type of ring. What do I do?" Her voice bordered on panicked with a hint of terror.

"Do you not want to marry him?"

"I do. God, so much. But what if I'm wrong? Or what if he's holding it for Daniel or someone? What if he changes his mind?"

"Whoa. Where is all of this coming from? You and Knox are solid. You've been so good together for months. I thought all the craziness was behind you."

"I thought so, too." She was quiet for a minute, focusing on the road instead of sharing her thoughts. "I love him."

"But?"

"But nothing. I just... Dawson really messed with my head. And all the men before him. Knox has always felt like he was too good to be true. And marriage?"

"Do you want to get married?"

She nodded, rolling her lips in and clamping them between her teeth.

"You're so excited you're scared, aren't you?" I asked.

She swallowed roughly and nodded again. She found a parking spot near Book Boyfriends Unlimited and turned off the car. "I've always wanted to feel like I belonged somewhere. With someone. He's been so much a part of this town his whole life that I kind of worried everyone who didn't like me would change his mind."

"Oh, Haley. He loves you. It doesn't surprise me at all that he wants to marry you. But you have to let go of these fears. If you want to belong here, you do. You have been here for long enough that people know you. And people like you. Hell, even Madeline has come around and likes you."

Haley exhaled a laugh. Madeline was one of our previous boss's clients, one who hated Haley. But Madeline finally gave Haley a chance and learned the truth about who Haley was and became Haley's client.

"If Madeline can change her mind, you know the whole town loves you."

"I guess."

"Including Knox. He knows letting you go would be a huge mistake."

"You think?" Haley asked.

I nodded. "Now, tell me about the ring."

Haley exhaled. "It's stunning. Absolutely perfect for me. And way too expensive. He didn't need to spend as much as he did."

"You're worth it, Haley. Every penny. And I have no doubt Knox would agree."

"Thanks, Chelsea." She drew a breath. "And thanks for letting me freak out and not telling me I'm being stupid."

"Never."

Haley grinned and lunged over to hug me.

I laughed and hugged her back.

Haley pulled back and opened her door. I met her on the sidewalk, and we walked to Book Boyfriends Unlimited.

Before Finley let us in, Haley tugged my arm. "Should I tell the others?"

"That's up to you. Someone might know something and ruin any surprise Knox has planned. You know they're all going to be so happy for you, though. Whether you tell them now or later."

Haley nodded, a hint of fear shining in her eyes. "Maybe I'll keep it to myself for now."

"Have you told Sofia?"

Haley shook her head. "I was worried it might be a ring for her and didn't want to ruin her surprise."

"Then it's our secret for now."

I forced my lips into a smile and tried not to think about the other secret I was keeping. I wasn't always good at keeping things to myself. It felt gross.

"Hello, ladies," Finley said, letting us in with a hug each.

"How are you?" Haley asked Finley.

"Good. Things are quiet around here now that it's October."

"That's good?" I asked her.

Finley nodded. "For me it is. I used to fight it, but I can get more reading done and spend more time at home with George."

"How is George?" Haley asked.

"He's perfect," Finley said, with a dreamy sound to her voice. "He's keeping us running."

"Any siblings for George?" I asked.

"I asked the same thing!" Elise said when we made it to the section in the back of the store we used for book club.

Finley shook her head, but her cheeks turned pink.

"You're trying," Blake said, blowing Finley's attempt to hide the truth out of the water. "So are we! Maybe we'll have cousins the same age again."

"That would be so awesome," Finley said. "And yes, we're trying, but Trent didn't want everyone to know. We got pregnant with George by accident, and it's been a few months, so he's stressing."

"Every pregnancy is different," Zoey said. "And there's no reason to be worried."

"Try telling him that," Finley grumbled.

"I got pregnant with Cameron in a few months, but it was a little longer with Alexis. Nina was the biggest surprise. We were only together a few months before I was pregnant with her," Zoey said. "And if he's stressing you out, distract him. Do something that makes it about enjoying each other instead of trying to make a baby."

"Ooh, I like that idea. Ian's not stressing since it took us a while to get pregnant with Maddox, but it's always on our minds. Want to go shopping this week?" Blake asked Finley.

"I think I need to. Something to snap him out of it," Finley said.

"Mind if I tag along?" Melody asked. "We've been in a rut lately."

"Absolutely," Finley said. "Anyone else?"

"I'm always up for shopping for fun things to spice things up," Elise said. "Chelsea? Want to join?"

"What? Why would I want to come?" I blurted.

"I thought you had a date with your match last week. It'll be good to have something on hand for your next date." Elise waggled her eyebrows at me.

I shook my head. "I'm good."

"Didn't you have your lunch date last week?" Elise asked.

Crap. I forgot I told them about the date. "Yeah, I'm not sure about him."

"But you had a date?" Haley asked. "Was he cute?"

I nodded. "He's cute. He's nice. But I'm not sure I'm going to see him again."

"That sucks," Elise said. "Did you at least get an orgasm out of the date?"

"Elise!" Blake gasped.

"What?" Elise asked, looking shocked anyone would be surprised by her comment.

I just shook my head and laughed, hoping someone would change the subject.

"How are things with Derek?" Melody asked. Not the subject change I wanted.

"What? What do you mean?" I laughed nervously. Did

she know something? I thought our... whatever it was, was a secret.

Melody looked around the room at everyone else. All of them were staring at me like I was insane.

"I just meant have you talked and found some common ground yet? Last you mentioned him, you were not a fan." Melody spoke slowly and clearly.

"I... Um... Yeah, I mean nothing's changed. We still aren't friends. Um, Jude is great. But Derek's a... pain," I stammered.

"I was really hoping you two would get along. It makes no sense to me that he's so difficult. I know he liked the people who owned the house before you, but it's not like he was close to them," Melody said.

"Yeah, I... I don't know," I said, digging the hole I was in deeper. I needed to shut my mouth and let the conversation happen around me.

"He'll come around. He's a nice guy," Melody said.

"He really is. Cameron and Jude have been buddies since we moved here, and Derek has always been great. Hey, maybe I'll reach out to him and see if he can go to guys' night this week. Maybe the other guys can talk to him about how amazing Chelsea is and change his mind," Zoey said, looking around the room for agreement from the others.

Everyone nodded, silently agreeing to get their boyfriends and husbands to talk me up to the man I was kind of, sort of, possibly dating? Ugh. What a disaster.

"You guys don't need to do that. It's fine. He can't really do anything to me." My laugh was high and nervous, even to my ears.

I searched the others, looking for someone who was going to call me out, but none of them seemed to notice my overeager attempt at backing off Derek.

Except Haley. Her eyes narrowed, and her chin lifted. She was suspicious. She took another bite of cake, then took a bullet and said, "I found a ring in Knox's drawer."

"You what?" they all said, diving into Haley's news.

After our talk in the car about her not wanting to tell the others, I knew she did it to save me. It didn't matter that she didn't know what she was saving me from, she did it for me. Something that was confirmed when she caught my eye and winked at me.

Which meant she would ask for details. Crap.

I tried to come up with something during the rest of book club, but every thought was muddied by the truth. I didn't like lying, and lying to my friend and business partner felt wrong. Which was why I spilled the whole story to Haley in the car on the drive home.

"Whoa, wait, you slept with Derek?" she shouted when she parked in my driveway.

I nodded.

"This requires wine. And more time. Can I come in?"

I nodded. "Yeah. I think I need someone to talk to."

"That doesn't sound good," Haley said.

I shook my head. "It's not all good."

I unlocked the door and flipped on lights. Dozer hurried out to greet us, barking and jumping on Haley before circling around us and guiding us toward the kitchen.

Haley gave Dozer attention while I grabbed a bottle of wine and poured us each a glass. I handed hers over, and we backtracked to the living room.

"Start over. What is going on?"

I took a breath and told Haley the whole story, from being paired on Book Boyfriends Wanted and talking for months on there to our limited interactions since I moved in. I told her about his jealousy, which she knew about, then him asking me out and our lunch date turned sex on the couch. And finally his request that we keep our relationship secret, and my fear that he was embarrassed by me.

"Oh, Chelsea, he'd be a fool to be ashamed of you."

I exhaled a mirthless laugh. "We both know not all men are confident in who they find attractive. He could easily hate himself for wanting me."

"Okay, some men are assholes, and I agree that it's very possible. Do you really think that's what it is? How was the sex?"

I gave her a look that said everything I couldn't find the words for.

Haley laughed. "Okay, amazing." She waved her hand in a circle, indicating my face. "I like that look. And men don't put that look on the face of a woman they don't find really attractive. You said he's been watching you in the backyard?"

"That's what he said. That when I let Dozer out, it makes him crazy."

"Aside from that being just a little creepy, I think that's all good."

"I never knew he could see into my yard. I should have, but I've never seen him at the windows and assumed he wouldn't just stand there and watch me. If I'd known he could see me, I would have put something else on."

"Sounds like it all worked out. Except you're still freaking out."

I exhaled a long breath. "Isn't it a bad sign that he doesn't want anyone to know?"

"Not if it's really because of his kid."

"But how do I know if that's really what it is?"

Haley smiled. "You're not going to like my answer."

"What?" I grumbled.

"You have to trust him."

"You're right. I don't like that answer," I told her.

She just laughed. But she was right. I had to trust him. If I wanted to be with him.

13

DEREK

I saw Chelsea once in the week since our lunch date. Once. It felt like she was avoiding me. I sent her messages and asked if we could see each other again, but she wouldn't commit to anything.

At least, not anything that worked for me and made it possible to keep our relationship a secret from Jude.

When Zoey asked if I wanted to drop Jude off Thursday night so I could go to guys' night at O'Kelley's, I was tempted to skip out on the guys and find Chelsea. Very tempted. But Zoey's offer also came with the offer for Sebastian to go with me to guys' night.

So much for that plan.

"Jude! Are you ready?" I called up the stairs.

"Coming!" Jude's footsteps above me were followed by him racing around the banister and running down the stairs. The smile on his face was big. He didn't ever get to go out on a school night, and the fact that he could not only go out but would be spending time with Cameron had Jude thrilled.

Zoey had offered to have Jude over before, but when she

was pregnant, then when Nina was a baby, I didn't take her up on the offer. It didn't seem right to leave her with another kid so I could go out and have a drink with friends. She wasn't my wife, and she didn't need to take care of my kid.

But now that Nina was two, and Zoey insisted having Jude over would make the evening easier for her, I agreed.

"Cameron said he got a new video game. We're going to play it tonight," Jude said as we walked outside. "I told him about Dozer and asked if he can come over here sometime. Hopefully Ms. Chelsea will let us play with Dozer. If Cameron can come over."

"I'm sure she'll be happy to let you guys do that."

"She's so cool, Dad."

"I didn't know you saw her that much."

"When she's not working, she brings Dozer outside when I'm home so we can play in the front yard. She knows you have rules." His tone said he thought my rules about him not being in anyone's backyard were ridiculous.

Maybe it was time to ease up on that one as far as Chelsea went. "Maybe I can talk to Mrs. Walsh about you going into Chelsea's yard. Since she's right next door and the yard is fenced and we know her a little."

"Really? That would be so awesome. Ms. Chelsea makes me keep Dozer on his leash in the front yard, but if we could run around in the backyard, that would be so cool."

"I'll talk to Mrs. Walsh," I promised.

"Sweet."

It had been a long time since I let Jude go anywhere that I wasn't. Most of his activities were ones I attended. Which was part of why he didn't do much. Middle school was bringing changes for both of us. I hadn't been able to stop thinking about Mr. Laurel said when I talked to him about Jude getting off the bus without supervision. Jude was growing up. He was going to be independent. He was going to need more freedom. I didn't have to like it, but it was going to happen whether I liked it or not, so I might as well at least get on board with it.

I parked in front of Zoey and Sebastian's house, barely turning the truck off before Jude was jumping out and racing toward the door. It opened when he was halfway up the walk, Cameron smiling and waving Jude inside. They disappeared as I rounded my truck.

"You want to come in?" Sebastian asked, appearing in the door the boys had left open.

"Yeah, I'll come say hi to Zoey. If that's okay."

"Of course," Sebastian said. "Those boys are terrors."

I chuckled with him, his smile giving away how he really felt.

Zoey was walking down the hallway toward the front door when I got to the porch. "Hi, Derek. I figured you had to be close since I heard the footsteps to the dungeon."

"Dungeon?" I asked.

Sebastian shook his head. "That's what she calls the game room. We keep it dark so the effects are better."

"And it's in the basement," Zoey added.

"Jude's so excited to be here. Thank you for having him."

Zoey smiled. "Any time. He's a great kid and always respectful and kind. He even keeps Cameron from picking on his sisters, which is a challenge."

"I'm glad to hear he's no trouble for you."

"Never," Zoey said.

"You ready?" Sebastian asked me.

"Yep. I'm guessing Jude's forgotten I exist, so tell him I said bye if he comes up for air before we get back."

Zoey laughed and nodded. "I'll let him know. I have

pizza for them to eat when they get hungry, and I know the new game will keep them busy."

"It definitely will. Thanks, Zoey."

"You're welcome. Enjoy your night."

I nodded and waved, heading to my truck so she and Sebastian had a minute to say goodbye without me watching them. Sebastian climbed into my truck a few seconds after I did.

"You sure you're good to drive?" he asked.

"Yeah. I have to drive home after anyway, so it makes sense for me to drive now."

"Thanks, man. That's not why Zoey offered to have Jude over, though."

"You make it sound like there's a reason she did offer." I hadn't considered an ulterior motive, but now that he put it in my head, it was all I could think about.

"The women think they're so smart. They orchestrated this to try to talk you into not hating your neighbor, Chelsea."

"Why do they think I hate her?"

Sebastian's brows jumped at my question, either suggesting I was crazy for asking the question or crazy for hating her.

"Well, the notes on her door and the threats about calling the cops to start with."

"I apologized to her for that."

"You did?"

"Yeah. We're all good now."

"Does Chelsea know that?"

"What do you mean?"

"This whole plan was crafted Sunday night when they were at book club."

"Seriously?" That was a surprise, and a little frustrating.

Especially after last week. We slept together. I told her I wanted to see her. And she was telling people I hated her?

"You sound surprised by that. Are you sure Chelsea knows you're all good?"

"I don't know how she couldn't know that after—"

"After what?" Sebastian asked.

I drew a breath and let it out slowly. So much for keeping our relationship between the two of us. I gave Sebastian a look that said everything I wasn't opening my mouth to say.

"You slept together. Well... That doesn't always mean things are good. Zoey and I were sleeping together for months before we got back together. I was so pissed at her. I told myself I hated her. But I wanted her so much that I was willing to try to fuck her out of my system. Didn't work, clearly. I married her."

"That's not what this was."

"Then what was it?"

I put my truck in park and turned it off. "We were paired together. On that app. We were talking for a while, but she wasn't like the other women I met on there who were just a quick roll in the sheets. I liked talking to her. I had no idea it was Chelsea until we met for lunch last week."

"Okay, this story needs drinks and more ears."

"I can't tell all of them about this."

"Dude, that's why we're here. We talk about our women, or the one we want to be ours for the single guys, and we help each other figure out how to not fuck it up. Trust me, you need this."

Sebastian's hand was on the door handle, waiting for me to agree. I nodded, and he opened the door, getting out and waiting for me on the sidewalk.

I felt like I was walking to the firing squad. They all liked

Chelsea. She was one of the women their women hung out with. For all the things I liked about raising Jude in a small town, having the tight-knit group who all watched out for each other was a challenge.

Because I wasn't in the group. I was on the fringe. Included when it was convenient, but not someone who was invited to most things.

And I was walking in to the base camp, about to tell all of them one of their own was at risk. That we were involved. In the group and outside didn't work. Ian and Blake worked. Ramsey and Melody worked. Zoey and Sebastian worked. Me and Chelsea?

At least I had my own truck so I could go home when they kicked me out.

Sebastian led the way to the bar, grabbing a seat on one end and leaving me to the open stool in the middle of the fray. Thrown to the wolves.

The looks exchanged down the line told me they were all in on the plan to get me to like Chelsea. Which meant they all liked Chelsea, and I was right. I was so screwed.

"He knows why we're here, and he has an update," Sebastian said once everyone said hello and the conversation that was in progress when we arrived faded away.

"An update?" Ian asked. He was sitting to my right. We'd spoken a few times about being small business owners in town. I liked and respected Ian, but he had pull. One word from him, or almost any of the men there, and I'd be out of business.

I opened my mouth to tell them what was going on and found the words wouldn't come. It wasn't so simple as we were sleeping together or so complex as we were together. Our relationship was somewhere in between, and it was something I wanted kept quiet until I knew what it was.

"He slept with her," Sebastian said for me.

I glared at him.

He shrugged. "You need help. They were paired and talked for a while, then met for lunch last week. I haven't gotten more than that out of him, but he didn't want to tell anyone about it, so start prying."

I growled and shook my head and debated standing up and walking out.

Hudson slid a drink in front of me.

"I'm driving."

"I know. No alcohol, but it tastes good and will chill you out," Hudson said.

I raised a skeptical eyebrow at him.

He just chuckled. "That app gets you every time."

I exhaled, knowing that was the best reply I could have gotten to Sebastian's exposé on my relationship with Chelsea.

"Melody said you don't like Chelsea. That Chelsea told them all about the notes and everything. What changed?" Ramsey asked.

"I... The old owners of the house were quiet. Never made any noise. Jude's bedroom is on that side, and the night she moved in, he didn't sleep. The noise kept him up half the night," I told them.

"That's our bad," Hudson said. "A bunch of us were there and didn't think about how loud we were being."

"Sounds to me like you need new windows," Knox said.

"Probably, but I didn't before she moved in," I said.

"That's not on her," Ramsey said. "But I repeat, what changed?"

"Jude had a half day a few weeks ago. I didn't know about it, and Mrs. Walsh didn't know about it, and Jude ended up on my porch, locked out," I confessed. No one outside the shop knew about that day. I felt like a shitty parent, and telling the others about it was not easy to do.

"Those half days are ridiculous," Sebastian agreed. "If Zoey wasn't home full time, I think we would have had the same thing happen more than once."

"But Zoey is home. You have a wife, someone to pick up the slack and take care of things when you aren't there," I said, trying and failing to hold back my frustration.

"True. So you want to marry Chelsea?" Sebastian asked.

"No! I... She found Jude that day, took him to her house and fed him and entertained him and made sure he was okay. I haven't left her a note since then." I ran a hand over my head, trying to clear the idea of Chelsea as my wife. I wasn't interested in tying down another woman who had no interest in sticking around.

"Sounds like a good thing," Ian said. "But there's more. Spit it out. What happened?"

I looked at him, searching for judgment and finding only curiosity. "Jude adores her dog, so she's been hanging around in the afternoons with him and Mrs. Walsh, letting Jude play with the dog. I didn't know she was the woman I was paired with, but when we met, she thought I was repulsed by her."

Every man in the group tensed with those words. All of them were married to or involved with women who were curvy like Chelsea. Women they were all ready to defend if I didn't correct the assumption Chelsea jumped to.

"She's wrong. She left before I could tell her that, and I followed her home and... told her she was mistaken."

The grins that lifted the lips of every man there told me they all understood the details I wasn't sharing at that moment.

"This was a week ago?" Ramsey asked.

I nodded.

"And then what?" Ian asked.

"I asked her if we could keep things between us."

They all groaned.

"There we go. That's the issue," Hudson said.

"Why? I have a son who's never known his mother. He's already getting attached to Chelsea, and I wanted to protect him. Make sure Chelsea and I were going to work out before telling Jude. I've never introduced him to a woman."

"I get it," Xavier said, leaning forward to speak for the first time that night. "When you're the only parent they know, you have to protect them. Did you explain to Chelsea that's why you wanted to keep it quiet?"

I nodded. "Yeah, of course."

"How many times have you seen her since then?" Ian asked.

"None."

They were all remarkably silent with that admission.

"I've reached out. I've asked if she wanted to get lunch, but she always says she's working. Jude said he's seen her after school, but she's always home by the time I get home," I told them.

"She's avoiding you," Xavier said. "She thinks you're full of shit. That you don't want people to know you're dating."

"Why would she think that?"

"How long after sex did you tell her not to tell anyone you were there?" Ian asked.

I shrugged, knowing I didn't really want to answer the question.

"Too soon," Ian said. "If you're not willing to tell us, it was too soon. Look, I get it. You want to protect your kid. But if you want Chelsea to give you a real chance, you need to make an effort to see her when it doesn't sound like a mid-day fuck."

"That's not—"

"Maybe not. Maybe you meant that was when you could get away. But she heard you're only interested in secret sex when no one will know," Hudson said.

"I never meant for it to come across that way."

"What we say, what we mean, and what they hear are not always the same thing," Xavier said.

"That helps," I grumbled.

The others laughed at me.

"Now you can fix it. You can be clear with her. More clear. Hell, go see her right now and explain it to her," Ian said.

"I can't. Jude is with Zoey, and I need to take Sebastian home," I explained.

"Sebastian is covered," Ramsey said. "Any of us will be happy to drive him home to make sure you get things right with Chelsea."

"But..."

"What? What else is holding you back?" Knox asked.

"What if she still doesn't believe me?"

"Then you tell her until she does," Ian said. "Sometimes they need to hear things a few dozen times before the lies they've told themselves are silenced by the truths you tell them."

"That's deep," I told him.

"It's experience. Blake didn't want me when we got together. She thought I was someone I wasn't. She convinced herself she wasn't enough for me, and she kept me at arm's length. It took a while to make her believe I was in love with her and wasn't going anywhere," Ian said.

"Not that he was sure about their relationship," Ramsey

added. "Ian had plenty of moments where he was positive Blake was going to walk away for good."

Ian nodded. "Every damn day I'm thankful when I wake up and she's next to me because every damn day I'm waiting for her to realize she could do so much better than me."

"She's not going anywhere," Hudson told Ian.

Ian grinned. "I hope not. If she does, I'm following her."

Hudson held his beer bottle to cheers with Ian's. They shared a nod and a look that said their wives were loved fully.

"Go see Chelsea," Ramsey said. "And if you ever need someone to watch Jude, Mel and I would be happy to."

"Us, too," the others said.

Maybe I wasn't on the outside.

But I was more interested in if Chelsea would give me a chance than securing my friendships with the men in the room in the moment. I could talk to the guys later.

"Sebastian, you good?" I asked, catching his eye.

Sebastian lifted his bottle. "Good luck."

"Thanks. All of you."

"One rule," Hudson said.

I stopped and looked at him.

"You have to come back next week and fill us in," Hudson said.

I looked down the line of men and nodded. "Deal."

14

———

I parked in my driveway and stared at Chelsea's house. Had I read everything wrong? Or were the guys right, and I fucked up?

Given my track record vs. theirs, I had a feeling they were right.

I walked across the grass to her front door. I pressed the button for her doorbell, noticing it for the first time. Did she install it because of me? Because of the notes? Or was it always there?

The door whooshed open while I was asking myself those questions, and there she was. Her hair piled high on her head in a messy bun, brown waves curling down her collarbones and teasing her breasts. Breasts contained in a tank top and covered with a sweater that did nothing to stop my memory of the way they looked naked. My gaze continued lower to her waist and legs, curves and more curves wrapped up in cotton that looked almost as soft as she was.

"Did you need something?" she asked, pulling me out of my fantasy of stripping her naked and having her right then and there. I wasn't there to fuck her. I was there to prove to her I wanted more than that.

But fuck, it was hard to remember that when she was standing in front of me, looking like a walking temptation.

"Can I come in?" I asked.

She peeked out the door, seeing my car in my driveway, and took a step back.

Dozer lived up to his name, snoozing in a large dog bed next to the couch. Her TV was on, a show I didn't recognize playing on the screen. I looked around her living room, seeing the place for the first time, even though I'd been there twice.

"I like your home," I told her. The couch was a dark blue color with pink, green, and purple pillows. A gray blanket was draped over the cushions like she'd been curled up under it until I disturbed her night. The coffee table in front was solid wood and matched the cabinets in her kitchen. Lamps on the end tables gave the room a soft glow that added to the intimate feel of the space. Cozy. Soft. A place you could relax and forget about everything.

"Thanks," she said, her tone offering me zero guidance in how she felt.

"Listen, I think I messed things up with us."

"With us?"

"Yeah. Last week. I told you I wanted to keep it quiet, but I was told that might have sounded like I was trying to hide our relationship."

"I'm not sure how else that could be interpreted." She crossed her arms over her chest, then released them and pulled her sweater tighter, covering her chest before crossing her arms again.

I took a step toward her. "Jude's mom left when he was too young to remember her. For a few years, she would come back and visit, but he doesn't know her as his mom. I mean, he knows she's his mom, but he doesn't have a relationship with her. She's a stranger who shows up sometimes. He doesn't ask to see her or ask why he doesn't have a mom."

She didn't say anything, just shifted her feet and kept staring at me.

"When he was in kindergarten, he saw me talking to his teacher. She was young and pretty and friendly, and Jude adored her. He asked me if she was going to be his mom. Said all the other kids had moms, and since he didn't, could she be his mom because he liked her?"

"Oh, Jude," she whispered.

"Yeah. So, I have been careful since then to keep my distance from women. Not that I haven't dated some, but Jude's always my priority. He comes first."

"And I told you I understand that."

"I know." I nodded and shifted my feet. "I was ambushed tonight."

"What?"

"I went to guys' night."

She nibbled on the inside of her cheek and avoided my gaze.

"When I picked Sebastian up, he asked why I don't like you. When I told him what happened last week—"

Her head snapped up at that admission.

"He pretty much had the same reaction. The other guys did, too. Because their wives and girlfriends told them four days ago that you made it seem as though we don't like each other."

"You asked me not to tell anyone. What was I supposed to do?" she snapped.

I took another step toward her. "I shouldn't have asked

you to keep it from everyone. Not wanting Jude to know and not wanting you to talk to your friends are different things. I'm not used to having people around to talk to, but it wasn't fair of me to ask you not to tell your friends. I know in a small town, it's likely Jude will find out before I'm ready for him to, but I didn't intend for you to feel like I was hiding us."

"Derek, there is no us. We slept together once. We've never been on a date. We have no idea where this is going to go. If anywhere."

"Isn't that what dating is about? Finding the answers to that?"

"Sure, but dating requires seeing each other. Getting to know each other."

"I've been trying to talk to you. You've been avoiding me."

"Don't put this on me. You made me feel like shit." Her chest rose and fell with her shaky exhale.

"Dammit," I breathed. I reached out, letting her see my hand before I moved close enough to touch her. I tucked a strand of hair behind her ear, letting it slide through my fingers.

Her eyes closed. Her lips pressed together. She swallowed roughly. "Don't do this."

"I fucked up more than I realized, and I'm here to apologize. I want to know you, Chelsea. I want to get together with you. But yes, I want to keep it from my son who has never had a mother and already likes you."

"Did you really tell all of them what happened?"

I nodded when she looked up at me. "Ian, Ramsey, Xavier, Sebastian, Hudson, and Knox were there. I have no doubt they will tell everyone else, including their wives and girlfriends."

"And you're okay with that?"

I cupped her jaw and curled my fingers to try to get her to move closer. She took half a step toward me. I nodded. "I was only thinking about Jude when I asked you to keep this between us. I never meant to hurt you or make you think I didn't want you."

"Okay," she whispered.

"Can I kiss you, Chelsea?"

"You're asking?"

"Yes, because I need to know you trust me. That you're okay with this. If you're unsure, I have more work to do."

"More work?"

I nodded. "I'm not here tonight to fuck you. I'm here to make sure you know I want to and that I'm going to, if you're willing, but not tonight."

"Why not?"

"Because I want you to know that's not what this is for me."

"What is it?"

I smiled. "It's me getting to know the woman who ignites my body with tiny shorts and skintight tanks and the woman who makes me laugh and ignites my brain."

"That's a really good answer," she breathed.

"It's the truth."

"Good." She lifted on her toes and pressed her lips to mine, shocking the breath out of me.

I inhaled past her, drawing in the subtle scent of her as I tilted my head to taste her. I licked her lips, groaning when she sighed and let me in. My hands tightened on her body, aching to wander.

She didn't have the same reservations. Her hands slid around my back and drifted to my ass. She squeezed and drew me closer, gasping when she felt the thick line of my erection against her belly.

I took advantage of her gasp and deepened our kiss, plunging my tongue into her mouth and backing her up to the wall. I fucking loved that she had a wall with nothing on it. A wall I could use to make her crazy.

My hands slid south to return the favor, molding and squeezing her ass. I slid one hand to her thigh and lifted her leg to give myself a spot to settle between her thick thighs. I thrust against her, a surprised moan making her pull back from our kiss.

"I thought... you said... no sex," she gasped, pausing with each stroke.

"This isn't sex. All our clothes are on, and I'm not inside you. That doesn't mean I don't want you to think about me when you go to bed tonight. Or when you wake up in the morning. Or any time you walk in that door."

"Oh, God," she whisper-moaned. "How are you making this feel so good?"

I rubbed against her again, my height giving me the leverage to rub along her clit with each stroke. Her clothes added to the friction, and it was clearly working for her. "Next time, I make no promises about not fucking you, Chelsea. Next time, I'm going to strip these clothes off of you and look at this beautiful body again. Next time, you're going to come so hard your eyes cross and you never doubt how much I want you."

"I'm... halfway there... now."

"Good. Time to finish." I slammed harder, speeding up my pace so she didn't have a second or two in between to recover. I pulled her leg higher, spreading her thighs wider.

She trembled, the leg on the floor shaking with the effort of holding her body upright.

"Lean on me, beautiful. I can hold you up."

She hesitated until I stroked against her again, then her body sank onto mine.

I held her, my eyes nearly crossing. Her giving herself to me, trusting me to take care of her, was almost as powerful as the orgasm I was racing toward. I was going to come with her, in my jeans, like a kid, and I fucking loved it.

"Come on, Chelsea. Let go, beautiful. Come for me."

She moaned and shook, then she threw her head back and let her release take over. Her eyes closed. Her breasts bounced. Her entire body shook.

I clenched my jaw and fought the urge to follow her, barely holding back before I came with her.

She was deadweight in my arms, the orgasm taking the last of her reserves.

I sank to the floor with her, holding her in my arms while she panted and trembled.

"Oh, my God, that was insane," she breathed.

"That was stunning," I told her.

She shook her head and laughed softly. "I... Did you come?"

"No, beautiful."

She looked up at me. "I... I'm sorry."

"Why in the world would you be sorry?"

"Because I didn't make you come."

I laughed, pulling her against me. "Oh, beautiful, I was close, but I wanted to watch you. I will replay that over and over again for a very long time. Especially later tonight in my bed with my hand wrapped around my dick, wishing it was your hand."

Her gasp told me my words turned her on.

"I've been thinking about you for months, and having actual experience with you to call to mind has only made it easier for me to come with your name on my lips. I like to think about your breasts bouncing free, and the way you stretched to take me in, and how your whole body shakes when you come. Oh, Chelsea, you are always making me come."

"I..."

"Is that too much? Does it offend you to know that?"

She shook her head. "I do the same."

"Oh, fuck, Chelsea. One day, I might have to have you show me."

She nodded, tentative.

"You've never done that for anyone, have you?"

She shook her head.

I kissed her softly, tasting her lips and memorizing the feel of them against mine. "You don't have to."

"No, I... I think it would be okay."

I smiled. I wouldn't ask her again, but I would definitely hope she'd bring it up one day.

We sat on the floor for a few more minutes. She wiggled, and I let go of her so she could get up.

"I should go get Jude. He's at Zoey and Sebastian's."

"Oh, God. And they know you came here?"

"I told you, Chelsea, I'm not ashamed of you. At all, beautiful."

"Okay."

"Are you working tomorrow?"

She shook her head and stood, adjusting her clothes. "I'm off."

"I hope I'll see you. If you want."

She nodded. "I would like that."

"Good. Have a good night, beautiful." I kissed her once more, then I went to get my son.

THE NEXT AFTERNOON, I parked in my driveway and heard the sound of laughter in Chelsea's backyard. My lips lifted. She didn't push them out. She waited so I could see her.

I set my bag inside my house, then went to Chelsea's yard, calling out before I opened the gate to let myself into her yard.

Dozer came racing toward me, barking and protecting his people. Jude was right behind him, laughing at Dozer. "That's my dad!"

Dozer stopped and turned back to Jude. He looked between us, like he was trying to figure out what was going on, then stood in front of Jude.

"Come on," Jude told the dog. "Let's race."

Dozer barked at Jude and waited until he took off to follow Jude back into the yard and allowed me to enter.

"He's not so sure about you," Mrs. Walsh said. "He's very protective of Jude."

"I would hope he's protective of Chelsea," I told her. I took a seat on the patio, next to Chelsea.

"He's not as protective of me as he is of Jude," Chelsea said. "I think after the way they met, Dozer decided Jude needed protection."

She didn't mean anything by the words, but it still bothered me that Jude ended up on the porch alone. "I don't think I'll ever be able to tell you how grateful I am that you found him that day."

She turned to me and grinned. "I guess you have yourself to thank, then."

I narrowed my gaze at her. "What do you mean?"

"I was on my way to your house that day because of another note you left on my door. So, it seems like it was thanks to you being a jerk that I found your wonderful son on your doorstep."

I smirked at her, seeing the humor in her brown eyes. "Then I guess it was a good thing I was a jerk."

"I'll never understand young people," Mrs. Walsh said. "But if you two can agree not to kill each other, I think I'm going to walk home and have those wonderful leftovers you gave me, Chelsea."

"I hope you enjoy them," Chelsea said, putting her blanket aside and standing to walk Mrs. Walsh out.

"I'll definitely enjoy it," Mrs. Walsh said. "You have a good night, Derek. Bye, Jude!"

"Bye, Mrs. Walsh," Jude said, hurrying over to say goodbye to her properly. He stopped in front of her and smiled. "Thank you for being with me this week. And for letting me hang out with Dozer."

"You're so welcome, Jude. I am enjoying my time out of the house." Mrs. Walsh patted his cheek, and to my surprise, he didn't argue or move away from her.

"I can walk you home," I told Mrs. Walsh.

"I'm already up," Chelsea said. "You stay here and relax. Unless you need to get home."

I held her gaze and shook my head. "I don't have anywhere else to be tonight."

Her lips curled up in a smile that she fought from getting too big, but I saw it. She was happy with my answer.

Jude ran back to Dozer, who paused long enough to know his person was okay, then the two of them ran around while Chelsea and Mrs. Walsh walked out the front.

Jude threw a ball for Dozer, then Dozer brought it back and dropped it in front of Jude, never once fighting him or coming anywhere close to hurting him. Jude laughed when

Dozer flew over a flowerbed to get the ball that bounced on the other side.

A bird swooped low and taunted the dog. He dropped the ball and growled, chasing the bird to the edge of the yard, paws going up on the fence as the bird left the yard.

"Dozer!" Chelsea shouted from behind me.

The dog dropped to all fours. He hung his head and his tail, slinking toward her like he knew he did something he shouldn't have done.

I watched as she glared at him.

He laid down on the grass in front of her and put his head on his paws.

"You're going to get hurt or hurt someone. We've talked about this," she lectured the dog.

He howled softly at her, like he was agreeing.

"Does he understand you?" I asked.

She shrugged, then jerked her head toward Jude. "Go play. And be good," she told Dozer.

Dozer licked her hand, then took off toward Jude again.

Chelsea returned to the seat she'd been in before I arrived. The one next to me. "He seems like he does sometimes. I don't know."

"It's good he listens to you."

"It would be nice if he wouldn't do it to begin with. I'm waiting for the fence to come down between our yards. I'm saving up to replace it in the spring. I promise."

"I... I am sorry I've been such a jerk of a neighbor."

She smirked and raised an eyebrow.

"Yeah, I know. I keep apologizing, then acting like a jerk again. Jude is all that matters to me. The guys last night also told me I need new windows. That would help the sound. So Jude can sleep better."

"I'm trying to be quiet at night."

"I definitely didn't hear anything *coming* from your house last night."

She gasped, catching my joke. "Derek."

"I was thinking about it, though."

"I didn't hear anything from your house either."

I nodded toward Jude. "Young ears."

She breathed a laugh. "The first time... you know... Dozer freaked out and started barking like crazy. I try to keep it down so he doesn't think I'm dying or something."

A laugh burst from me. "Are you serious?"

She giggled and nodded. "It totally ruined the mood."

"No wonder he looked at me like he was ready to attack last week."

"And today," she added.

"Do you think he remembers me?"

She shrugged. "I'm not sure, but I'm glad he can't tell his best friend what he saw."

I looked at Dozer and Jude, laughing and playing. "Yeah, thank God for that."

15

CHELSEA

I was freezing. It was cold outside, and I'd been out for hours. But every time Derek looked at me like he wanted to devour me, I forgot all about how cold it was. Mostly.

Sitting on my patio and talking to him while Jude and Dozer tired themselves out was exactly what I'd hoped to find when I moved to the neighborhood. Not that I expected it in the form of a sexy single dad and the sweetest kid on the planet, but I was definitely not upset by that part.

"What are you thinking?" Derek asked.

I smiled and looked over at him. "That I'm glad we finally found some common ground."

"Common ground?" He raised one eyebrow in question.

I shrugged. "I was wondering if I was going to have to move. This is what I hoped to find when I bought this house. A community."

"You seem to be pretty ingrained in the community."

I nodded, pulling the blanket tighter around me. I did not dress for the sinking sun and the chilly temperatures. "I've lived here my whole life, but I've always been Cathy and Ken's daughter or Elise's cousin or Debby's employee. I wanted to be Chelsea. I wanted to stand on my own. My own place with my own community."

"Why wouldn't you want to count on the connections you have? Let the people who know you be a part of your community."

"It's not that I don't want them to be. Elise, my cousin, we were really close growing up. When she went to college, we grew apart. Until a few years ago, we hadn't gotten close again. So, all the people she had in her circle weren't a part of mine. They were her friends."

"Okay?"

"When we got closer again, they welcomed me in, but they're still her people. When I moved in, most of them were people she invited to help."

"But they came."

"Yeah, they did. But... it's just different. I like them, but it's like any other relationship. When something goes wrong, people pick sides."

"Do you think Elise is going to stop talking to you again?"

"No. That's not what I'm saying." I paused, trying to figure out how to explain it in a way that made sense. "I want... I want my own people to call. Haley and Sofia, and Knox and Daniel by extension, are my friends. I'm getting to know the others, but they came because of Elise."

"I think I get what you're saying. You want the people in your world to be there because of you and not because of someone else."

I nodded, knowing I sounded like a fool. Did it matter how I met someone? Was it really an issue?

Maybe not, but I also knew I would question it.

"What about me?"

"What about you?"

"Do you think I'm only here because of my connection to all those men?"

I raised a brow. "Are you?"

He shook his head slowly, his eyes darkening even more. "Definitely not thinking about anyone besides you right now."

"Dad, I'm hungry," Jude said, jogging over to us with Dozer on his heels.

"Okay. I think Ms. Chelsea is cold. We should head home and get dinner."

"Can Ms. Chelsea and Dozer come over for dinner?" Jude asked.

I looked up at Derek just in time to catch the panic on his face. He erased it quickly, but not before the look was seared into my mind.

"We can't tonight," I answered before Derek could say anything.

"Aw, man," Jude said.

Derek tried to catch my gaze, but I carefully avoided looking at him.

I smiled as Jude kneeled in front of Dozer and wrapped his arms around my dog's neck.

"I'll see you soon," Jude promised.

Dozer barked his agreement.

"Bye, Dozer. Bye, Ms. Chelsea," Jude said, waving as he made his way toward the gate.

"I thought you didn't have plans tonight," Derek said when Jude was out of earshot.

"I didn't want you to feel like you had to have us over. I know that's the opposite of what you want."

"Why do you think that?" he asked.

"I... I saw the look on your face when Jude asked, and

you made it clear before that you don't want him to know about us."

"Dinner with a neighbor isn't the same as a date."

"Derek, it's okay. Go spend time with your son. We'll find a time we can get together." I forced a smile that had to fool him. It had to.

He sighed, knowing he wouldn't change my mind. "I will make it up to you."

"There's nothing to make up. Have a good night."

He drew a breath. "I really want to kiss you right now."

I smiled. "Soon."

"I'm going to hold you to that," he said. He stayed another few seconds, then swore and followed Jude out the gate.

I waited until I heard the door close to their house before I released the breath I was holding.

Dozer whimpered.

"Yeah, I wasn't ready for them to leave either."

I DIDN'T SEE Derek and Jude on Saturday since I was working all day. I intentionally left after they did so I didn't run into them outside. Yes, I was hiding. I hated myself for it.

Sunday, I spent the day inside. I knew if I skipped book club, I'd get shit for it, especially after Derek told all the men about us sleeping together, but I was still deep in my feelings and confused.

I wasn't surprised in the least when Haley showed up at my house twenty minutes before book club.

"I was going to go," I grumbled when I opened the door.

"You were going to try to make an excuse." She looked

around my living room and waved her finger at the mess. "What happened?"

I spent all day on the couch and hadn't cleaned up nearly enough. Dozer didn't mess with anything, but it was still a disaster. "Busy day?"

Haley pursed her lips and shook her head. "Eating ice cream and pizza and drinking wine?"

"Don't judge me."

"You definitely need book club. Are you ready to go?"

"I can't go like this," I argued.

"Go change. I'll clean up." Haley shooed me toward the stairs.

I grumbled but followed her orders and stomped my way up the stairs.

I closed my bedroom door and drew three deep breaths. Haley was right. I needed to get out of my head and be around people. But like I told Derek the other night, they weren't really my people. I had Haley and Sofia, Elise and my family, but all the women were still new to me. I still had the urge to impress them so they would like me. So they would decide I was worthy of their friendship.

I brushed my hair and tied it up in a messy knot. It looked horrible, but when it was up, it was passable. I changed out of the sweats I'd been wearing all day, thankful I had an unbreakable habit of showering first thing in the morning. I pulled on a pair of jeans and a tank top that was soft and cozy and would give me a little touch of comfort. I added a sweater over it and debated on jewelry before deciding that was trying too hard. I grabbed a pair of warm boots since the weather got even colder over the weekend.

Haley had the living room clean by the time I got downstairs. The trash was gone and the coffee table was clean. Even Dozer looked relieved.

"Thank you," I told her.

"You're welcome. Now, tell me what happened."

"It's nothing."

"It's not nothing, but if I've learned anything about this group, it's that sometimes things don't come out the way you intend. If you tell me now, I can make sure you tell the story you want to tell."

"It's the same thing. He needs to put Jude first, and I get that, I really do, but it's not easy to be brushed off and to know it doesn't matter how I feel."

"Why doesn't it matter?"

"Because Jude has to matter more."

"I get that, but you should still matter."

"Not when what I want is in conflict with what Derek thinks is best."

"What does that mean?"

I sighed. "Jude and Mrs. Walsh were over here Friday afternoon. When Derek got home, he came over. We were all in the backyard, and Jude asked if Dozer and I could have dinner with them."

"Okay? What's wrong with that?"

"Derek looked like Jude asked if we were getting married. He panicked. Jude didn't notice, but I saw the look on Derek's face, so I told Jude we had other plans."

"But you didn't."

I shook my head. "No, and Derek knew that, so he asked me about it."

"And what did you say?"

"I told him the truth. And he didn't argue with me. He said it wouldn't be a date, but I knew he didn't want me there."

"I'm sorry, Chelsea. So, is that it?"

I shrugged. "All of this is just harder than I expected.

Maybe because he's right there, but we don't actually have time together."

"Do you want to be done?"

I thought about her question and shook my head slowly. "No. I don't."

"Then let's go figure out a game plan."

"Are you sure I should tell all of them?"

"Yes. Now, let's go."

I didn't argue with Haley again and let her lead me to her car. I thought I saw the curtains move at Derek's house, but I didn't stop to look closer.

Haley and the others let me get into Book Boyfriends Unlimited and sit down with a piece of cake before they dove in.

"So, you and Derek are not enemies, huh?" Elise asked.

I was happy she was the one bringing it up. My cousin was sarcastic and snarky, but she wasn't cruel. "I don't know what we are," I admitted.

Haley filled them all in on what happened Friday night, then Zoey told everyone about Thursday night when Derek came over after guys' night. I filled in some of those blanks since Zoey only knew Derek came over and not what we talked about.

Then it was open season on my love life.

"Being a single parent isn't easy," Goldie said. "And I know you're not saying you disagree, but can I offer some perspective from his side?"

I nodded.

"Whenever I dated anyone, I kept them from Paul completely. As he got older, I might tell him I had a date, but never who it was with. When Patrick and I started seeing each other, it was really hard because he and Paul had already met. It felt like I was walking a tightrope, balancing them and everything else."

"But you managed to do it," Haley said. "You kept them separate until you felt like it was the right time to introduce Patrick as more than your employee."

"I did," Goldie confirmed. "But Paul is older. I was able to talk to him about being in a relationship and know he wasn't going to get too invested in it until I was ready for him to know what was going on."

"You're also Mom," Karissa said. "And Paul still has Dad in his life. For Jude, it's kind of like what Xavier and McJenna went through. J never knew her mom, so she was ready to latch on. When we met, it was like you and Jude. I adored J, and she immediately attached to me. Obviously, since X and I had history, J already had a reason to hope we would end up together, but it's different when they have that gap in their life and are, maybe not intentionally, but they're looking for someone to fill it."

"I think that's how my boys were with Hudson. Especially Joey. Hudson was his hero, this guy who was always there for him and would do anything for him," Anna said. "Matty was the same when he started going to O'Kelley's and got to know Hudson. I was the holdout who wanted nothing to do with him."

"That didn't last," Finley teased Anna.

Anna grinned. "No, it didn't. But it wasn't easy to let a man into my life. Not after the way Nick hurt all of us. I don't really know Derek, but that could be on his mind, too."

"It definitely is," I said. "He told me about his ex. As far as Jude goes."

"He hasn't talked about how he felt about the divorce?" Goldie asked.

I shook my head.

The divorced women exchanged a look.

"What?"

"He might not be ready to move on. He might still be holding out hope that she comes back. That could be a part of why he doesn't want Jude to know about you," Anna said. "That's how I was the first few times Nick left. I told myself he'd be back, and he always was. Usually it was for money and sex, but he came back. The boys were embarrassingly old before I accepted that their dad was not the man I thought he was and that we were better off without him in our lives."

"I don't…" I wanted to defend him, but I wasn't sure I could.

"Derek's never mentioned his ex to us," Melody said. "Aside from saying she's not in the picture. We've known him for years and she's only been around a few times."

"Same here," Zoey added. "I'm not sure I agree that he might be hoping she comes back. It's possible, but that's not the impression I get from him."

"But until you ask, you don't really know," Goldie said.

I nodded, knowing she was right and wishing I hadn't gone to book club. It definitely did not make me feel better. Even though the cake was really good.

KNOX ARRIVED mid-day Tuesday to install my new backdoor. He wanted to wait until it was a little warmer in the day to swap the door out. Not that it was much warmer, but better than first thing in the morning after our first snowfall.

"Hey," I said, opening the door and waving him in. "I'm not sure what you need access to."

"Good afternoon. You're all good. I think I might take the

door around to the back. Just to make it easier. No twists and turns to navigate."

"Sounds good."

"Teddy is here, too. I'm not sure if I mentioned he was coming. I needed an extra set of hands."

I shrugged. "Works for me. I don't think I'd be much help."

Knox laughed. "You doing okay?"

"Haley tell you to ask me that?"

He shook his head. "No. You just don't have your usual spark."

"I'm good."

He looked at me closer. "Want me to kick your neighbor's ass?"

I snorted. "No. He's good. I'm the one who needs to get my head on straight."

"Offer stands. I think I could take him. If I catch him by surprise."

I laughed and shook my head at Knox's grin.

"We'll get started so you can get back to your day," Knox said.

"Yes, busy day of sitting on my couch."

Knox chuckled. "It's good to have downtime, too."

I nodded. Knox went out the front, and I went to the back to unlock the door and make sure there was nothing in their way on the patio.

I turned the heat off inside the house so I didn't waste money trying to warm up the outside air. I was not ready to admit my dad was right and I should have replaced the door when I first moved in. It only took three weeks from when Knox helped me pick it out until the new door came in and Knox added the dog door to it, but winter was racing toward us.

I curled up on the couch under two blankets to fight off the cold. Dozer laid on my feet, shivering from the cold and his anxiety. Every time there was a noise, Dozer whimpered and lifted his head to look at Knox and Teddy.

They got the old door out quickly, and Knox came into the living room to let me know they had to repair the doorframe after Dozer's attempt to escape the doggy door.

"I'm not surprised," I told him.

Knox chuckled and rubbed Dozer's head. "He was scared. Needed to get away."

Dozer yawned and barked his answer.

Knox laughed. "I get it. Teddy went back to the store to grab what we need. He should be back soon. I didn't want to leave you with a hole in your house."

"Thanks. You want a drink or something?"

"I'm good. I'm going to sit on your patio so I don't get dust all over your house."

"Don't be silly. It's freezing out there. You can sit in the house."

He gestured to his clothes. "I'm kind of a mess."

I waved to Dozer. "Have you met my dog?"

Knox laughed. He grabbed a chair from the kitchen, a wooden one that would be easy to wipe clean. Still thoughtful even after I told him not to worry about it.

"So, listen, I know you didn't ask for my opinion, but I think Anna's wrong about Derek still being hung up on his ex."

"I just don't know," I admitted.

"I get it, but I also know a lot of men aren't as in touch with their emotions as women. We don't dwell on things like that. I'm not a dad, but I think there's a difference between a man who strings his woman along and a woman who leaves. They've been divorced for nine years? I don't think Derek's the type to hope she's coming back after all that time."

"But he hasn't told me anything about it."

"Did you tell him about your most painful breakup?"

"Well, no."

Knox gave me a pointed look. "It's not fun to talk about the things you see as failures. He wants you to like him. Why would he share his worst moments with you? Especially the one that has another woman walking away from him?"

"I never thought of it that way."

"Maybe that's not what it is." Knox stood and wiped the dust from his chair. "All I'm saying is don't jump to conclusions just yet."

"Thanks, Knox."

"You're welcome, Chelsea."

Teddy appeared at the back door, calling for Knox, who obviously heard Teddy before he appeared. Knox went back to work, the two of them making quick work of the doorframe and door and leaving while Knox's words still played in my mind.

16

———

I stayed inside the rest of the day, coaxing Dozer to use the new doggy door. He was worried, and resisted heavily, but after a little while, he tentatively tried it out. And didn't panic.

It was a victory! My house was still standing and my dog was able to get outside to use the bathroom without me opening the door. I showered Dozer with praise and told him how good he was and gave him an extra treat for using the new door.

I heard Jude get off the bus that afternoon, but they didn't stay outside, going into the house as soon as the bus pulled away. A part of me felt guilty for not going out to see Jude and Mrs. Walsh, but it was too cold for all of us to be outside for long.

That night, I got a message from Derek.

STONECOLDDAD

Jude was disappointed he didn't see you and Dozer outside today.

CUTHAIRDONTCARE

I had a new door installed and was cold all day. I'll explain to Jude next time I see him.

STONECOLDDAD

It's okay. He just mentioned your car was in the driveway but you weren't out. He talks about Dozer constantly.

CUTHAIRDONTCARE

I think Dozer missed playing with Jude today, too.

STONECOLDDAD

Who would have thought my son and your dog would become best friends?

CUTHAIRDONTCARE

Both are pretty awesome.

STONECOLDDAD

True.

CUTHAIRDONTCARE

LOL

STONECOLDDAD

I missed you today, too. I've gotten addicted to sitting with you in the afternoon and talking to you.

CUTHAIRDONTCARE

I enjoy that, too.

STONECOLDDAD

When can I see you?

My heart skipped. Dammit. I wanted to be tough and not react, but I wanted to see him. I wanted to be with him.

I drew a breath before I answered because my first thought was whenever you want, but that was the wrong answer. A relationship had to be a partnership. Both of us needed to be in this if it was going to work.

Which also meant I needed to know about his ex, and if he was still hung up on her. And I needed to talk to him about my past relationships. Good and bad.

CUTHAIRDONTCARE

I work the rest of the week.

STONECOLDDAD

What about lunch?

Lunch. Again.

I drew a breath. Anna and Goldie said lunch wasn't a slight. It was convenient. It was an opportunity to get together without having to explain it to Jude.

Lunch was a good option for a single parent.

CUTHAIRDONTCARE

I can do lunch. I take an hour at one every day.

STONECOLDDAD

Tomorrow?

CUTHAIRDONTCARE

Works for me.

STONECOLDDAD

Perfect

CUTHAIRDONTCARE

Where do you want to meet?

STONECOLDDAD

My house. If you're okay with that. No one will think anything of our cars being in our own driveways at the same time.

CUTHAIRDONTCARE

I'll see you tomorrow.

STONECOLDDAD

Can't wait.

I closed the app and sucked in a sharp breath. It was like holding back tears on the phone, except there was no rationalization for holding them back when texting.

Except I did. And they fell as soon as I set my phone down.

He was still hiding me. Hiding us. He didn't want people to see us together around town. Or he just wanted sex. Either way, I wasn't sure how I felt about it.

Was I supposed to bring my own lunch, too? This was getting to be too much frustration and confusion for me. Maybe it was better if I ended things now.

But I didn't want to. I wanted to get to know him. I wanted to know if the chemistry I felt when we were together would translate to other parts of a relationship. If we would get along when we weren't hiding.

Maybe it would get better. Once Derek felt safe telling Jude about us. Once Derek was ready to share our relationship.

If he was ever ready.

I couldn't let it stop me. Not yet. It had only been two weeks since we started seeing each other. I owed him time.

I just hoped I didn't regret giving it to him.

I PACKED A LUNCH. I wasn't sure what to expect, so I packed a lunch. When I pulled into my driveway, I debated what I should do, but I decided it made more sense to bring my lunch into his house than leave it in the car and have to go back out. Especially because a trip to the car would increase the odds of a neighbor spotting me going to Derek's house instead of my own.

I crossed the strip of grass between our driveways and went to his porch, knocking on his front door when I got there. It was hard to believe it had only been a month since I found Jude in that same spot, and everything between Derek and me changed.

Derek whooshed the door open, ushering me inside before he spoke. I'd never been inside his house, and I took a second to look around before he was pushing me against the door he'd just closed and covering my body with his.

I dropped my handbag and lunch, my keys jangling to the floor on top of both before I reached up and cupped his jaw, holding him in place.

His tongue split my lips, tangling with mine as I sighed. This was why I ignored the voices that told me to be wary of him. This was why I pushed away the uneasiness. When he held me, I could feel how he felt. How he wanted me. It was only later, when I wasn't in his arms, that those doubts crept back in and told me the way I felt wasn't enough.

"Hi," he whispered against my lips. "And sorry for jumping you as soon as you walked in."

I smiled. "I wasn't complaining."

He grinned back and leaned in, kissing me again. Softer. Sweeter. Like we weren't limited to an hour of time together. An hour we'd already broken into with driving home.

"Are you hungry? I made lunch. I wasn't sure... You brought lunch?"

I followed his gaze to where my lunch bag laid on the floor. I reached down and grabbed it and my handbag. "Well, we didn't really say what we were doing for lunch, and I don't do well if I skip meals since I'm on my feet all day. So, I brought a sandwich, an apple, and a bag of chips. I figured worst case I could eat in my car on my way back to work."

My voice trailed off as I spoke, realizing how I sounded to him. He invited me to lunch, and I brought my own. Not trusting him to provide food for me.

"I'm sorry. I... This is all new to me."

Derek sighed. "I know. I haven't been very good about things. A secret relationship is probably not how your best relationships have started out."

"Well, I mean, it's not how any started out, but I meant more along the lines of I don't date a ton. My last serious relationship was a few years ago, and it was convenient, in some ways."

"Were you in love with him?"

I shrugged. "I was in love with the idea of him. We were friends in high school. He went away to college, but he moved back here a few years after. His mom and my mom were friends, and they gave us each others' numbers. He asked me to dinner, and we ended up dating for about six months."

"What happened?" Derek looked more curious than worried.

"He was too boring for me. That sounds so horrible, but it's true. I wanted to go dancing or to a movie or even to dinner, and he wanted to plan things out in advance. We didn't work in the end."

"I... Are you trying to warn me off getting too attached to you?" Derek asked, his tone a little harsher than I expected.

"Warn you?"

Derek leveled me with a glare. "I'm not spontaneous. I have a son. I have to plan things, Chelsea. If you're here to tell me this isn't going to work because I can't drop everything—"

"That's not what I was trying to say. I was just trying to tell you about my last relationship. I told you I haven't dated much and was being honest with you." I looked at him expectantly, hoping he would get the hint.

He didn't.

He nodded once, then turned away, frustration clear in the taut lines of his back.

I sighed. "Are you over your ex-wife?"

"Excuse me?" he growled.

I raised an eyebrow and crossed my arms over my chest. "You said she didn't want to be a mom, but you never really talked about how you handled it."

"Are you asking me if I wanted to walk away from my son so I could keep my wife?"

"No. I... I didn't mean it like that."

"Then how did you mean it?"

"Never mind."

"No, I want to hear this. I'm really curious what your question was trying to find out."

"I'm trying to find out if you're hoping your ex-wife comes back to you."

He held my stare for a long moment before he grimaced. "No. Sasha was... I loved her. She was everything to me when we met. When we were together. But any woman who could walk away from her own child, a child she said she wanted and tried for and planned for and swore to protect and love her whole life..."

The look in his eyes was one of pain, but I wasn't sure if the pain was for Jude or because of Sasha.

All I knew was I couldn't ask.

"Not every person is meant to be a parent. I know

that. I get it. Sasha told me she didn't want kids when we got married, and I was disappointed, but I loved her enough that I tried to get over it. Her friends started having kids, and she changed her mind. She said what the hell, let's do it. Not the most excitement I'd ever seen from her, but I believed she would fall in love with being a mother once Jude arrived. That she'd look at him and feel like a piece of her that had been missing was finally in place. She never felt like that. She felt like having him took a piece from her instead. A piece she couldn't get back as long as she was here trying to be a mom and wife."

"What if—"

"Chelsea, I'm sorry, but we only have an hour together. I really don't want to spend it talking about my ex-wife. She hasn't been a part of my life for years. She's not coming back, and even if she did, I don't want her back. I don't have any interest in a relationship with her."

"Okay," I whispered.

"Are you hungry?"

I nodded, forcing a smile.

Derek led me into his kitchen, through the living room like mine. His house was similar but not the same. He had a formal dining room that looked like it doubled as an office and creative space. The walls were lined with pictures Jude had drawn, the skill level changing with the pictures and telling me they were done over many years.

The kitchen was bigger than mine and updated. A window over the sink overlooked my yard. Derek stood there, staring out with his back to me.

"I was standing here the first time I saw you. I was drinking my cup of coffee and almost dropped it. You were so beautiful."

I didn't reply, letting him live in his memory. He turned to me, his eyes blazing with desire.

"You still take my breath."

I sucked in my own breath, feeling spirals of desire wind through me.

"Are you hungry?" he asked.

I wanted to say no, but my stomach rumbled and gave me away.

Derek grinned and pulled something out of the oven. I hadn't even noticed the scent in the air until he opened the oven.

He set a sheet pan full of vegetables and beef chunks on the stovetop. He grabbed a can of ranch seasoning and sprinkled it over the hot food, giving it a good coating.

"This is one of my go-to dinners for us. Easy and delicious. I hope you like it."

I accepted a plate and scooped food onto it. We sat at the kitchen table. I blew on the food and took a bite, groaning when the flavors hit my tongue.

"Wow, that's good," I mumbled.

"Good."

We ate in relative silence. I felt guilty for ruining the short time we had together, but I was happy I got some answers from him.

I finished my food and put my plate in the dishwasher. I had twenty minutes before I needed to be at work, but Derek wasn't saying much. Staying there longer felt like a bad idea. Until he started talking.

"I don't talk about Sasha a lot because she's not a part of our lives. Jude doesn't ask about her. She's gone. She chose to be gone. If she died, I think it would have been easier. That sounds horrible, but she didn't want us. The first few years were painful. I did wait for her to come back. I told myself she'd realize what she was missing. Even when the divorce papers came, I thought she'd come back. But after nine years? I don't want her, Chelsea. I want you. And I know I'm not being fair to you. I am asking a lot of you, and I'm not giving you much in return."

"What do you think I need that I'm not getting?" I leaned against the counter.

"You deserve to be shown off. To be paraded around town. Inviting you here makes it seem like I'm hiding you, but I promise I'm not."

"I know."

"Do you? Because there is only one reason I'm not taking you out and telling the whole town you're mine. And that is my son."

"I understand."

"I hope you do. I really hope you do. Even when we're public, I'm not going to be able to drop everything and go places. Not without Jude. One day he'll be able to stay home alone, but I'm not there yet."

"Derek." I crossed the room, curling onto his lap and praying he had really strong chairs.

His hands slid over my thighs, caressing me through my jeans. His cock twitched against my leg.

"I'm willing to be patient about all of this. I'm not trying to push for you to do something different. But I do worry I won't be patient enough for you. And I worry that I'm seeing things that aren't there. Like if you're as interested in this as I am."

"Then I need to show you how I feel more often." He kissed my neck. "And tell you how much I want you." He nipped my jaw. "And convince you I'm worth the wait."

He claimed my lips and inhaled fast as he parted my lips. One hand went into my hair, the other holding my thighs where I sat. He tugged my hair to tilt my head back and nibbled his way down my throat.

"Can I fuck you before we go back to work, Chelsea? I want to watch you come. See you lose your mind. Know I'm the man you smell like for the rest of the day."

"Yes," I moaned.

"Stand up, beautiful," he growled.

I crawled off him. He was on his feet and backing me against the countertop in the next breath. His hands pulled at my top, tugging it up before he broke our kiss to free it from my body. His hands cupped my breasts, rubbing my nipples before lifting them to his mouth. He nudged my bra to the side and sucked one nipple, then the other, making quick work of any remaining sanity I had that told me this was a bad idea.

It was a good idea. A very, very good idea.

I unbuttoned and unzipped my jeans, shoving them down with my panties, not caring that he wasn't going to see the lace panties I wore just in case we ended up here.

"On the counter," he said.

"I'm naked."

He grinned. "Oh, I'm aware. Hop up."

I jumped, barely clearing the edge and landing on the cool countertop. I squeaked, reminding myself he'd just wiped the countertops down so it was clean.

Derek stepped out of his jeans and set a condom on the counter next to me, then he kneeled in front of me.

"Derek."

He looked up at me and reached for one of my boots. He smiled, his eyes heavily lidded. His gaze trailed up my legs and settled between my thighs.

"Not today, but one day. When we aren't rushing back to

work." He dropped my boots to the floor, then pushed my panties and jeans off with them.

I was on his countertop in his kitchen in my bra only, both cups pushed to the side and my nipples on display.

And I couldn't have cared less.

I needed him.

He rolled the condom down his length and dropped to his knees again. Before I could say anything, he yanked me forward, bringing my core to his mouth.

"Derek," I moaned as he licked me.

His tongue spun around my clit and flicked it once before he rose to his feet. "I couldn't wait another day to find out how good you taste." He leaned into me and kissed me hard. "Delicious."

I groaned, finding my taste on his lips an aphrodisiac I never knew existed.

His fingers teased the sensitive flesh between my legs, pulsing and plunging and plucking at me until my hips got into motion. I fucked his hand, shamelessly riding it until my orgasm started.

"Derek," I whispered.

"Come, beautiful. Let me feel you."

He slammed into me when he told me to come, and my orgasm burst inside me, a kaleidoscope of rainbows the only thing I could see. He grunted, slamming into me, pulling me to him as he chased his own release.

"Oh, fuck," I whimpered, another orgasm sneaking up on me as Derek hit a new spot.

"Yes, Chelsea. Come with me. Fuck, Chelsea."

My body responded to his demands and squeezed him, triggering a release for both of us.

He grunted and stilled, the pulsing of his orgasm

blending with my aftershocks and sending shivers through me.

He kissed my neck, his face buried there. His breath was hot on my skin, but I didn't want him to move. I wanted to stay there the rest of the day and pretend the world outside didn't exist.

A faint chime reached my ears. My alarm. The first one of two.

"Is that your phone?" he asked, his lips still against my skin.

I nodded. "So I didn't lose track of time and end up late."

"Smart. I didn't think of that."

"I'm always late unless I have alarms. I have another one in five minutes."

"Another one?"

"That's my leave now or else alarm."

He chuckled. "It's good to know yourself."

I nodded. "But it's not good to leave right now. I never understood the appeal of skipping out on work until now."

Derek kissed me again, working his way from my jaw to my lips. His kiss was sweet and sexy and seriously tempting. "I don't want to go either. I think we should make this a regular thing. And find a way to see each other more. If you're up for it."

I nodded. "I would like that."

He smiled. "Me, too."

17

DEREK

I COULD NOT STOP SMILING THE REST OF THE DAY AFTER LUNCH with Chelsea. Or the next day. Ricky gave me shit about it, but he didn't say anything to anyone else.

I knew I wasn't going to be so lucky when I went to guys' night. Sebastian studied me and shook his head at me when I dropped Jude off to play with Cameron for a few hours. Zoey just told me to be good to Chelsea.

"Am I not?" I asked, wondering if there was a reason for her comment.

"I didn't say that, but she doesn't seem... experienced with relationships."

I shook my head. "She's not. We talked. It was good."

Zoey raised an eyebrow. "Talked?"

I chuckled. "Yeah, talked."

"Okay, time to go," Sebastian said, shoving me toward the door and stepping between his wife and me.

He kissed her fully on the mouth and whispered something I was too far away to hear. He turned to me with a smirk of his own and followed me outside.

"You're lucky," I told him.

Sebastian nodded. "Hell, yeah."

I shook my head at him and drove toward O'Kelley's. I was determined to make it through an entire evening without rushing off to see Chelsea. I needed to. It wasn't fair to Zoey or Sebastian for me to use them as free babysitters so I could get laid.

It was like Chelsea said about her cousin's friends. I wanted to have people who were there for me because they wanted to be, but the other side of that was I didn't want to abuse that relationship.

Especially for sex.

Even the best sex of my life.

"So things are going well?" Sebastian asked when I parked.

"Yeah, they are."

"So Chelsea asked you about your ex-wife?"

"How the fuck did you know that?"

Sebastian snorted. "They all talk."

I scrambled out of my truck and met him on the sidewalk. "Does everyone know everything in this town?"

"Yeah. Pretty much. You've been here long enough you should know that. It's how we all knew you were single this whole time. Nothing's secret around here."

"It didn't use to be this bad."

Sebastian clapped me on the back. "It means people care. About both of you. They want you to be happy, and they like you together."

"How do you know that?"

"Because if they didn't want you together, you wouldn't be." He left me with that comment and walked into O'Kelley's.

I followed him, wondering if he was right. I took a seat next to Sebastian at the bar, shell-shocked.

"You broke him," Hudson said. "What did you tell him?"

"The truth. That if people didn't want him and Chelsea together, they wouldn't be."

James smacked Sebastian's shoulder.

Sebastian turned and glared at James, his fists balling. "I don't care if you're a cop, I'll kick your ass."

James smirked. "Bring it, lighthouse boy."

Sebastian rolled his eyes and chuckled.

"Knock it off," Hudson scolded James. "Tell Derek he still has control of his life."

"No can do," James said. "That's why no one knew Trinity and I were together for a long time. I didn't want any of you fuckers messing it up."

"Oh, please. You were just happy she was giving you the time of day and afraid she'd tell you to shove it if it became public knowledge," Ian said with a laugh.

"Isn't that what you did with Blake?" James countered.

"Fuck yeah, it is. She was ashamed of me. Thought I was an asshole," Ian admitted.

"It all worked out," Hudson said. "For all of us. Because it was right. Derek, ignore these fuckers."

"I don't think I can. Why does anyone else care who I'm dating?" I asked.

"It's not that they care who you're dating, it's that they care if you're dating the wrong person," Trent said. "I fucked up with Finley more than the rest of these guys did with their women. Hudson was there to set me straight, more than once. I hated him for it, but he was right because I wasn't the man she deserved. Once I pulled my head out of my ass and admitted that I wanted her in my life, Hudson didn't back off. None of them did. Because a change of heart so I could get in her pants wasn't good enough. That wasn't all it was, but they didn't know me. They were protecting her."

"Is that what this is? Protecting Chelsea?" I asked.

"Partly," Knox said. "I offered to kick your ass the other day."

"Seriously? I thought we were friends." What the fuck?

"I was only partly serious. Trying to gauge how pissed she was," Knox said.

"And?"

"She declined my offer. I took that as a good sign that she wanted things to be okay with you."

"When was this?"

"When I installed her new backdoor."

My brows went up. I spoke to her after that. She said she was inside because of the cold, and she worked the few days after that. Was that just an excuse because she didn't want to see me? "Okay, so why is everyone protecting her? I thought after last week we were all good."

"She's worried about your ex," Patrick said.

"I know. She asked me about her. I told her there's nothing for her to worry about."

The silence that met my answer didn't feel like it was comfortable. It was loaded with tension and things no one wanted to say.

I looked at Knox. I thought, hoped, he would tell me the truth. "What am I missing?"

Knox sighed and shook his head, glaring at the others. "You all suck." He focused on me. "The women put it in her head that you're not over your ex. Even if you talked to her, I'm not sure it's enough. This is likely an uphill battle for you. Something you're going to have to reassure her about more than once. Since you're not willing to go public with her, dates out and being seen with her, asking her to park at her own house, she thinks you're ashamed of her."

"I'm not!" I protested.

"Good, but she's going to need to hear that. A lot," Knox said.

"A lot," Rowan said. "Trust me."

"I can't see her all the time because I have Jude."

"Being a single parent isn't easy," Hudson said. "I didn't do it, but I saw Anna. It was hard. I know it's hard. But if Chelsea matters to you, she needs to know you want to be with her when you can't. Mornings when you're getting Jude ready for school. Afternoons when you're at work. Late at night when Jude is sleeping. Not just the dirty stuff. Unless that's all this is for you."

"It's not," I growled.

"Then make sure she knows. Because otherwise you'll never have to worry about Jude finding out because this will be over before you have a chance to tell him about it," Hudson said.

STONECOLDDAD

It was really hard to stay at guys' night tonight and not leave early so I could see you.

CUTHAIRDONTCARE

I had a date with my couch and a glass of wine tonight.

STONECOLDDAD

Just a glass?

CUTHAIRDONTCARE

Yeah, more than one and it feels pathetic.

STONECOLDDAD

You could never be pathetic.

CUTHAIRDONTCARE

Thanks. There are times.

STONECOLDDAD

I know asking this is a risk, but are we okay?

CUTHAIRDONTCARE

Why is it a risk to ask that?

STONECOLDDAD

Because if we're not, I should know. A part of me feels like we're good, but I missed a lot of signs with my ex. I don't want to make the same mistake with you.

CUTHAIRDONTCARE

We're okay.

STONECOLDDAD

Okay doesn't give me a great feeling. Is there something I can do to get an upgrade? 😊

CUTHAIRDONTCARE

What signs did you miss?

I sighed. I opened the door, but I didn't like talking about Sasha. Ever. She was a part of my past. A part that made me feel like I failed.

STONECOLDDAD

I was so in love with her that I didn't see how she changed when Jude was born. Even before that if I'm honest. She was stunning when we met. Full of life. Bright and happy and magnetic. No one could resist her. Wanting to be around her and wanting to have her attention.

CUTHAIRDONTCARE

Including you.

STONECOLDDAD

Yeah. I fell hard for her. Just like so many others. But she wanted me. She chose me.

CUTHAIRDONTCARE

You were the lucky one.

STONECOLDDAD

It felt that way. And when she said she wanted to try for kids, it felt like everything I'd ever wanted was happening. Before that, she always said no. I was getting everything I wanted.

CUTHAIRDONTCARE

You said it didn't go well.

STONECOLDDAD

Hindsight is a bitch. At the time, I was so happy that I missed everything. The way she held her breath when they would check for the heartbeat. The way she cried at the ultrasounds. I saw it all as joy, but it was fear. It was hope that she'd miscarried dying when she saw the baby.

CUTHAIRDONTCARE

That's horrible. Why would someone try to get pregnant then wish for their child to not survive?

STONECOLDDAD

Her best friend had a hard time getting pregnant. Took years. She had three miscarriages before she carried a baby to term. I think Sasha expected her pregnancy to be the same. Maybe she wasn't hoping for a miscarriage, but I think she was pregnant before she realized she didn't want a baby.

CUTHAIRDONTCARE

Wow.

STONECOLDDAD

I haven't wanted to get involved with anyone since. Jude already lost one mother who didn't want him. I can't bring someone else into his life who will walk away.

CUTHAIRDONTCARE

I understand.

STONECOLDDAD

I'm not keeping you from him because of you. It's all about him.

CUTHAIRDONTCARE

And you.

STONECOLDDAD

Me? No. I am an adult. I know relationships end. Jude shouldn't have had to learn that lesson so young.

CUTHAIRDONTCARE

I get it, but you can't tell me there's not a part of you that worries about it. I do, and I'm not divorced.

STONECOLDDAD

What are you worried about?

CUTHAIRDONTCARE

When this ends. When you decide you're no longer interested. Having to see you every day and pretend I'm okay. Jude coming over to see Dozer and dying inside because I wish things could be different.

STONECOLDDAD

What if it works out? What if that never happens?

CUTHAIRDONTCARE

I've never had that happen, so I don't know.

STONECOLDDAD

Can we agree not to plan for this to end? That we're going to get to know each other and spend time together and enjoy whatever this is and go from there?

CUTHAIRDONTCARE

I can try.

STONECOLDDAD

I've never had it work out either. But I'm not ready to give up on us just yet.

CUTHAIRDONTCARE

Yet?

STONECOLDDAD

I'm going for honesty here.

CUTHAIRDONTCARE

I hear it's the best policy.

STONECOLDDAD

I hear that, too.

CUTHAIRDONTCARE

I should get some sleep. I have to work in the morning. But hopefully I'll see you soon.

STONECOLDDAD

I hope so, too. Good night.

CUTHAIRDONTCARE

Good night.

I smiled at my phone. The guys were wrong. Things were good with Chelsea. And they were going to stay that way.

I was disappointed to not run in to Chelsea before work the next day. I was hoping she would be around when I got home, but her car was still gone. Long day.

I let myself into the house and found Mrs. Walsh and Jude in front of the TV.

"What are we watching?" I asked.

"I'm so sorry, Derek. I was tired today and agreed to a little more TV than usual," Mrs. Walsh said.

I shook my head. "It's not a problem. We watch a lot of TV. There are some pretty good shows."

"I just feel bad for not playing a game or something with Jude."

"Winter is long, Mrs. Walsh. I imagine there will be a lot of TV watching. Usually that's what we do."

"Well, I'll see if I can find some other options, too." She pushed to her feet, looking slower than usual.

"Are you feeling okay?"

"I'm definitely getting tired. The shorter days take it out of me. But being here is good for me."

"Are you sure?"

"Absolutely. I do have an appointment next Tuesday, though. I tried to move it, but the next time they could get me in is in three months."

Shit. Tuesday was when I was supposed to meet with a new vendor for tires. The company was a start-up in Massachusetts and wanted to see if we would stock their tires. "I'll try to move some things around so I can be home."

Mrs. Walsh was far too astute and saw my hesitation. "I can take the appointment in a few months."

"No. Absolutely not. If you have something you have to

do, we are not going to stand in your way. On top of that, three months puts you in the middle of winter and there's no way of knowing if you'll luck out with a good weather day."

"I did have that thought, too."

"We'll figure it out," I assured her.

"You could ask a friend, or a neighbor, if they could help out." Mrs. Walsh nodded her head toward next door and raised her eyebrows.

I glanced at Jude, who was engrossed in the show he was watching. "She's working today. She has a lot of late days."

Mrs. Walsh shrugged. "Yes, but she's home a lot of afternoons, too. She adores Jude, and if she's around, it might be an easy solution for you."

I nodded, trying to come up with a reason I didn't want to ask Chelsea. There wasn't one. I still held back, though. Why?

"Maybe a friend, then?" Mrs. Walsh suggested, as if she knew I was hesitating when it came to asking Chelsea.

"I'll figure something out," I told her.

She smiled and patted my arm. She didn't miss a thing. "I should head home."

"You are welcome to stay for dinner," I told her. "You're always welcome."

"Thank you, and I know. But I have a delicious dinner waiting for me. Chelsea brought it over yesterday. She made more than I could eat one night, so I get to have it again. Lasagna. I'm a big fan."

"That was nice of her." There was a lot I didn't know about the woman I was seeing. A lot she didn't share. A lot I wanted to know.

"She's a wonderful person," Mrs. Walsh said, shrugging into her coat.

"Jude, Mrs. Walsh is leaving."

Jude jumped up from the couch and came over to us. He hugged Mrs. Walsh and thanked her for being there when he got home.

She grinned and hugged him back. "It was my pleasure, Jude. I'll see you next week."

"Bye!" Jude said, returning to the couch.

Mrs. Walsh smiled. "He's a good boy. You've done an amazing job."

"Thank you," I said. The compliment was hard to take but appreciated. I put my coat on and told Jude I'd be right back, then followed Mrs. Walsh outside.

"Ooh, it's gotten so chilly. I'm not looking forward to the winter," she said.

"Have you thought about going south?"

She shook her head. "Oh, no. This is home. I love it here, even if the weather doesn't always love us back."

We stopped at the end of my driveway when we saw headlights coming toward us. A blinker flashed, telling us the driver was turning.

My heart kicked. Chelsea.

Mrs. Walsh waited until Chelsea pulled in, then turned around.

I wanted to hurry Mrs. Walsh home so I could have a minute with Chelsea, but that was rude.

"Good evening, Ms. Chelsea," Mrs. Walsh said.

"Good evening. Are you heading home?" Chelsea grabbed her handbag and joined us at the edge of the drive-way. She glanced my way and smiled.

"I am. I have your delicious lasagna to warm me right up." Mrs. Walsh rubbed her hands together.

Chelsea's face lit up at the compliment. "Oh, good. I was hoping you would enjoy it."

"Oh, so good. You gave me way too much, as usual."

"It's hard to cook a small amount of lasagna. I froze half of it as it was."

"Well, I am appreciative of the meal. It's not easy to cook for one."

Chelsea laughed. "I agree. I'm happy I can share with you."

"I'm always willing to eat."

Chelsea and Mrs. Walsh laughed at the joke, as if there was more to it than I knew. I cleared my throat, not intending to break up their conversation, but it had that effect.

"I should get home and let you two get out of this cold. Tomorrow?" Mrs. Walsh asked Chelsea.

"I'll see you at ten."

Mrs. Walsh nodded, then started across the street. Chelsea made a move toward her house, and I asked her if she had a minute. If I could knock on her door. She agreed.

"So you're going to ask her?" Mrs. Walsh asked.

"I know you're not as oblivious as you want people to think."

"You two are good together. I will not interfere, ever, but I want you to know I think she's good for both of you."

I smiled, trying not to let that sink in. I wasn't ready for Chelsea and Jude to get too close. As our neighbor and Dozer's owner, sure. But as the woman I was seeing? We weren't there.

Mrs. Walsh seemed to sense my thoughts and said, "Don't *what if* things to death. Everyone deserves a shot at happiness."

"Thank you, Mrs. Walsh."

"Have a good night, Derek."

"You do the same."

I waited until her door locked before I jogged down her

driveway. Chelsea met me on her driveway when I made it across the street. Her arms were crossed and her hands buried in the fabric of her coat.

"I didn't mean for you to wait outside for me," I told her.

"It's easier if I go inside once. Dozer likes to come outside if I go out again. The door in the back has helped, but when I get home, he wants to go out."

"I won't keep you then."

"You asked if I had a minute. I didn't want to delay whatever it was you wanted to say."

"Mrs. Walsh has an appointment on Tuesday. She can't get Jude. I know it's a lot to ask, and you can say no, but—"

"Yes," she blurted. "I can get him off the bus, if that's what you're asking."

"Are you sure? I wouldn't ask, but I have a meeting and can't get here that early. I don't know your schedule. I don't want to throw things off for you."

"I'm off Tuesday. It's not a problem at all." She exhaled a shaky breath.

"Are you okay?"

She nodded and chewed her lip. "I thought you wanted to talk to tell me you were done. That this was over."

"Shit. I'm sorry. I... It never occurred to me that's what you would think. I'm really sorry, Chelsea."

She smiled at me. "It's okay. I... It's fine."

I glanced around and didn't see anyone out. No curtains moved. Houses were lit from the inside and quiet from the outside. I stepped closer to her, cupping her jaw with my cold hands.

The lights from our houses illuminated the shimmer of tears in her eyes. "I'm not done with you yet. Not anywhere close. I'm sorry I made you doubt this."

She forced another smile and relaxed. Her breath shuddered out of her.

I dipped my head slowly, giving her plenty of time to pull back. She didn't, and I closed the gap between us, getting a taste of her cold lips.

She sighed into me, circling her arms around my waist.

I pulled her in tighter and delved into her mouth. I couldn't get lost in her like I wanted to, but I hardened anyway. I inhaled deep, carrying her scent into me.

I pulled away with a groan. "One day I won't have to leave you on the driveway and walk away."

She smiled again. "Just not today."

I shook my head and stepped back, letting my hands fall from her face. "One day. Thank you for helping me out on Tuesday. It means a lot."

"I'm happy to."

I glanced at my house, knowing I'd been gone longer than usual and Jude would be looking for dinner soon. "I should go. Talk later?"

She nodded. "I'll be here."

"Good night, Chelsea."

"Good night, Derek."

18

CHELSEA

IT DIDN'T MATTER HOW MANY TIMES I CHECKED THE TIME Jude's bus would be there, I was still worried I was going to miss him. Derek said Jude could come to my house, so I was outside on the driveway. Waiting.

Dozer sat next to me, whimpering every so often. He didn't understand what we were doing.

The bus came around the corner and ambled down the street. It stopped a few times to let other kids off, then stopped in front of Derek's house.

Jude jumped off the bus and ran right over to Dozer, who jumped up to greet his buddy.

"Hi, Dozer! How are you?"

Dozer barked his greeting as the bus pulled away. Dozer tugged at his leash to get closer to Jude.

"How about we go inside and you guys can visit?" I suggested.

Jude nodded, standing and rubbing Dozer's back on his way to the door. Jude waited for me to open the door, even though it was already unlocked, then stopped to take off his shoes. I toed my boots off and unclipped Dozer's leash so he and Jude could greet each other properly.

Jude threw his arms around Dozer's neck and whispered, "I've missed you."

My heart melted at the profession meant only for Dozer's ears.

Dozer seemed to hug Jude back, resting his head against Jude's shoulder for their hug.

"Can I take him outside, Ms. Chelsea?"

"How about a snack first? Are you hungry?"

"Yeah. Do you have any cookies?"

I grinned. "Always, Jude. We always have cookies. How about an apple with your cookies?"

"I like apples."

I nodded, following the boys to the kitchen. Jude took a seat at the table, and I set the plate of freshly baked cookies in front of him. He grabbed one and took a bite.

"Oh, man, that's good. It's warm, too."

"I just made them. I made some for Dozer, too."

"He can have this?" Jude asked, holding the chocolate chip cookie above Dozer's nose.

"Not that one," I said quickly, before Jude handed it over. "They're treats that are safe for dogs. Do you want to give him one?" I picked up the tray of cookies for Dozer and held it out to Jude.

"Yeah! That's so cool. Can I ask him to do the tricks I taught him?"

"Of course. We've been practicing so he wouldn't forget."

"He's smart. He'll remember," Jude said with confidence. He stood in front of Dozer and straightened his shoulders. "Dozer, sit."

Dozer dropped his butt to the floor.

"Good. Now, down."

Dozer flopped, sprawling on the floor.

Jude grinned. "Awesome. Roll over."

Dozer kicked his feet and rolled over.

"Good boy. Dozer, shake!"

Dozer jumped up and shook his whole body with Jude, wiggling their butts and shaking.

Jude collapsed into a puddle and held the cookie up to Dozer.

Dozer snatched it, knowing it was one of his and not one of Jude's. He sat down and ate the cookie with Jude on the floor with him.

"You're such a good boy," Jude said.

I smiled at the two of them. After the talk Derek and I had last week, I was feeling both better and worse about what was going on between us. I understood his hesitation after his marriage. But I also knew if a person didn't open themselves up to good things, they never came.

I struggled with the idea of having a future with anyone, but I wanted it. My struggles came from the way I'd been treated and the less than spectacular relationships I'd had.

Derek was different. He wasn't one of the men who saw me and said no. He still wanted me. But I wasn't hoping for a future just because he was there. That wasn't fair to either of us. No, I liked him. I liked Jude. I liked being able to talk to Derek, and the sex was better than any I'd ever had.

But we were a long way from dating to forever. I meant it when I told him I was already waiting for the day he'd walk away. The day I'd have to look him in the eye and pretend I wasn't broken inside.

I was going to hate that day.

"Can Dozer and I go outside?" Jude asked, bringing my attention back to the moment.

"Sure. But not for too long. It's pretty cold today."

"Thirty minutes?"

"I think I can agree to that. Then homework?"

"And then maybe we can go out again?"

I smiled. "You're a good negotiator."

"My dad says the same thing."

I laughed. "It's a good skill to have."

"I think so, too." Jude went to the front and put on his jacket and sneakers. He walked through the house with Dozer on his heels, opening the door to the backyard. I heard him tell Dozer he had a cool door to use before the door closed between us.

I kept an eye on them as I cleaned up the kitchen, checking every few minutes that they were okay. I went outside for a few minutes, but unless I ran around with the boys, it was too cold for me to sit out.

"Fifteen more minutes," I told Jude.

"Okay!" Jude called back.

"I'm going in. It's too cold for me."

Jude laughed. "Okay, Ms. Chelsea."

I closed the door and watched them for another minute before going back to the kitchen. I busied myself getting things ready to make dinner and was about to start when the boys burst inside.

"Did you have fun?"

"Yeah, it was awesome."

Dozer ran to the cabinet where I kept his treats.

"Do you want to give Dozer a treat?"

"Another cookie?"

"Not just yet. How about two of the treats in the cabinet?"

"Okay." Jude grabbed the treats I pointed to and tossed two to Dozer, who caught them in the air.

"What homework do you have today?" I asked Jude, a subtle reminder he agreed to do it when they came in.

"Math, science, and reading."

"That doesn't sound too bad."

He shrugged and traded his jacket and sneakers for his backpack. "Can I sit on your couch?"

"Of course. You can use the coffee table if you want. Or you can sit here. Whatever is easier for you."

"Thanks, Ms. Chelsea."

"You're welcome."

I assembled the casserole I was making for dinner and slid it into the oven. Then I started on the chicken soup. I liked to cook a few meals at a time on the days I had off since when I was working, the last thing I wanted to do when I got home was cook.

"That smells really good," Jude said, walking into the kitchen an hour later.

"Thank you. I have chicken, broccoli, and rice in the oven, and this is chicken soup."

"My dad's chicken never smells like this."

I laughed. "It's all about the spices. Do you want to taste the soup?"

"Can I?"

"Sure. It's just broth, vegetables, and spices. It needs another hour or two before it's done, but the chicken is cooked, so it's safe to eat. The vegetables take a while."

I took a ladle and scooped a bit into a small bowl. I handed him a spoon and set the bowl on the table so he didn't burn his hands trying to hold on to it.

"Make sure you blow on that. It's hot."

Jude nodded and got a spoonful, blowing on it before he tasted the broth. "Wow. That's so good."

"Thank you."

"Can I have this for dinner tonight?"

"Sure. It should be done before your dad gets here."

"Thanks, Ms. Chelsea." Dozer sat next to Jude while he finished the small bowl of soup. When he was done, he asked if they could go back outside.

"Sure, but I think this is going to be the last time for today. It's getting dark and I don't want you two getting too cold."

"Okay. Can we stay outside for forty-five minutes, then?"

I raised an eyebrow at the negotiator and nodded. "Sure. But not a minute more."

"Thanks, Ms. Chelsea!" Jude called. He took off to the front for his shoes and jacket again, Dozer on his heels. Jude talked to Dozer the entire time, telling him they were going to play a little longer.

Dozer followed along, barking happily at the excitement in Jude's voice.

I stirred the soup and checked the casserole. The casserole was almost done, so I put the broiler on so the top would get crispy. It wasn't long before I was able to pull that out of the oven to cool.

I sat at the table and looked through the books for Serenity Salon for the last month, double checking that everything was paid as expected and that all charges came through. Haley and I were meeting in the morning to talk about the shop and the projects we wanted to tackle through the winter months when things were a little slower.

It still made me smile when I thought about the salon. It was ours. Mine and Haley's. We could do whatever we wanted to with it. Which meant ideas were always coming up. It was fun to dream, even if some of those dreams weren't going to happen anytime soon.

Like expanding the shop and adding two more chairs.

Haley and I talked about it and both agreed it would be nice to do, but it wasn't something we had the financial backing to make happen. Maybe one day. If the building next door ever went up for sale.

Until then, we were looking at maintaining the space we had, updating what we could, and helping our friends and neighbors look and feel their best.

I stirred the soup again, stabbing the vegetables to test how close they were to done. Pretty close, so I started the water for egg noodles to go into the soup. It was how my mom always served it when I was a kid, and my favorite noodle in chicken soup.

When the noodles were done, I strained them and added a drizzle of olive oil to make sure they didn't stick to each other. I tossed the oil through the pasta and put the strainer back in the pan to keep the noodles warm.

Jude and Dozer came in a few minutes later. The smiles on their faces said the cold didn't bother them at all.

"Does he get another treat?" Jude asked me.

"He does. Did he use the bathroom?"

"Yeah, he peed. Is that okay?" Jude looked at me like he worried he did something wrong.

"Yep, that's perfect. Thank you, Jude."

"Okay, good. So, two treats?"

"Yep. Thank you."

"You're welcome." Jude gaze Dozer his treats, then took off his jacket and sneakers. He rubbed his hands together and came back to the kitchen. "Can I have some soup now?"

"You can. It's ready to eat. Do you like noodles?"

"Oh, yeah."

I held a bowl while Jude got his soup and added noodles to the top. I put it on the table and poured him some water, then got my food and joined him.

"How did your homework go?"

Jude shrugged.

"Does that mean you didn't finish?"

"I did, just I don't think I did some of it right."

"I can help you if you need it."

"You can?" he asked.

I nodded. "I might not know everything you're learning, but I can try to figure out what you're supposed to do. Want me to look when we're done eating?"

"Yeah. Thanks, Ms. Chelsea."

A knock on the door had me checking the clock. Earlier than I expected for Derek, but I couldn't think of anyone else who might be there.

"I'll be right back," I told Jude. "Dozer, stay."

Dozer moved in front of Jude to protect him from whoever was at the door.

I opened it when I saw Derek's truck in his driveway. "Hey," I said.

His gaze slid down my body, taking in my yoga pants and oversized sweater. It was warm and comfortable, although not my most attractive article of clothing. "Hi."

"Um, come on in. Jude's eating some chicken soup. I hope that's okay."

Derek followed me inside as I kept talking.

"I baked cookies earlier, and he played outside with Dozer. I think he was cold, and I already planned to make the soup. He said it smelled good, but I should have asked you if it was okay."

"It's fine, Chelsea. Thank you. For feeding him and getting him off the bus today. Really, it means a lot."

I smiled, relieved he wasn't mad.

"Hey, Jude," Derek said, catching sight of his son at my table.

"Hi, Dad." Jude got up and hugged Derek, Dozer on his heels the whole time. Jude went back to the table and dove back into his soup. "You should have some soup, Dad. It's really good."

"I'm sure Ms. Chelsea doesn't want to feed both of us."

"I don't mind," I told him. "But if you need to go, I understand."

He held my gaze for a long moment. A moment I was sure would end with him leaving. To my surprise, he shrugged out of his coat and joined Jude at the table. "Let me try a bite of that."

Jude covered his bowl so Derek couldn't get to it.

"Hey!"

"It's mine. You can get your own," Jude said with a laugh.

"I already have some here for you," I told Derek. "There's plenty more. I eat it for a few days, then freeze the rest so I have it for a little while."

"That's a really good idea," Derek said. He took a bite and groaned. "Wow, this is good."

"That's what I said. I told Ms. Chelsea your chicken never smells this good."

Derek paused with his spoon halfway to his mouth. "Hey!"

Jude shrugged. "It's true."

Derek chuckled and shook his head. "Kids won't hold back."

"That's one of the good things about them."

"True."

"How was work?" I asked him.

He paused, like he was surprised by the question.

"You said you had a meeting. Did it go well? Am I overstepping by asking?"

Derek shook his head slowly. "No. No, you can ask.

Sorry. I'm just not used to being asked." He glanced at Jude. "I can't remember the last time I was asked how my day was."

"I ask you," Jude argued.

Derek smiled at his son, and I saw the incredible resemblance between them. Usually I thought Jude probably looked like his mother, but when they both smiled, he was all Derek. Same cheeks, same narrow eyes, same smile. Jude's brown skin was a few shades lighter than Derek's, but their hair was the same color. Eyes, too.

And now that I knew them both, I could say they were both kind, sweet men who would make someone very lucky one day.

"You do ask me, Jude. You're right. And thank you. My day was good. My meeting was a success. A new tire manufacturer wants to stock some of their tires with us, and it looks like a good product, so I agreed to a limited supply for now with the potential for more. And I decided to hire an office manager to help out. I posted the job online today."

"That's a lot for one day," I said.

Derek nodded. "It is. You know how busy it is when you own the business. A lot of decisions rest of you alone."

"Well, Haley is my partner. We make all our decisions together."

"That could be tough. What if you don't agree?"

"We talk things through. I'm more of an idea person. I have a hundred ideas for things to do to the shop at any time. It's a huge benefit when a client wants a cut but doesn't know what they want, but when it's the business, it can be more of a challenge. Haley is more rational and practical. She says she was always an emotional person who led with her heart, but she has learned to slow down and make choices from a more rational perspective."

"I can see how it's valuable to have both sides."

I nodded. "It works well for us. We are good together."

"You're lucky to have someone like that in your life."

"Yes, I am."

Derek and I stared at each other for a long moment. Long enough that I got lost in his eyes and forgot we weren't alone.

Dozer made a noise, startling Derek and me. Derek wiped his mouth on his napkin and finished his soup in record time. I tried not to be hurt when he ushered Jude out the door.

I busied myself cleaning up the kitchen and putting away the food I cooked so I'd have dinner for a few days.

An hour later, I got a message from Derek.

STONECOLDDAD

Come over. Please. Jude's in bed. Front door is open. Sorry I ran out. If I stayed another minute, I wouldn't have been able to hold back from kissing you.

I want to see you. I know I'm asking a lot. Again. If you don't come over, I understand. But I hope you do.

He was a fool if he thought I could resist him.

CUTHAIRDONTCARE

On my way.

19

——————

WALKING INTO ANOTHER PERSON'S HOUSE WAS REALLY uncomfortable. Especially sneaking in.

The door was unlocked like Derek said, but I still felt weird. I'd only been inside one other time. I closed the door behind me, turning the knob to make as little noise as possible.

"He's a pretty good sleeper," Derek said, startling me with how close he was.

"I didn't know you were right there," I hissed.

He chuckled. "You don't have to be a ninja."

"I don't know. It's not like I've been here when he was sleeping before." I toed off my sneakers and hung my coat on an empty hook near the door.

"I know. And I'm an asshole for asking you to come over when it's late and it's cold and I'm being a selfish dick and want to see you." The look on his face told me how he felt. How wrong he thought it was that he was making me go to him.

"I wanted to see you, too," I admitted.

"That makes me feel better." He reached for me, winding his fingers through mine. "Come here."

His voice was raspy, needy. I didn't hesitate to obey it. I wanted to be close to him. To be in his arms and to feel him against me. Sex was out of the question with Jude right upstairs, but I wasn't going to turn down a few kisses. And whatever else Derek had in mind.

He kissed me gently, his lips lingering against mine without pushing for more. He wound our arms behind my back, anchoring me to him. He thickened between us, pressing his erection into my stomach and guiding me toward the couch.

We sat next to each other, and I immediately felt the loss of him. He held my hand and reached with his other hand to turn on the TV. "In case Jude wakes up. I don't want him to hear us talking, or anything else."

"Does he wake up often?"

Derek shook his head. "No. If he can get to sleep, he's usually out for the night. He usually only has trouble when he can't get to sleep."

"Like when I moved in."

Derek nodded, drawing his lip between his teeth.

"I don't want to cause problems for you and Jude next summer, but I also want to be able to use my backyard."

"I know. And I've been thinking about that. I was wrong to get upset with you for something that every other person on this street can do without any issues. I've been looking at options. I'm definitely going to replace the windows in the entire house because they're horrible."

I pulled my hand from his and rubbed both up and down my arms, nodding. "It is kind of chilly in here."

"I know. It has been since we moved in, but I didn't have

the money to do anything about it. Kids are expensive, and buying a business is almost as expensive."

I laughed with him, softly. "I guess that's good to know if I ever have kids."

"Do you want kids?" His tone was curious.

I nodded. "Yeah. I'm getting close to an age where it won't be a realistic option to have biological ones, but I know there are a lot of kids who need someone to be there for them."

"Have you considered adoption?"

"It's really tough as a single person, and there are a lot of families looking to adopt. I'm more likely to foster, but with my work schedule, that's not a great option."

"I know what you mean." Derek rested his arm on the back of the couch. His fingers brushed my hair, teasing the strands. "I know raising Jude would have been easier if I wasn't doing it alone. Sasha wasn't the right person for us, and I know her leaving was a blessing in many ways. At the time, I was angry and hurt, but looking back on it, I know it would have ended the same way. She would have left, but if she tried to stick around longer, we would have hated each other."

"You don't hate her?"

He shook his head slowly. "I could never hate her. I don't love her the same way, but she gave me Jude. He's the most important person, and no matter what I think about her, I'll always be grateful that I have him."

"He's lucky to have you."

"I'm lucky to have him, too." He leaned over and kissed me quickly. "And you."

I smiled. "I feel the same."

He held my gaze for a long moment, his eyes never

straying from mine. "This is why I always asked you to lunch. It's killing me to sit here with you and not lead you up to my bedroom and make you come."

I shivered with a moan, wishing for the same. "Maybe we should schedule another lunch date soon."

He shook his head. "Well, yes, but I want to take you on a real date, too. With fancy food and nice table settings where I pick you up and drive you to dinner, then bring you home and lay you out on my bed. Where your scent lingers for days on my sheets and I get hard every time I lie down."

"One day," I said, knowing it wouldn't be anytime soon. I wasn't mad about it. Not anymore. I wasn't happy, but I wasn't mad. He kept showing up. He didn't disappear. He was proving to me what we had was real.

"Soon," he said. "I'll ask Sebastian and Zoey if they can take Jude for a sleepover sometime."

"I don't want you to feel like I'm pushing you to do that."

"No. You're perfect. You're amazing. And I want you so bad I'm barely keeping myself from risking it all and dragging you up the stairs, anyway."

I shook my head. "No, we can't take that risk. I want you, too, but I understand why you're protecting Jude. He's a great kid. Smart, too. He won't be fooled forever."

"No, he won't be." Derek groaned. "Come here. At least let me feel you."

He urged me on top of him, pulling one leg to his opposite side so I straddled his hips. I lowered onto him, jumping at the thick ridge I landed on.

"I told you I wanted you."

I lowered myself down again, settling onto his erection and moaning softly at the contact.

"Even through our clothes, you feel good."

"So do you," I whispered. My hips moved, rocking over his erection and sparking bolts of pleasure through my entire body.

His hand went up my back and into my hair, tugging me down to kiss him. One hand gripped my thigh and guided my hips to a faster rhythm, his hips meeting mine with each stroke. "Fuck, Chelsea."

"I might... I might come," I whispered against his lips.

"Yes. Don't hold back. Please."

I rocked against him, the sensations washing over me. Muted and almost out of reach. I wanted to slide my hand down and rub my clit, but I wasn't ready to do that in front of him yet.

He moved his hand from my thigh to my core, pulling my yoga pants away from my body so he could slide his hand between us.

My stroke faltered, the feel of his fingers enough to send me to a different place. A better place.

"Oh, shit," I breathed.

"Good?"

"So good."

He rubbed my clit awkwardly, his hand at a weird angle but neither of us caring. He brought my lips to his again and rubbed faster, faster, until I was coming with a gasp and a whimper that had me wishing for more.

"I love watching you come," he whispered a minute later.

"That was so damn good."

"More?" His hand was still trapped between us.

I went to move when I heard a noise from somewhere else in the house. A noise that reminded me we weren't alone. It wasn't a lunch date, or a date at all. It was a secret interlude while his son slept upstairs.

It was hot, but it wasn't safe.

"I should go," I said regretfully.

We both dragged our gazes from the stairs, where the sound came from. Maybe we were wrong, but it was too risky.

"Yeah," he said, sounding as thrilled as I was. He eased his hand from my pants in the most awkward post-orgasmic encounter of my life, which was saying something, then licked his fingers in the hottest post-orgasmic encounter of my life.

Damn, the man knew how to keep me coming back for more.

"I can't wait to get that straight from you."

I shivered. Wow.

He smiled. "We're going to have that date soon. All night. No kids, no dogs, just the two of us and a bed."

"And dinner. You promised me dinner."

He laughed. "And dinner."

I climbed off his lap, hating that I was leaving him to take care of his own orgasm. "Um..."

"You do not owe me, Chelsea. Never have, never will. Like I said before, it won't take me long once I start replaying that memory."

My knees weakened at the lust-filled tone of his voice. A full night with him was going to be... Were there words? I was going to need to make up new ones.

"I'll see you soon," he promised. He walked me to the door. "I'm going to watch you until you get home. Unless you want me to walk you."

I shook my head. "I'll be good. Thank you, though."

"I feel like a jerk not walking you home."

"Nope. It's barely thirty feet. And you can see me the

whole time. Plus, I imagine you don't want to leave Jude home in case he needs something."

He sighed. "You're right."

"Thank you for tonight."

"A real date soon. I promise."

"Sounds good."

He kissed me one more time, lingering and sweeping his tongue through my mouth and making me regret not taking him up on the offer to sneak up to his room. When he pulled back, we were both breathing hard. The look in his eyes said he was thinking the same thing I was.

Which meant it was time to go. No good decisions ever came after orgasms and kisses that could only lead to orgasms.

"Have a good night," I said.

"I already did."

I smiled and waved, then stepped onto his porch. I hurried to my house, unlocking my door to get inside before the cold seeped through my coat. I turned back and waved, spotting Derek waving back, then went inside and locked the door.

"Hey, do you know Natalie Edwards?" I asked Haley on Monday morning.

Haley thought for a minute, then shook her head. "I don't think so. Should I?"

I shrugged. "She's in my book for today, but I don't know her. The name isn't familiar to me."

"Me either. I guess we'll see when she shows up. What time is she coming in?"

"She's my first appointment."

"Oh, I wonder if she's Daisy's friend. You know what? She probably is."

"Who's Daisy?"

"Daisy Lincoln. I told you about her. Knox made the display for her store last spring. Lincoln Toys?"

"Oh, yeah, I vaguely remember that. You think Natalie is a friend of hers?"

"Well, Daisy is my first appointment. Last time she was here, she said she was trying to talk her friend into coming. Said she doesn't stop working to take care of herself. Daisy said she was going to try to get her friend to come in with her because it might be easier."

"Is this like going to the bathroom together when you were in high school?"

Haley laughed. "Probably something like that."

"Have you met her friend?"

"Nope, but if she's a friend of Daisy's, she's cool with me."

"I guess we'll see."

We finished the rest of our morning routine and opened the doors fifteen minutes early so our customers didn't have to wait outside when they showed up. Two women walked in together, one blonde with a bright smile and the other brunette with a ponytail and a scowl.

It wasn't hard to guess which one was there by force.

"Daisy! Hi!" Haley gushed, hurrying to the blonde and pulling her into a warm hug. "How are you?"

"I'm good!" Daisy replied. "I'm so glad we were able to get in at the same time. This is Natalie, and you can see she's so excited to be here."

Haley turned to me before smiling at the brunette. "Nice to meet you, Natalie. Chelsea said you're on her schedule, and she is going to take excellent care of you.

She's a master, and she can make anything come to life. Trust her."

Natalie scowled at her friend, then flashed me a tentative smile. "My lack of desire to be here has nothing to do with you, and I assure you, it is not personal. I can't remember the last time I had a haircut. Period."

"She usually snips her split ends with kitchen scissors," Daisy provided.

I tried to contain my reaction, but my eyes widened and I gasped, and they all noticed. "I'm so sorry."

Daisy laughed. "That was my reaction when I saw her do it the first time! She needs help."

"I run a summer camp. No one cares what I look like," Natalie argued.

"The parents might only care if you are keeping their kids safe, but the people you ask for funding, and the mayor when you meet with him, might struggle to support your initiatives if you look homeless," Daisy countered.

Natalie's scowl deepened. "I don't look homeless."

Daisy raised a brow at her friend. "You don't not look homeless."

Natalie rolled her eyes. "I'm here. I agreed to this. Let's just get it done."

Ringing endorsement, but I wasn't there for the praise. I was there to make her feel like the best version of herself, even if she didn't know she wasn't already.

"Natalie, are you open to me washing your hair first?"

"Sure," she said with a dismissive shrug.

"Excellent." I led her to one shampoo station while Haley led Daisy to the one next to it. "You run a summer camp?"

Natalie's hazel eyes lit up for the first time as she leaned back toward the sink. "I do. It's my baby. I have a degree in elementary education, but I didn't love teaching. I still wanted to work with kids, and my favorite thing when I was a kid was summer camp."

"It sounds like it's a perfect thing for you." I shampooed her hair while she spoke.

She nodded. "I work at the community center during the school year, mostly in the afterschool program. I was there for a few years before Amelia pushed me to start my summer camp. They still have a good program, but they didn't have space for all the kids who needed a place to go."

"That's pretty cool. It makes sense there would be more kids who need a place over the summer. My neighbor's son was at the afterschool program earlier this year, but he's on the older side and begged to go home."

"That happens," Natalie said. "Usually those are the kids who need a spot in the summer. Going home after school and being alone for a few hours or having a friend or neighbor stay with them is easy. Being home alone all day while their parents work is a whole different thing."

"I imagine it is." I thought about the half day when I met Jude. "Do you have kids, Natalie?" I rinsed the last of the conditioner from her hair as she shook her head.

"No. I always wanted kids, but it helps if you have sex."

I snorted a laugh. "True." I pointed to my chair for her to have a seat. I dried her hair with the towel, then pulled it free to get a better look at her hair.

It was long, nearly to her waist. The ends were uneven and not overly healthy. I'd definitely seen worse, but with the right cut, she would look like a whole new woman.

"What are you thinking? Or do you not have any ideas what you want?"

She shrugged, avoiding my gaze in the mirror. She had a thought, but was afraid of it. I'd seen that look before.

"You can tell me. I'll be honest if I think it won't work for you."

"I know Daisy means well, but this is so far outside my comfort zone. I look at what others do, and I like it, but I need something I can pull out of my face. Something that can go into a ponytail when I'm playing basketball with the teens or when I'm painting with the little ones."

I fluffed her hair and studied the way it reacted. "It looks like you have a little curl to it, something that'll come out if I take some of the weight off of this. If you're willing to go shorter, you tell me how short."

She nibbled her lip, then dug her phone out of her pocket. She showed me a picture that was drastically different. Layers that framed the woman's face, curtain bangs brushed to the side, and lots of layers through her hair.

"Is this what you want?" I asked Natalie.

She shrugged and shoved her phone back into her pocket like she couldn't wait to hide it again. "I like it, but I don't know if I can pull it off."

"It would be stunning on you."

She met my gaze in the mirror. "Can you do it?"

I nodded once.

She nodded in reply. "Do it."

"Are you willing to donate your hair? I know we didn't talk about it, but you have enough to do it, if you want. It won't change the end result, whatever you decide."

"I can do that? Even though it's not all that healthy?"

"Absolutely."

"Yes, please. I would love that. It makes me feel like this is even more worth it."

"You got it." I went to work transforming her. I tied her hair into a ponytail and cut the first twelve inches off the bottom.

Daisy gasped, but Natalie didn't flinch.

With the weight gone, her hair started to lift immediately. I worked quickly, taking off more and more inches, crafting the style she asked for and completely changing the look of the woman in my chair.

I worked in silence, knowing the cut was important. The chatter around the salon drifted in and out of my ears, but Natalie didn't join in any of it either. She was watching me carefully, catching glimpses in the mirror when she could.

Haley finished Daisy's cut first, and the two of them turned to watch me work.

"Nat, you look so good," Daisy said. "I told you this was a good idea."

Natalie pressed her lips into a smile for her friend but didn't say anything. I wasn't sure if that was good or bad, but it was too late to go back now.

I finished the cut and dried her hair, avoiding my instinct to reach for the curling iron. Natalie needed to know her hair could look good without her having to spend a ton of time on it.

When it was dry, I fluffed it a bit and swept her bangs to the side, like the picture. I checked that every strand was right, then I stepped out of the way for Natalie to get her first complete look.

"That's not me," she breathed. "Holy shit, how did you do that?"

I smiled for the first time in ninety minutes. "Do you like it?"

She touched her hair and shook her head. "I... I love it. It's stunning. I look like a whole different person."

"Wow," Daisy breathed. "You really do look amazing. I knew this woman was under all that hair."

Natalie rolled her eyes at her friend but smiled. "Thank you for bringing me here. I needed this more than I knew."

"Good. Next, I'm going to get you to sign up for online dating," Daisy said with a sparkle in her eyes.

Natalie groaned. "Please help me."

Haley laughed. "You should use Book Boyfriends Wanted. It's where I met my man, and where Chelsea met hers."

"Really?" Daisy said. "I signed up for that one, but I wasn't sure."

"Oh, it's good. You should definitely use it," Haley said. "Right, Chelsea?"

"I have my first official date coming up, so I really can't complain about it."

"You do?" Haley shouted. "Yay! Congratulations. How are you making that work?"

"Sleepover."

"Ooh, good idea. He's a smart man. And he's a single dad," Haley explained to Daisy and Natalie.

"You're going to have to share those details next time we come," Daisy said. "For now, we both have to get to work." She turned to Natalie. "My treat."

"You don't have to—"

"I know," Daisy interrupted her. "But I want to. It makes me happy to see you looking that happy."

"You're the best friend ever," Natalie said.

Haley and I shared a smile. It was good to have friends like that.

"Hey, you two should come to book club sometime," Haley suggested. "A bunch of local women meet Sunday nights at Book Boyfriends Unlimited. You should join us."

The two of them exchanged a look and shrugged. "Sounds good," Daisy said.

"Excellent," Haley said. "And thank you."

"Oh, no, thank you both. This was the perfect start to our day." Daisy hugged Haley, then me. Natalie followed suit, then they both waved as they headed out the door, Natalie still touching her hair.

"Another amazing experience for our clients," Haley said, wrapping her arm around my shoulders.

"We make a great team," I said.

"Hell, yeah, we do," Haley agreed.

20

DEREK

"Hey, boss! You have a visitor!" Jason called from the waiting room.

I got up from my desk and fought the smile on my face as I pictured Chelsea showing up to surprise me at work.

Not Chelsea.

My smile slid just enough for Mayor Omar Knight to notice. One brow lifted. "Sorry to disappoint you."

I laughed off his comment. "No disappointment. Just thought you were going to be someone else."

"A female someone else, I'm guessing based on that."

I chuckled. "Maybe. But we're keeping things quiet because of my son." I exhaled. "You didn't come here to ask about my relationship status. What can I do for you, Omar?"

"I'm not sure if you have time, or are willing, but I'm thinking of buying a car, and I wanted someone I trust to take a look at it."

I nodded. "Of course. Is it outside?"

"Yep. Nothing like overstepping and using my power to influence others. Shit, I sound like the man I took over from."

"You are nothing like Mayor Levine. And asking a friend who owns a garage to look at a car is pretty much what anyone would do, regardless of their position or power."

"Thanks, Derek. I appreciate that."

I followed Omar outside and whistled when I saw the car he parked in the lot. I knew immediately which one it was because none of the rest of my customers drove electric blue muscle cars. It wasn't the first thing I'd guess would suit Omar either, but I was not one to judge. Especially when the car was a head turner.

"Yeah, I had a hard time resisting when I saw her. But I need someone who's not going to be emotional about it, who knows a hell of a lot more about cars than I do, to tell me if it's a smart buy or not."

"First question is, why are you looking at her? Purely leisure and pleasure or are you planning to use it as your daily driver?"

"Leisure. I plan to keep her in the garage and only take her out when the weather is decent. She's got a lot of miles on it, but I'm hoping she'll last for a while."

"She's gorgeous."

"Yeah, she is."

I gestured to the door. "Mind if I get in?"

"Of course not. Whatever you need to do."

I sat in the driver's seat and cranked up the engine, listening for any hesitation or unusual sounds. I revved the engine, checking on the RPMs. I left the car running and popped the hood, taking a look underneath to get a picture of how everything looked.

A sharp whistle split the air. I turned and saw Ricky wiping his hands on a rag and approaching. "You keep all the fancy ones for yourself. Guess that's why you're the boss."

I snorted and shook my head. "Just doing a favor for a friend. Omar's thinking about buying her and wants a level-headed opinion."

"And he came to you?" Ricky joked. He shook hands with Omar. "Nice to see you again, sir."

"You, too, Ricky. Feel free to poke around. She looks like a great buy, but I might already be in love and can't see that she's got eyes for every other man around."

Ricky laughed. "Every other man definitely has eyes for her. She's a beauty."

"That's what I said."

Ricky leaned under the hood with me. We checked all the fuels and the easy stuff. There were a few things I'd recommend, but nothing major. Ricky laid on the ground and checked out the tires, then asked Omar if he'd be open to us rolling the car into the shop.

"You are welcome to whatever you need to do, but I feel bad I'm pulling you away from other jobs."

"I'm good," Ricky said. "Finished the last one a little early and have a free bay for thirty minutes or so."

"Pull it in," I told Ricky, getting out of the way so he could drive the stunner around back and into a bay.

"She's a gorgeous car," I told Omar. "So far, I don't see anything I'd worry about. Lucky find."

Omar laughed. "Yeah, it was. I don't even know how I got so lucky, but she popped up and I jumped on the chance to check her out."

"Local?"

Omar nodded. "Not far. The owner recognized me when I got there and said I could take her for a drive. Said he knew how to find me if I didn't come back."

"People around here are different, aren't they?"

"Yeah. I kind of like it. Better than other places where they don't trust a single person for anything."

"True. Especially ones who look like us."

Omar pursed his lips into an agreeable smile. "Yeah."

I held the door for Omar to go in ahead of me, then led him right onto the shop floor. Ricky pulled into the bay and climbed out of the car. He grabbed the remote to lift the vehicle into the air so we could get a good look underneath. Make sure there were no significant issues we couldn't see from above.

Ricky stopped the lift when we got to him. He locked the lift and hung the control on the post.

The three of us looked at the car, not finding anything major. Wear and tear that was expected for the age, but nothing worse. There was some rust, but again, not worse than expected for how many miles were on the car.

"If you don't buy her, I'm going to," Ricky told Omar.

Omar laughed. "If you guys say she's that good, I think she's sold."

"Probably for the best. My wife would kill me if I came home with this car. We're out of garage space as it is."

Omar nudged me. "Guess there's an advantage to being single."

"There's gotta be something," I agreed with him.

Ricky shook his head. "Don't let this one fool you. He's not entirely single these days. Just wants people to think he is."

"It's not like I'm moving in with her."

"Not yet."

I rolled my eyes.

Omar smirked at our interaction. "Well, one failed marriage was enough for me. I'm good with staying single."

"You'll change your mind when you meet the right

woman," Ricky said, the truth of a man in love with the woman of his dreams.

"How long have you been married, Ricky?" Omar asked.

"Thirty-eight years. Wouldn't change a day of it. Even the bad ones. Emily is my world, and I'll do anything for her."

Omar nodded appreciatively. "Good for you. And her. A good relationship should be like that. I hear."

We all chuckled. I understood what he was saying.

"All right, well, I'll let you two get back to work. Sorry for taking up so much of your time. Derek, want to ring me up?"

"We didn't do any work. Nothing to charge," I told him.

"Aw, come on. I didn't come here for a freebie." Omar looked between Ricky and me.

I looked at Ricky. "I didn't see you pick up any tools. Did you do any work on this vehicle?"

"Nope. Not a thing," Ricky said. "All good."

I shrugged. "Nothing to charge."

Ricky lowered the vehicle to the ground. "Although I won't say no to taking this baby out for a ride one day."

Omar extended his hand to Ricky. "That I can definitely agree to. Date night with Emily? You let me know when you want to borrow her."

"Seriously?" Ricky asked.

"Of course. She's a fun vehicle for me, and I'm not above sharing her. I know you'd take excellent care of her."

"Absolutely, sir. Without a doubt."

"Then we have a deal. You let me know."

"I will. Thank you, Mr. Mayor."

"Omar, please."

"Omar," Ricky said. "Thank you."

"You got it."

"You want to pull the car around, Ricky?" I asked him.

"Yeah, I got her."

"Thank you."

Omar followed me into the waiting room and outside while Ricky drove the car around again.

"That was really cool of you," I told him.

"I'm happy to. A car like this doesn't need to sit in a garage and never get driven. It should be shown off. Like a woman." He cocked a brow at me.

"Yeah, yeah. I know. I already told Chelsea we need a proper date. A friend is going to keep Jude overnight so I don't have to worry about the date going really, really well and having to end it before we're ready."

"With the right woman, I don't know if you're ever ready for it to end."

"True. And she's definitely not an exception to that."

Omar's brows went up. "So, this isn't new?"

"It's new, but not so new that we've never stolen time together."

"Well, good for you. I hope it works out."

"Thanks, Omar. I do, too. Enjoy the new car."

"I will. She's the only woman I'm bringing into my life these days."

I laughed with him as Ricky climbed out of the car and stared at it. He almost ran into Omar because he was looking at the car. They exchanged a few words and smiled, then shook hands, and Ricky joined me to watch Omar drive away.

"That's a hot car," Ricky said.

"Yeah, she is."

"Think he was serious about letting me borrow her sometime?"

"Yeah, I do. He's not the kind of man who's going to say something like that if he doesn't mean it."

"Awesome. Gotta tell Emily we have to schedule a date

night."

I laughed. "Enjoy." Ricky headed toward the shop as my stomach growled. "Hey! I'm gonna run home and grab some lunch. I was running late and didn't grab anything. Call me if you need me."

"Will do, boss."

I jogged to my truck to get out of the cold. I didn't wait for it to heat up before I was pulling out of the lot and on my way home. I didn't want to take too long away from the shop.

But that thought fled when I saw Chelsea's car in her driveway.

My feet carried me to her door instead of my own. Food could wait. Seeing her couldn't.

She opened her door with a smile. "Hi. I—"

I backed her into her house with my hands on her face and my lips pressed to hers.

She gasped against my lips and backpedaled without stopping. Her back hit the wall just inside her front entrance and I covered her body with mine, not letting my lips leave hers.

I licked my way inside her mouth, tasting her and grabbing as much flesh as I could. One hand on her thigh, the other cupping a breast. The one on her thigh moved to her knee and lifted, bringing my throbbing erection into contact with her heated core.

"Derek," she gasped.

"Do you want me to stop?"

She shook her head. "Upstairs. Bedroom."

"Fuck yes."

We'd never been in a bed, and I wasn't going to complain about her genius idea. She led the way upstairs, my hand firmly in hers as we raced away from her nosy dog. She passed one door and went into another one.

The room was Chelsea in bedroom form. Sensual and intoxicating. Lush bedding and enticing fabrics. Clothes were everywhere, as if she tried on everything in her closet that morning and discarded all the options.

"Sorry. I had trouble finding something to wear this morning."

"Want to try again?"

"Excuse me?"

"To find something to wear. You can model for me."

Her cheeks pinked, and I ached to know how far down her neck that flush went.

"I have a hard time with clothes. If they are comfortable, I hate the way they look. If they look good, they're uncomfortable."

"Good thing you don't need any clothes right now."

A slow smile lifted her lips. "Good point. Neither do you."

I grabbed my shirt and tore it off. "Already on the way."

She tossed her shirt onto one of the piles, then paused and watched me hook my thumbs in the sides of my jeans.

As soon as my pants hit the floor, hers followed. I kicked my shoes off and shoved my jeans to the side.

"Condom," I said, reaching for my jeans.

"I have some," she said, her voice fading at the end. "I noticed what kind you used and asked Haley to get some."

"Haley?" My brows shot up.

Chelsea shrugged. "She's in a relationship. I figured no one would think twice about her buying condoms. If I bought them, the whole town would be trying to figure out who was crazy enough to be sleeping with me."

"Lucky enough," I growled. "Anyone who can't see that is the crazy one."

She smiled tentatively. "You could have anyone. Why me?"

I tucked a strand of hair behind her ear. "I didn't want to want you. You were a temptation. Too young, too beautiful. But when you stayed with Jude... You took care of my son without asking for anything. After how horrible I was to you. I knew you were a different person than the one who had a crazy dog who was tearing up the fence between our yards and kept us up all hours of the night. You're not just beautiful. You're kind and smart and creative and talented. You amaze me with the way you see things. You make me want to be a better man."

"Wow," she breathed.

"Is that too much?"

She shook her head slowly. "That's the most beautiful thing anyone's ever said to me."

"I don't want you to doubt why I'm with you. I had reservations, sure. You're the same age Sasha was when she left. It messed with my head."

"I didn't know that," she whispered.

I shook my head. "I didn't know it would be an issue until it was. But I was determined to resist you anyway, so it didn't matter."

"Are you still determined to resist me?"

I moved closer to her, reaching for her and shaking my head. "Not even a little." I brought her naked body to mine. We both exhaled a rush of breath, our mouths crashing together.

Hands found skin, softness met hardness. She wrapped her thick fingers around my cock, and I hissed.

"Fuck, you feel good."

She stroked me twice, then dropped to her knees.

"Chelsea," I groaned.

She looked up at me as she took my dick into her mouth. Watching it disappear between her thick lips was only a precursor. I wasn't going to come in her mouth. I needed to be inside her for that. But fucking hell, she was good with her tongue.

"Jesus," I ground out. "Chelsea."

She didn't let up, stroking me with her hands and cupping my balls before working me with her mouth.

I wasn't going to last, but I had no choice.

"Stop," I barked.

She looked up at me, pulling back until her lips popped free. "I'm sorry. I didn't mean to upset you."

"Oh, beautiful, the only thing you did was make it even more impossible for me to resist you. I'm about five seconds from coming in your throat, and that's not what I want right now."

"What do you want?" she asked, her face lighting up in anticipation.

"I want you on this big bed you have, and I want to hear you scream."

"But Dozer," she whispered.

"On the bed, beautiful," I commanded her.

She listened while I closed and locked her bedroom door.

She smiled. "If you think that'll stop the crazy dog, you haven't been paying attention."

"It'll slow him down. Now, where are those condoms?"

She opened the nightstand drawer and revealed an unopened box of the brand I preferred. And the right size. I was relieved, and awed. No one had ever bought condoms for me before.

I grabbed one, hating that I would only get to use one, and tore it open. I rolled it on, knowing when I had her ready, I wouldn't want to stop to put it on. Then I settled between her thighs to return the pleasure she gave me.

"Derek," she gasped.

"If you don't want this, I won't, but I have wanted another taste of you since the first time I licked you."

"Are you sure?"

I looked down at her pretty pink flesh outlined by dark hair and throbbed. She was glistening and already plump. "Without a doubt."

She scooted up the bed and made room for me to lie on the mattress with her.

I pressed her thighs wider and inhaled deep, drawing her scent into me. I was going to smell like her all day, and there was nothing I wanted more.

I licked her, catching the juices already dripping from her body. Her hips lifted from the bed with the first lick.

She was close. God, this woman. She was ready for me. As ready as I was for her.

I pressed two fingers into her, groaning when they slid in without any resistance. She met each stroke, her hips working my fingers. I added a third one and focused my attention on the swollen nub buried in her folds.

"Derek," she whispered.

"Come, Chelsea. Don't hold back on me."

She bucked her hips, chasing my tongue. Her core squeezed my fingers. She teetered. Right there. Hanging on. Pulsing. Dripping. Ready, ready, ready.

I sucked her clit between my lips and flicked my tongue over it. My fingers curled deep inside her.

And my beautiful woman screamed. Oh, she screamed like she'd never had an orgasm like the one I was giving her.

"Derek! Oh, shit. Derek. Yes. Oh, yes. Yes!"

Her body flooded, soaking the sheets as her body made space for me.

I wanted to be a gentleman and give her more, but I was going to come without her if I didn't get inside her immediately.

I positioned myself at her entrance, waiting until she opened her eyes and nodded before I pressed into her.

Her body curled, like the pleasure was so intense it tightened every cell of her.

"Fuck, you feel good," I whispered.

"My thoughts exactly."

I stroked into her, bottoming out deep inside this woman. This woman who took all of me and didn't fight me. This woman who met me at every turn. Who captivated me in every possible way.

"Who are you?" I breathed.

She smiled and cupped my cheek. "I'm your pain-in-the-ass neighbor."

I chuckled with her. I turned my face to kiss her hand.

My hips drew back, pulling me out of her. I eased back in, needing a slow pace so I didn't go off before I got her worked up again. I held her gaze, watching the marvel that was Chelsea in the midst of an oncoming orgasm.

Her eyes brightened, then darkened. Closed, and opened. Her cheeks flushed, then her body down to her waist. She shifted her hips, rubbing herself against me on each stroke.

But there was something else. Frustration.

"Touch yourself," I whispered.

Her eyes snapped to mine. Unease lingered.

"I want to see you. Please, Chelsea."

"I've never..."

"I know. You don't have to, but I... You don't have to."

I didn't want to be disappointed. It wasn't fair to her that I was asking her to share something with me she'd never shared with another man. But I wanted a piece of her no one else had. I wanted to see her pleasure herself, feel her come with me inside her, and know no one else had ever witnessed the same majesty.

And I knew it would be majestic. It was Chelsea. It was—

Her fingertips brushed my dick.

"Chelsea."

"Don't say it."

"Thank you," I whispered.

The look on her face said that was the best thing I could have said.

I leaned back so I could watch her fingers. She pinched her clit, then she rubbed her fingers over it.

The responding tightening of her body clenched my dick as I stroked into her.

"Oh, fuck," I groaned.

My reaction urged her on. She stroked faster, her fingertips brushing me every so often.

I watched, fascinating by the way she rubbed her wet flesh and made herself crazy.

"Derek," she whimpered.

I moved my hand to join hers and rubbed with her. Our fingers intertwined and rubbed her clit, her orgasm crashing over her and dragging me under with her.

I slammed deep, my eyes crossing as I came hard. I didn't have time to prepare for my orgasm. To bite back the sharp edge of pain that came with the pleasure.

But it was perfect. It was Chelsea. It had never been better.

21

———

I laid there with her for a few minutes, time losing all meaning as I smelled and felt her body wrapped around me. She sighed happily, like she was feeling the same I was.

Stay.

I had no interest in leaving. Now or anytime soon. Even though I knew responsibility was there. Hanging on the outside of my awareness. Telling me I needed to return to work.

"That was amazing," she breathed.

I wasn't sure if she knew she said the words aloud until I grunted an agreement.

Her arms tightened around me, then went slack.

I took it as a sign that she was ready for me to get up, so I pushed off her. "Bathroom?"

"Across the hall," she said.

I nodded and opened her door, laughing at Dozer standing guard. He looked up at me and cocked his head. "I didn't hurt her."

He barked, then moved past me to get into the bedroom.

I chuckled and made my way to the bathroom. I took

care of the condom and washed my hands, then went back to her room where she was sitting on her bed, still naked.

"You are making it hard to go back to work."

She laughed softly. "Well, I need to get back, too. I have a client coming in thirty minutes."

"I'm sorry I took up your entire break."

She smiled, the look in her eyes one of pure pleasure and zero regret. "I'm not going to complain at all."

"Did you eat? I have stuff at my place for sandwiches."

"I already ate, but thank you. I'm just going to use the bathroom."

I moved aside to let her by, enjoying the view as she walked, her curves on full display for me.

I grabbed my clothes from the floor and got dressed while she used the bathroom.

She walked back into her room naked and quickly dressed before leading Dozer and me downstairs.

"Are you free Saturday night?" I asked her when we stopped at her front door.

"This Saturday?" she squeaked.

I nodded. "Yeah. I asked Sebastian, and he said Jude could stay with them Saturday night. If you're available."

The flush on her cheeks answered before she nodded. "I'm available."

"Good. Don't make plans for Sunday morning, either."

Her eyes widened.

I leaned in and kissed her hard, delighting in the way she melted beneath me. Saturday night was going to be a lot of fun. "Thank you for letting me invade you for lunch."

"You're welcome anytime."

I chuckled. "Good to know."

I said goodbye and jogged across the driveways to my

house. I made a quick sandwich and carried it to my truck. Chelsea was already gone.

On the way back to work, I ate my sandwich and wondered what I should plan for our date. Dinner at my place and sex wasn't enough. It was what I wanted, but Chelsea deserved more. She needed to know I was in this. That I didn't want to hide her, even though I did want her all to myself.

No one in the shop noticed when I got back, so I went to my office and reviewed the applications I had for new office managers. In just over a week, I'd gotten a dozen applicants. Some were more promising than others, but one surprised me.

"Hey, Jason. Can you come in here?" I called into the shop.

The other guys teased him, his ears turning red as he approached me.

I led the way to my office and asked him to close the door when he walked in.

He fiddled in the seat, definitely uncomfortable.

"Why didn't you tell me you were interested in the office manager job?" I asked him.

His face took on the same red tone as his ears, and his head ducked even farther down. "I didn't think you would want me to take it. My girlfriend said I should apply, anyway. Good experience writing a resume."

"It is, and it's a damn good resume. I wanted to hire someone who already knows the place, the work, and the employees."

"I didn't know that."

"I only posted the job because no one said they were interested. I mentioned it a few times."

Jason nodded. "After I screwed up with Jude and that call, I…"

"That's forgiven and forgotten, Jason. It was a mistake, but it wasn't something intentional. You weren't negligent."

"Yeah, but—"

"If you had this job, it would mean more responsibility. It would mean counting on you to make sure things are done. I want to hire someone so I have more time with my son."

"I get it. And I understand if I'm not the right person for the job."

"I am not going to tell you it's yours right now. I would like to interview you and a few others, but my preference would be someone who's been here a while. Someone I know and trust. Someone like you."

"Yeah?" He grinned for the first time since he walked into my office.

"Yeah, Jason. It's a huge factor."

"Okay, well, thanks, Derek."

"It's no guarantee."

"I get it. I know. But I really appreciate you considering me for it."

"You're a good guy, Jason. I'll schedule time for us to sit down during your next shift. Is that okay?"

"Yeah, sounds good."

"Thanks. Get back out there. I know you're in the middle of something. Sorry I dragged you away."

"All good. I'm almost done."

"Thanks, Jason."

Jason left my office door open and hurried back to the shop. He walked out smiling, and he wasn't the only one.

His resume was impressive. He had a business degree, which I didn't know, and was a certified mechanic. He had references from two former employers included with his resume, something the posting said could be requested but wasn't required to be included. The fact that he included them showed initiative.

I looked back through his employee record since he started working at Stone Auto Repair. He'd never been late to work, never called in. He took his vacation time, which I encouraged, and he worked a lot of overtime and was always open to whatever schedule was set for him. He was a model employee.

But would he make a model office manager?

I knew the tasks I wanted to hand over, the things I needed help getting done. It required attention to detail and organization.

Jason was able to get both a closer look and an unfair look as a current employee. No other candidate would be someone I could evaluate in the same way. But no other candidate was someone I could consider so heavily either.

I liked the idea of hiring Jason. But I'd gotten a lot of applications and felt I owed it to them to consider every one of them.

I looked at Jason's schedule. He was already fully assigned to work for his next three shifts, so I blocked off an hour next Tuesday for an interview. I made a note to speak to him before he left so he would know when it was.

With that done, I reached out to the four best candidates besides Jason and set interviews with all of them for the end of the week and early the following week. If any of them were half as good as Jason, I'd set second interviews for the end of next week and try to get someone hired.

Pressure eased from my shoulders. After debating for so long about hiring someone, having the process underway and the interviews scheduled made me anxious to get someone in the job.

I went out to the shop and let myself get lost in the work for the rest of the day. It was good to get my hands dirty and to see a project finished. And when I went home, I knew I was making the right choice hiring someone.

"Do you want to spend the night with Cameron on Saturday?" I asked Jude the next day, after I confirmed with Sebastian again that they could keep him.

"Really?" Jude asked.

I nodded. "Yep. Sebastian reached out and asked if you could spend the night."

"Yeah! Can I?"

"I wouldn't ask if you wanted to if I wasn't willing to let you."

"Do I have to go to work with you on Saturday?"

"Unfortunately, yes. But it might be one of the last Saturdays."

"Why?"

"Because I'm going to hire someone as the office manager. Someone who will likely work most weekends so I don't have to."

"So we can do things instead?"

"Yeah. What kinds of things would you want to do?"

"Go to the movies, the park. Maybe have friends over. Can we get a dog?"

"I don't know about that last one, but we can do the others."

Jude scowled. "I knew you were going to say that."

I chuckled. "Let's see how things go. It's been a long time since we've had weekends free."

"So, maybe we could get a dog?"

"Maybe one day. I make no promises, though."

"Yes!" Jude cried, pumping his arms in the air.

I laughed. It didn't take much. Just a dog and a few weekends where he didn't have to go to work with me.

Even better news, when Saturday morning came, Jude didn't argue at all about going to the shop. He was ready when I asked him to be, and he climbed out of my truck and went right to Ricky to help him start the day.

I missed too much, and I was ready for that to change.

The day was painfully slow for me. I was ready for it to be over so I could see Chelsea, but it took forever. Every vehicle had an issue, every customer was short on patience. It was a long day, and only longer when I thought about Chelsea and my plans for the night.

I made us reservations at a nice Italian place, one I'd never been to but she was a fan of Italian food. It was too cold for something like a walk outside, but I got us tickets to see a movie at MacKellar Theater. A movie meant we wouldn't have a lot of time to talk, but I planned to keep her up all night. To learn everything there was to know about her.

When the last customer of the day pulled out, I sighed, feeling like we'd won some kind of war we weren't prepared for. The weary looks on the other guys' faces said they all felt the same.

"Thank you, everyone. That was a hell of a day, and you all did amazing."

They grumbled their thanks, and I knew I had to do something for them. Something special. Next week, when they were all recovered.

Jude followed me to the truck after we checked the doors and made sure everything was locked. He climbed in, bouncing in his seat like he wasn't exhausted.

"Are you ready for Cameron's?" I asked him.

Jude nodded. He'd packed his things the night before and had his bag in the back of the truck so I could drop him off on my way home. I was going to shower before I picked up Chelsea, but there was no reason for Jude to wait to go to Cameron's.

"Cameron said we're going to have pizza for dinner. And play games. He said we might go out for ice cream, too. We're going to watch movies all night long. What are you going to do, Dad?"

I hesitated. I'd never told Jude when I was dating, but it was different with Chelsea. I was already thinking about talking to Jude about her, and if I was going to do that, I needed to tell him I was dating first and get his reaction.

"I have a date, actually."

"With Ms. Chelsea?" he asked.

"What... Why would you ask me about Chelsea?"

Jude shrugged. "I just figured it was her."

"Why?"

"I saw you two kissing on the couch. She was sitting on your lap and you were kissing her."

"When was this?"

"I don't know. After we had dinner with her last week, I think. Why? Do you not like her anymore?"

"No, I..." How did I explain it to him? He was still young. Relationships and sex and dating were foreign concepts. He didn't understand, and I didn't want him to.

Before I could say anything, Jude continued, "I love Ms. Chelsea. She's great. She's funny and she's smart and she bakes me cookies and she lets me stay with her so I don't have to go to that afterschool program."

"Yeah, I..."

"I think you should date her. Then she can be my mom. Would that mean she and Dozer could move in with us?"

"That's..."

"Oh, we're here!" Jude shouted.

I pulled into Sebastian and Zoey's driveway and turned off my truck. Cameron ran outside with Sebastian and Zoey right behind him.

Jude opened the door and jumped down, then climbed back in to grab his bag from the back. He and Cameron talked on top of each other about all the things they were going to do.

"I think they're excited," Zoey said, appearing next to me. "I'm glad this worked out."

"Yeah," I said, my throat tight. I cleared it and pressed my lips into a smile. "Thanks so much for having him."

"He's a pleasure. They have so much fun together. Amber is coming over, too. That way, both older kids have a friend for the night. We're ordering pizza and watching movies and letting the kids be kids."

"Jude's really excited. He's been looking forward to this."

"Cameron, too." Zoey looked closely at me. "Are you anxious about tonight? You look like something's bothering you."

"I'm good. Fine. Just thinking about work."

Zoey rolled her eyes and laughed. "You sound like Sebastian."

"I guess we're all the same."

I glanced at Sebastian, who was talking to the boys and making plans. He waved, but he didn't come over.

Good thing, because he wouldn't have been as easy to push off as Zoey.

"You should go," Zoey said. "Get ready for tonight. We'll be here all day tomorrow, so no rush on when you want to pick him up."

"Thanks. I appreciate that."

"Enjoy your night," Zoey said.

"Thanks." The boys were still talking, so I called out to them. "Hey, Jude, I'm going to go."

"Okay." He raced around the truck and gave me a hug. "Bye, Dad." He met Cameron in the front, and the two of them ran inside.

"Thanks again," I told Zoey and Sebastian.

"You're welcome. Any time," Zoey said. She looped her arm through Sebastian's and led him inside.

He waved and followed her.

I climbed back into my truck and backed out. I waved when Ramsey honked his horn and pulled away so he could drop off Amber.

I drove home on autopilot. My mind kept replaying Jude's words.

I love Ms. Chelsea.

I think you should date her.

Then she can be my mom.

The first woman I dated, and he was marrying me off. He wanted a mom. A woman who was there for him. Someone to count on.

Jude had already decided. Which was what I was afraid of. He saw us. I was careless and reckless and I risked my son's heart.

It had to stop. He came first. Always. And getting his heart broken was not an option.

I parked in my driveway and looked over at her house. I was supposed to be at her door in an hour to get her.

I couldn't do it. I backed out and left.

22

CHELSEA

I BOUGHT A NEW DRESS. HALEY DID MY HAIR. I PUT ON makeup. I stopped at new shoes, but I pulled out a pair I didn't wear often from the back of my closet. I was ready. And I looked fucking amazing.

Dozer watched me the entire time I was getting ready. I made sure he had extra water and that he was fed a little early so he wouldn't be hungry. The doggy door was unlocked so he could go out on his own.

I had a clean pair of underwear and comfortable clothes in a bag by the door. It felt presumptuous, but Derek said he wanted me in his bed, so I was prepared for it. I wasn't going to want to put my dress back on in the morning. Even to walk across the driveway.

A glance at my phone told me he would be there soon. Butterflies flew around in my stomach, making me anxious and excited at the same time.

It was a date. A real date. Our first one. I was so ready for it.

I sat on the couch and drew a breath. My phone buzzed

with a text, and I grabbed it, expecting it to be from Derek, telling me he was on the way.

HALEY

Good luck! Have fun. I can't wait to hear all about your date tomorrow at book club.

ME

Thanks! I can't wait to tell you.

She sent a heart. I locked my phone again, noting the time. Five minutes late. I peeked outside. His truck wasn't there.

It was fine. Maybe he got hung up at work. Or dropping Jude off. I could wait five minutes.

I turned on the TV and flipped channels. Nothing good was on, not that I was paying any attention to the TV. I glanced at the door, then my phone.

Thirty minutes passed. Forty minutes.

I looked outside again. His truck still wasn't there.

Did something happen? Was he in an accident?

The butterflies were sinking in my gut instead of fluttering. I grabbed my phone, sick of waiting.

There were no messages from Derek, which made me more anxious. I opened Book Boyfriends Wanted. I pulled up his name and our previous conversations.

CUTHAIRDONTCARE

Did I get things mixed up? I thought you were going to be here at 7.

I stared at the screen. Nothing happened. No message saying he read my text. No bubbles telling me he was texting back. Nothing.

CUTHAIRDONTCARE

Are you okay? I'm worried.

Still nothing.

I chewed on my lip and debated. He was taking Jude to Zoey and Sebastian's house. I had Zoey's number, but I'd never called her. If I did, and everything was fine, I'd feel like an idiot. But if not…

I called Zoey before I second guessed the decision.

"Hello?"

"Hi, Zoey?"

"Yeah. Chelsea?"

"Yeah, hi. I'm so sorry to bother you, but um, have you seen Derek?"

The background noise grew quieter. "He dropped Jude off two hours ago. I thought you two were going out tonight."

"Yeah, um, I thought so, too. I haven't seen him, and his truck isn't here."

"Hold on." The phone went silent on the other end, like she put me on mute.

I pressed my ear to the phone, as if I would be able to hear something through the line.

"Chelsea?" Zoey said, her voice sad.

"He's not coming, is he?"

"I have no idea what happened. Sebastian called him. He answered because he thought something was wrong with Jude. Sebastian asked what's going on, and he wouldn't say. Just said to tell you… he can't."

"He can't? That's all he said?"

"I'm really sorry, Chelsea. Are you okay? Is there anything I can do?"

"No. I'm… thanks, Zoey."

"Chelsea..."

It didn't matter what she was going to say, I already hung up.

He can't. More like he didn't want to.

I swallowed the lump in my throat and closed my eyes against the building tears. I was not going to let him take that from me. Take anything from me. I thought he was the one. I fell for him, and I thought he was the one, and I was wrong.

Because he *can't*.

"Fuck him," I breathed.

I looked around my house and suddenly couldn't be there. I thought of him pushing his way inside four days earlier and leading him to my room. Kissing me in the living room, sex on the couch, orgasms against the wall. Sitting on my patio and laughing, him telling me he wanted me.

He *can't*.

I grabbed my bag and walked out. I couldn't sit there. I couldn't do it. I got in my car and backed out of the driveway before I put my seatbelt on. I had to go. Fast. Before he came home from wherever he was.

He can't.

I drove home, to my parents' house. I parked in the driveway and walked up the front walk with my bag over my shoulder. I realized when I got halfway there I never packed another pair of shoes.

Too late now.

I rang the doorbell, not wanting to risk walking in on my parents doing something I didn't want to see. I looked up and down the street, as if Derek was going to follow me.

Ha. He couldn't show up when he was supposed to. Why would I think he'd show up when he's not supposed to?

"Chelsea?" Mom exclaimed when she opened the door.

"What are you doing here? Come in, come in. You have to be freezing."

"Thanks," I mumbled.

"What's going on? Why are you in a dress?"

"I don't want to talk about it."

Dad came around the corner just in time to hear what I said. He exchanged a look with my mom. "Want some dinner?"

I nodded and let my mom lead me to the kitchen. She sat me down at the table. Dad dished me up some dinner.

They talked while I pushed the food around on my plate. I wasn't hungry, but I needed food. I stabbed a piece of chicken and stuck it in my mouth. It was a little dry, but I had a hard time caring.

I ate my rice with the chicken. Broccoli came last. By the time I was done, my parents had finished, but they didn't leave me.

Plates were cleared, and a pint of ice cream came out. My dad handed me a spoon and said nothing else. He and Mom went to the living room to watch a movie.

I stared at the ice cream. It wouldn't make everything better, but it would be good.

I picked up the pint and the spoon and followed my parents. I curled up in the oversized chair next to the fireplace, the one I always sat in when I was in high school. The movie started, and I took a scoop of ice cream.

It was cold, and sweet, and perfect.

I didn't need a boyfriend. I had everything I needed right there. Ice cream, a movie, and my parents.

Maybe I could live with them until I sold my house.

I finished the pint of ice cream. The sugar soothed all the broken parts of me. For now. It wouldn't last, but if I could get through all the *right nows*, maybe eventually I would be okay.

"We're going to go to bed," Mom said, handing me the remote. "Are you staying?"

I nodded.

Mom kissed the top of my head. "I'll make sure the house is locked. Go to bed whenever you're ready. The sheets on your bed are clean."

"Thanks, Mom. You, too, Dad."

"Good night, sweetheart," they both said.

"Good night."

I watched them walk up the stairs, their murmurs too low for me to understand. It wasn't hard to guess they were talking about me and wondering what sent me to their house on a Saturday night. In a dress and heels.

I refused to cry. It built up inside me, but I wasn't going to let it out. I deserved better than being stood up on our first real date, and I wasn't going to cry over a man who couldn't even bother to tell me he wasn't coming.

He can't wasn't good enough.

I put the spoon in the dishwasher and the empty pint in the trash. I ran the dishwasher for my parents, then I carried myself upstairs, being quiet so I didn't bother them.

I brushed my teeth and changed into the clothes I planned to wear home the next morning. I stuffed my dress into my bag, hating that I spent so much on something to impress a man who didn't care. I was done with Derek Bailey. And I was done with men.

I laid down in bed and stared at the ceiling. With a deep breath, I reached for my phone and deleted Book Boyfriends Wanted. No more men.

I set my phone on the nightstand in my childhood bedroom and forced my eyes closed. It was going to be a long night of debating what I did wrong. A night with no answers.

MOM AND DAD were drinking coffee when I came downstairs the next morning. I set my bag near the front door. Neither of them said anything when they looked up from the paper and smiled.

I fixed a mug of coffee and sat down at the table. I sipped my coffee, letting the warmth sink in and soothe me.

"What are you doing today?" Mom asked as I put my mug in the dishwasher.

"I need to get home. Check on Dozer."

"Oh, I didn't even think. Do you think he was okay?"

I nodded. "He had food and water, and I left the doggy door open so he could go to the bathroom. I'm sure he was fine, but I should go."

"Are you okay?" Mom asked.

I nodded. "I'll be fine. Thank you for letting me stay here last night."

"Any time," Dad said.

"I made the bed, but I didn't strip it. I can if you want me to."

Mom shook her head. "It should be fine. It doesn't get much use."

I hugged both my parents, then went to the door.

Mom followed me. "Are you sure you're okay?"

I hugged Mom again. "No, but I'm sure I will be."

Mom pushed the hair back from my face. "Come back if you need to."

"I will. Thanks, Mom."

"I love you, Chelsea."

"I love you, too."

She held the door for me to get outside, then stepped out onto the porch behind me.

I hurried to my car so she would get out of the cold. It wasn't easy in my heels, but I did my best. When I got in, I started my car and waved to her, sighing when she went back inside.

I fastened my seatbelt and backed out of the driveway. I wasn't ready to go home, but going out anywhere in the shoes I was wearing was not a great option. Too bad Cracked didn't have a drive-thru.

Derek's truck was in his driveway when I pulled into mine. I stopped and stared at it for a minute. I deserved an explanation, but I wasn't ready to listen to one. Not now, maybe not ever.

I went to my house, crouching down to speak to Dozer once I got inside. He was so excited to see me after his night alone that I felt guilty for leaving him.

"I'll never leave you again," I promised him. "You're the only man I need in my life. Just you and me."

He barked his agreement, then ran to his bowl in the kitchen, reminding me it had been hours since he'd eaten and he was wasting away.

I fed Dozer, then carried my bag upstairs. I took a shower, washing away my night and memories of Derek. I was done with him.

I dressed in my most comfortable clothes and debated hiding out for the day instead of going to book club. If I skipped, everyone would assume I was still with Derek. If I went, everyone would ask about our date.

It didn't matter what I did, I was going to have to explain it all, eventually. Might as well get it over with.

Plus, they would be nice to me. Elise and Haley would make sure of it.

I brushed my hair and tied it back in a long braid. I brushed my teeth and made sure my clothes were clean, even if they weren't fashionable. Caring was out the window, with my hopes of a future with Derek.

I checked the front, like an idiot, to make sure Derek wasn't outside before I went to my car. I kept my gaze from his house and forced myself not to hurry. He was the one who screwed up, not me. I refused to hide, but it didn't mean I wanted to see him.

There was no movement at his house, but his truck was in the driveway, so I knew he was home. I backed out and went toward town, parking a few storefronts down from Book Boyfriends Unlimited. By some miracle, I was the only one walking in when I did, so I didn't have to answer any questions before I got inside.

Finley hugged me and smiled brightly. "How are you?"

"Good. How are you?" I replied automatically. I was asked the question a million times every week by clients who were making small talk. I never answered honestly. Did anyone?

"I'm good. Trent's traveling this week, so I'm already dreading a full week without him. But my parents are going to help out."

"That's really nice of them. It's good to have people you can count on."

Finley chuckled. "It is. But I know anyone who walks in that door on Sunday night would do the same for me if I asked."

"You're lucky. To have so many people in your corner."

She stopped me and looked carefully at me. "You know

we're all here for you, too. If you ever need anything. You look like something's not okay."

"She's probably tired from her sleepover with Derek," Haley answered before I could say anything.

Finley held my gaze. The others made noise behind us, but Finley saw the truth. "Cake. Now. What happened?"

A slice of cake was shoved into my hand. I was led to a chair. A dozen faces surrounded me, all of them compassionate and understanding. A few ready to kick Derek's ass before they even heard my story.

I found Zoey in the crowd. She gave me a sympathetic smile. "Didn't you tell them?"

All heads turned to Zoey as she shook her head. "I would never. It's up to you what you want to tell people. Besides, I don't really know what happened."

"Well, that makes two of us."

"Back up. Slow down. You had a date with Derek last night. Your first. You were so excited. What is going on?" Haley asked.

I drew a breath and looked at my closest friend, my cousin, and the other women I'd come to trust. "He didn't show up."

"What?"

"That jerk."

"Fuck him."

"And he's okay?" Melody asked.

I nodded. "I called Zoey because Jude was staying with them."

"Sebastian called him when Chelsea called. Derek said to tell Chelsea he can't," Zoey said.

"Can't what?" Elise asked.

I shrugged. "Does it matter? He stood me up. He decided I wasn't good enough for him."

"I'll kill him," Elise said.

"I'll help," Melody said.

"What is wrong with men?" Blake asked.

I shrugged. "I wish I knew. I'm glad you all found good ones. I'm done. I deleted Book Boyfriends Wanted. Dating isn't for me."

"You can't let Derek steal your happiness. Your future happiness," Goldie said. "I get needing a break, but there are other men out there."

I shook my head. I shoved a bite of cake in my mouth instead of trying to come up with the words to explain how badly Derek hurt me. How broken I felt inside.

"You're in love with him," Anna said. It wasn't a question. It was a revelation for the room.

I swallowed roughly and nodded. Tears leaked free, running down my cheeks. I ignored them and ate more cake.

"Shit," Elise said. "You're never been in love before."

I shook my head.

"I didn't know you were together that long," Trinity said.

"It's only been a few months since we met," I admitted.

"I fell for Gavin faster than that," Piper said.

"I loved Nico instantly," Laura said.

"There's no timeline for falling in love with someone. And there's no timeline for getting over it," Blake said. "But I'm sorry, Chelsea."

"Me, too," said the others.

"Thanks. I... I wish I knew what changed, but I guess it doesn't really matter. He showed up at my house on Tuesday and asked me out. Said Jude would be with Zoey and Sebastian. It all sounded good. Like he was in this. Even from the first day, he went out of his way to make sure I knew he wanted me. I guess he just wanted sex and decided dating me wasn't worth the trouble," I told them.

"We'll get answers out of him," Melody promised.

I shook my head. "It's fine. I know you're all being nice, and I appreciate it, but you've known Derek longer than you've known me. I know you guys have to choose his side."

"Fuck sides," Zoey said. "You're our friend. Derek is the one who messed up here. If he led you on and screwed you over, that's on him. We're not willing to get answers because we're nice. We want answers because you deserve them. And we care about you, Chelsea. You're one of us."

"Whether you like it or not," Melody added.

I smiled and looked around. All of them were looking at me with the same expressions of kindness and care. I wasn't there because of Elise or Haley or Sofia. I was there because they wanted me to be.

I had my people. And I wasn't giving them up.

"Thank you," I whispered. "I promise to call before I show up to crash on anyone's couches."

"No need to call. Come over anytime," Elise said.

"Same," the others added.

"You're always welcome," Finley said, grabbing my hand and squeezing.

Forget Derek. I was going to be fine. Eventually.

23

DEREK

THE DOG BARKING NEXT DOOR DREW MY ATTENTION. I DRANK my coffee at the sink, watching for her to walk into the backyard like the creepy fucking weirdo I'd become. Trying to catch a glimpse of Chelsea.

Dozer ran around the yard, pausing to sniff every so often. He lifted his leg and peed on the fence that divided our yards. Seemed about right. I deserved that.

And I deserved to not see Chelsea. It was better that way.

"Dad, can I go outside and say hi to Dozer?" Jude asked, meeting me at the window to dump the leftover milk from his cereal down the drain. He put his bowl and spoon in the dishwasher, then looked up at me with pleading brown eyes and his hands clasped together.

I glanced back out the window and nearly collapsed with relief when I saw Dozer making a beeline for the house. "He's going inside already. Sorry, Jude."

"Can we invite them over for dinner this weekend? It's been forever since I've seen Dozer."

"What if we ask Cameron and his family if they want to go to a movie this weekend?"

"Don't you have to work?"

I shook my head. "Nope. I'm starting my new schedule this week."

"Really? So we can do something fun instead of having to go to your work all day?"

"Yep. What do you want to do?"

"See Dozer. Can we, Dad?"

I drew a sharp breath. It hurt to think about sitting down and talking to Chelsea. "We'll see. Brush your teeth and get your backpack. The bus should be here soon."

"Yes! Thanks, Dad."

I didn't remember agreeing, but apparently that wasn't what he heard.

Chelsea's car was gone when we got outside to wait for the bus. She'd been leaving early every day, like she was making sure she didn't run into us. Not that I was hoping to change that. Jude would want to talk to her, and I would have to pretend everything was fine.

It was better. Things would go back to how they were when she moved in. It would all be fine.

The bus rolled up the street, and I hugged Jude, telling him to have a good day. He waved and went to the bus. I waved to the driver, then got in my truck to start my day.

I had to focus. I was interviewing Jason for the office manager job. I met with five candidates so far. Two were easy nos. One man was stiff and awkward, which I could overlook, but he turned his nose up at shaking my hand because there was grease on my sleeve. Not my hand, my sleeve. He was clearly not okay with getting dirty. Another one was too friendly and casual, showing up for the interview in a tee and jeans. Okay, it was a maintenance shop. I could look past the casual appearance, but I drew the line when he tried to chat with me about local gossip.

Another two were okay. They weren't shining stars, but they weren't clear duds either. Both men were smart and had good resumes, but neither impressed me as much as the one woman who applied for the job.

Rachel knew her way around a maintenance shop and dressed for it, which impressed me before she even spoke. She wore a blazer with a cotton shirt underneath and tailored, dark pants with boots. She looked professional and put together, and she was experienced in not only managing an office but in dealing with a maintenance shop from ordering to pitching in and working on the cars. She was organized and smart, and even offered a suggestion when Mick interrupted with a problem that stumped him.

As far as I was concerned, it was between Rachel and Jason. But first, I had to interview Jason.

He started his day with two appointments that were scheduled before I was able to block his time. I told him not to rush and to come find me when he was free, and that it wouldn't count against him to be late or count for him to be early. The customers came first. Always.

Jason showed up two minutes before our scheduled time. He was in his work overalls, but his hands were clean and it was obvious he'd made an effort to ensure his overalls were the same.

He walked in and shook my hand, taking a seat in the vinyl guest chair opposite my desk.

"So, obviously, this is a little different since I know you, but tell me why you're interested in this job."

Jason drew a breath and leaned forward. "I've always enjoyed working with my hands. Putting something together, figuring something out. My dad skipped out on us when I was younger, so it was just my mom, my sister, and me. My mom is a true wonder woman. She can do anything, and she taught us to be the same. To defy all stereotypes about our genders and the way we grew up and everything."

"She sounds impressive."

Jason nodded. "She is. Incredibly impressive. She works hard, but she loves what she does, and she taught my sister and me to try different careers until we found what we enjoyed. As for why I want this job, I know what it would mean to the shop. I know it would mean expanding my skills in a new way. I've been working on cars since before I could drive them. I love doing it, but I have an eye for things like this job needs."

"In what way?"

"The office manager would be responsible for ordering supplies and making sure everything is not only available but available when it's needed. I have contacts with some of our suppliers. I know people in the community. I have ideas of others we should be working with, and I have thoughts about the way we structure our day and the work."

"What would you do differently?"

Jason launched into his thoughts. He shared ideas that impressed the hell out of me. When I took over Stone Auto Repair, I kept things how they were because I didn't have time to think about making large-scale changes, but Jason had half a dozen ideas already.

"What's the first thing you would change?" I asked after he laid out some of his ideas.

"I'd restructure the schedule. We have to have appointments for the walk-ins, the emergency repairs that can't be planned. I'd dedicate one bay to those things, with the intention of adding a second when necessary. I'd have two bays reserved for the appointments we have daily. Oil changes, tire rotations, alignments, state inspections. The last bay I'd use for the major jobs. Obviously, there would still be some overflow and movement between the jobs, but I think we could move cars through the shop faster if we did things like that."

"And the employees?"

"One day a week on routine, and then flex the rest of the schedule so they're always using their skills but have at least a day of easy work."

I rubbed my jaw and considered what he said. "I've never thought about what you're suggesting. It would be a major change."

Jason nodded. "It would be. But it would increase revenue by five percent, minimum, if we implemented it."

"How do you figure?"

Jason jumped in, laying out the numbers he knew off the top of his head. He explained his thoughts, and I had no argument against his idea.

We kept talking, half abandoning the interview and half asking questions I'd asked the other candidates even as I made my decision to hire Jason.

When the hour I'd blocked for him was up, I paused. "You've given me a lot to think about. And you've made my decision challenging."

"I hope that's a good thing."

I grinned. "It is. We'll talk later."

Jason nodded and shook my hand again before he went back out to work, leaving me to think about what I had to do.

I hated the idea of letting Rachel go when she was such a skilled and smart woman, but Jason was the clear leader. Rachel could come to the same conclusions and have the same suggestions if she worked at Stone Auto Repair, but she hadn't, and that gave Jason an edge.

An edge that was going to give him the job.

I called the two I had no intention of hiring first. I thanked them both for their interest in the job, but I explained a different candidate had been chosen. They were both understanding and thanked me for letting them know.

I debated on the next two. I knew neither of them were right, but they weren't horrible either. If Jason and Rachel both turned the job down, I would need to decide between the two that were just okay.

Or keep doing everything myself.

I couldn't do that. I had to choose.

"Boss, there's two people here," Mick said, sticking his head in for long enough to relay the message before going back to helping customers.

I got up from my desk, wondering what was going on now, and came face-to-face with two scowling men. "Gentlemen."

Knox Randall was a large man I considered a friend. Daniel Ryan was someone I didn't know as well, but I still liked him. But they weren't there as friends of mine. They were there because their girlfriends were Chelsea's best friends. And I was in trouble.

"We're taking you to lunch," Knox said.

"Let me grab my keys," I said, knowing I'd get stranded without a ride back to work if I counted on them to drive me.

Knox and Daniel were in Knox's truck when I walked out. He waved for me to follow them and led the way out of the parking lot.

My gut twisted on the drive, but I had to face them eventually. If this was the last conversation I was going to have with the two of them, I owed them the truth.

Knox parked in front of Will Work For Burgers. The three of us walked in silently, each ordering and paying before Daniel grabbed a table for the three of us and the interrogation began.

"Why is she not good enough?" Knox asked to start things off.

"Who said that?" I asked.

"Chelsea did," Daniel answered. "She said things were fine, then you changed your mind. Said 'you can't.' She's not good enough."

"That's not... I never meant for her to feel that way."

"How did you mean for her to feel when you stood her up for your first date? After sleeping with her for a month and telling her you wanted to be together?" Knox pressed.

I opened my mouth to answer when our names were called. The three of us went to the counter to grab our food, then returned to the most uncomfortable seat I'd ever been in.

I didn't like it.

"Jude told me he loves Chelsea," I admitted.

The two of them looked at me, then at each other, then back at me.

"And?" Knox asked.

I sighed. "That's what I wanted to avoid this whole time. Chelsea isn't his mother. She's not his anything. I don't tell Jude about dating because I don't want him to get attached, but he did. He is. He said he loves Chelsea and wants her to be his mom."

"Isn't that what you should want when you have a kid? A woman who makes him feel safe and comfortable and loved?" Daniel asked.

"I…"

"Listen, I'm not a parent," Daniel continued. "My parents got divorced when I was a teenager. After my brother died, they couldn't handle being together. Both of them dated some, but the people they dated were always ready to push me out the door. I wanted to go because nothing was the same, but I lost my brother, then both of my parents because they couldn't handle losing Michael. I would have loved it if someone came into one of their lives who made me feel safe and loved."

"I told her I was worried about that. About him getting attached and then things ending." I had to make them understand.

"But you ended them," Knox said. "You're the one who made that second part a reality. And Chelsea couldn't exactly stop Jude from liking her."

"Yeah, she's pretty great. Funny and smart and creative. What's not to like?" Daniel asked.

My fists clenched. My jaw tightened. I wanted to take a swing at him.

"You're angry because a man who's not single is complimenting the woman you just dropped. What the fuck, dude?" Knox growled.

I glared at them both, then took a bite of my burger. Daniel had no right to talk about Chelsea. To tell me how wonderful she was. I knew. Fuck, I knew.

But it didn't matter.

I chewed my burger and swallowed, glaring at the two men in front of me. "Jude's going to get hurt. He already had his mother run out on him. He was two-years-old when Sasha left. Two. Barely old enough to be a person, and she just left. You know how old she was? The same age as Chelsea."

"So you think all thirty-two-year-old women ditch their families? Walk out on the people they care about?" Knox asked.

"It's been my experience," I snapped.

"What about forty-three-year-old men?" Daniel asked.

My throat tightened.

"Because Chelsea isn't the one who ditched someone she cares about," Knox piled on.

"You are," Daniel said.

"Exactly," Knox picked up. "You're the one who made plans with her. You're the one who said she was special and that you wanted something real with her. You're the one who lied to her and fucking ditched her when she was sitting in her living room, waiting for you to pick her up."

"I've done some fucked up things in my life. I've made some big mistakes. I almost lost Sofia because I couldn't see the truth right in front of me," Daniel said. "I will always regret that I believed the lies of someone else instead of the truth of Sofia. But she forgave me. She was willing to see past my faults and give me another chance. And I'm going to spend the rest of my life making it up to her. If you don't want that with Chelsea, then no worries."

"But if you do," Knox said, "then you might want to start getting real about what the fuck is really going on. Because none of this is Chelsea's fault, and you know it."

Daniel nodded with Knox, the two of them executing the perfect mic drop moment.

Because they were right. Chelsea didn't do anything wrong. She didn't manipulate Jude into loving her. He fell for her because she's a good person. A good person who took every single cruelty I'd committed against her and looked beyond it. She never once held my sins against me, or Jude. She let us both in and cared for my son the way a loving person would.

And I threw it in her face.

I treated her like shit.

Because I was scared.

"What did I do?"

"My guess? You didn't think you could trust her," Daniel said.

Knox shook his head. "Nah. He didn't think he could handle it if she left. He's scared. Because he loves her and doesn't want to admit it."

Daniel and Knox were both quiet, watching me closely to see who was right.

Or just waiting for me to snap.

"He's right," I admitted.

"Who's right?" they asked together.

"I'm in love with her. But Chelsea has this whole town. She has people who adore her. She's kind and thoughtful and didn't even judge me when she had every right to. The only time she judged me was when she thought I didn't want her because of her size."

"You what?" they growled together.

"She was wrong. I set the record straight with her. I always wanted her."

"Then you need to do something to prove that to her because right now, she's done. With you and men and relationships. You hurt her. Big time, Derek. I like you, and we're friends, and that's not going to change, but Haley's never going to let you in our place if you don't fix this with Chelsea," Knox said.

"Neither is Sofia," Daniel added.

"I know. I need to fix it. I freaked out, and I was wrong, and it was all my shit and had nothing to do with her."

"Good. How are you going to do that?" Daniel asked.

I shrugged. "Got any suggestions?"

The two of them exchanged a smile that told me I should not have asked.

But at least they were going to help. I just hoped it was enough to convince Chelsea to give me another chance.

24

CHELSEA

I SAT IN THE VET WAITING ROOM AND RUBBED DOZER'S HEAD. Tension poured off of him. I didn't pick up on it the last time we were there. It was busier, and some of the other dogs barked at each other.

"Bulldozer?" the assistant called.

I stood, nearly tripping over Dozer. He was a little slow to move, pressed against my leg so close he was barely moving.

"Let's go," I told him, encouraging him to go to the friendly woman who'd called his name.

As soon as we were out of the waiting room, Dozer relaxed. When we were closed in a room, he almost sighed with relief.

"It's busy out there today. Sorry about that," the assistant said. "I'm Sheila. Dr. Harris is running a little behind."

"That's okay. We're not in a hurry," I told her. I was off for the day and had absolutely no plans.

"Thank you. Let me check out Mr. Bulldozer here. Great name."

"Yeah. Some friends' kids named him because he almost

knocked down my fence the day I got him, and then he passed out hard."

Sheila snorted. "Sounds like the right name for him. How has he been since he was here last? Looks like three months?"

I nodded. "He's been good. Since we don't really know his history, Dr. Harris wanted him to come back for an extra check to make sure everything is going well."

"He's very thorough."

"He is. That's why I came here. He's incredibly kind."

"I agree." Sheila smiled and reviewed her tablet, then turned her attention to Dozer. "How are you, sweetheart?"

Dozer barked in reply, and Sheila grinned at him.

"Oh, is that so? Well, I think that's a good thing."

Dozer replied, and the two of them had a one-sided conversation that Dozer was completely involved with.

Sheila was smart. While she spoke, she got his weight and checked his teeth, peeked in his ears, and did a general physical exam.

"He looks great to me. The bloodwork from last time showed us what shots he'll need, so I'll go get those ready. It's only two, but I know they're not any fun."

"He did well last time. A little jump, but you guys are so good that he didn't react much."

"That's great. I'll be back in a few minutes with Dr. Harris. I won't give Bulldozer any shots until the doctor confirms everything and is okay with him getting them."

"Thank you, Sheila."

She smiled and let herself out of the room.

The noise outside had Dozer freezing in place, but when the door shut again, he relaxed. He pranced around the room like he was in charge, not a care in the world.

My phone buzzed, and I dug it out of my handbag since we were just sitting there for a few minutes. It buzzed again.

Someone was at my door.

I pulled up my doorbell camera and gasped. Derek was at my house. He didn't ring the bell, but he was peeking inside.

What the hell was he doing?

The exam room door opened before I could see more, and I shoved my phone away to focus on the doctor.

"Who do we have here?" Dr. Harris asked. "Bulldozer, I think you're bigger since I last saw you."

Dozer jumped up, front paws on Dr. Harris's shoulders to give the man what appeared to be a hug.

"Dozer!"

"Oh, he's fine. He's just saying hello," Dr. Harris said. He hugged Dozer back, then spoke softly to him.

Dozer listened, dropping to the floor and pressing himself against Dr. Harris's side.

I shook my head. "He adores you."

"The feeling is mutual," Dr. Harris said. "Sheila said things look good, and I agree. He is healthy and strong. I think he's adjusted extremely well to life with you, Ms. Chelsea."

"Thank you. He's a great dog."

"Any issues?"

"Um, I think we're okay."

Dr. Harris raised his bushy gray brows at me and waited for me to elaborate.

"He used the bathroom in the house a few times. I had a doggy door, but it was a little too small for him, and he got stuck. I have a new one now, and he's getting used to it. The accidents were before."

"That's normal, unfortunately. And as long as they didn't

last, and it didn't appear as though he was doing it for any other reason, it's fine."

"Any other reason?"

"Sometimes dogs use the bathroom in the house because they're in pain or can't hold it. In pain, you would have noticed because he would have made a noise. If he couldn't hold it, that's usually because they aren't getting enough time outside for a bowel movement and get to a point where they can't stop themselves."

"Oh, no, neither of those. He loves to be outside, even in this cold weather."

"The winter could provide new challenges," Dr. Harris said.

I nodded. "I've been trying to figure that out. I have a fenced-in backyard. He usually goes out there, but it's not easy to clear if we get a lot of snow."

"Dogs can go in the snow. It might be new to him, and he might not love it. We have a few things we've suggested to patients that you could try." Dr. Harris looked over at Sheila, who was already handing him a sheet of paper. "Some owners like to create a pad for the dog, somewhere that's easy to clean but still outside. You can do small things or go big and create a whole adventure area in the backyard for him. There are a few companies you can check out, and there's a local contractor who does some of this. You could speak to him if you want to do something more permanent."

I looked over the sheet and smiled when I saw Knox's name and number. "I know Knox. I'll give him a call and ask him to come up with something."

"Good. He's very talented."

"Yes, he is." My phone buzzed again, but I ignored it.

"Sheila is going to administer the two shots. One in each leg. If Dozer has any issues with these, call us. Otherwise, I think we're safe to wait a little longer until we see him again."

"Six months?" Sheila asked.

"Six months," Dr. Harris echoed. "For his next shots."

"Sounds good. Thank you, Dr. Harris."

"You're welcome. Any time. Bye, Dozer." Dr. Harris rubbed Dozer's head and leaned down to give my dog a warm hug. He was a little slow when he stood up again, his face pinched.

"Are you okay, Dr. Harris?"

He took a breath and nodded. "Just fine. Hello to your parents."

I nodded, watching how slowly Dr. Harris moved when he left the room.

Sheila caught me watching him. "We've been telling him he needs to slow down. He won't. I'm worried about him."

"That's not good."

"I agree. But I'm keeping an eye on him. We all are."

"I hope he's just slowing down and not that anything is wrong."

"Me, too." Sheila squeezed Dozer's left flank and injected him quickly.

Dozer made a noise, but as soon as he did, Sheila was done. She repeated the process on the other side, and Dozer didn't react.

"All done," Sheila said. "Take care of this sweet one."

"I will. See you in a few months."

Sheila walked me up front, entertaining Dozer while I checked out so he didn't panic with the other dogs there. I couldn't imagine taking Dozer to the vet and not seeing Dr. Harris. I didn't want to even consider it.

I was almost home before I remembered Derek was in front of my house. If he thought he could show up at lunch and expect me to have sex with him after he made it clear he didn't want to be seen with me in public, he was way wrong.

His truck was in his driveway, but I didn't see him outside. Guess he gave up on his quest for a nooner. Screw him.

Dozer got out of the car and went to the front door, where a note was taped to the window.

My heart sank. Starting over. With nasty notes. Yay.

I grabbed it from the window and debated throwing it away without even looking at it, but I couldn't help myself. I opened the note.

> I'm sorry.
>
> I was wrong. I know this isn't enough to fix anything, but I didn't want to wait another minute to tell you how sorry I am.
>
> There's more I want to say, but I want to say all of it to your face. In person. Because you deserve to have someone who shows up.

I closed my eyes. It was not fair how easy that was. I didn't want to let him off the hook so quickly.

And I wouldn't. I deserved more than just someone who showed up. I deserved someone who didn't want to hide me from the world.

Dozer and I went inside. I tossed the note from Derek on the table and tried to ignore it. I tried to ignore everything I was feeling. Because the urge to cry was coming back.

But I was not going to cry. He was not going to get that power.

I made lunch and settled on the couch again. I was

halfway through a movie when I heard a noise in my backyard.

Voices. Male. More than one.

I grabbed my phone and called nine-one-one.

"Nine-one-one. What is your emergency?"

"Hi, um, there are people in my backyard."

"Okay, are you safe?"

"I don't know! I mean, there are people in my yard. I don't know what they're doing there."

Dozer barked.

"Tell me your address. Are you able to see them?"

I gave her my address and crept closer to the kitchen, hating that the door to the backyard had a window in it. I should have gotten a solid door. Something where no one could see inside the house.

Dozer barked again.

"Are you still there?" the operator asked.

"Yeah. I'm trying to see without them seeing me."

"Do you have an upstairs?"

"I do," I breathed. "But what if they try to come into the house?"

"I already have a car on the way to you. An officer should be there in three minutes."

"Okay. I'm going to go upstairs."

"I'll let the responding officer know."

I raced to the front of the house and up the stairs. I moved into the guest room next to the bathroom. If they looked, it was possible they could see me through the curtains, but they'd have to be looking.

I moved the curtain to the side so I could see without the gauzy fabric in the way. "They're gone," I cried. "My back-yard is empty. Oh, God, what if they're already in my house?"

"An officer is pulling onto your street right now. You should hear the sirens."

I held my breath and listened. The sirens were getting louder. "I hear them."

"Good. I'll stay on the phone with you until I have confirmation from the officer that it's safe for you to go downstairs."

"Thank you."

I heard more voices around my house, in the front this time. I went to my room, but I couldn't see anything beyond the bumper of the police car blocking my driveway.

"Ma'am?" the operator asked.

"Yes."

"The officer said you can come downstairs. It's safe. But he needs to speak to you."

"Okay. Thank you. I really appreciate you getting help here right away."

"You're welcome. Stay safe."

"Thank you."

I hung up the phone and let out a shaky breath. I hoped it was a cop I knew, and that they caught whoever was sneaking around in my backyard.

I opened the front door and walked outside. Knox, Daniel, and Derek were in handcuffs and sitting on the curb with James and Rowan smirking at them.

"Ma'am, these are the men we found on your property," James said, his voice official but laced with humor.

"Chelsea," Derek started.

"Don't speak," Rowan growled at him.

I looked between the five men. "What is going on?"

"I'd love nothing more than to bring these three in. Tres-passing, destruction of property, scaring the hell out of a woman because they're stupid." James crossed his arms and glared at the three of them.

"That's not a law," Knox said with a roll of his eyes.

"It should be."

"You'd have been arrested for that, if the rumors were true," Rowan said.

James smacked him on the back of the head.

Rowan growled at James. "One day."

James smirked.

"What the fuck is going on?" I screeched.

James and Rowan exchanged a look. Rowan stepped forward and gestured to the driveway. "Will you come with me?"

I had no idea why he wanted me to walk up my driveway, but whatever. I followed him, wrapping my arms tighter around myself to ward off the serious chill in the air.

Rowan opened the gate to my backyard and stepped to the side.

"What the...?"

"Derek wanted to apologize for what he did. I know he wants to say the words to you, but from what they told us, he wanted to surprise you with a safe place for Dozer to be in the winter. Somewhere that would mean he could go outside without having to worry about tons of snow or anything else."

"I was just looking at this. Knox builds these."

"Which is why he's here. I think Daniel's here for the entertainment."

I snorted. "Don't let him hear you say that."

"I'll tell him to his face. His hands were spotless. He hasn't touched a shovel."

I smiled, looking at what they started to do. Pet friendly synthetic grass was laid out in a wide path that twisted around my entire backyard. Framework was in place to support sheltered areas, one right off the patio and more scattered through the yard so Dozer could still play outside, but he would have spots that were free of snow to use the bathroom.

"They were trying to do this when you weren't home. I guess they started earlier and went inside Derek's house for a break and came back here without paying attention to your car in the driveway," Rowan said. "They didn't mean to scare you. They were trying to do something nice for you."

"Why?"

"You know why, Chelsea. You would do anything for Dozer, and it seems Derek would do anything for you."

"He can't stand the dog, and he doesn't want me."

"I think you're wrong on both counts. But again, he wants to tell you all of that."

I looked up at Rowan. "What should I do?" I whispered.

"Have you met Willow? I know better than to tell a woman what she should do."

I chuckled.

"I will say I think you know. If you don't know, you can take as long as you want to think about it. No one says you need to make any decisions about anything right now."

I nodded. "Thanks, Rowan."

"You're welcome, Chelsea."

I looked at the yard again, then walked back to the front. James was still standing guard over the three of them, on the cold curb in handcuffs. "You can let them go," I told James.

"We don't have to. I can take them all in. Book them, hold them overnight," James suggested.

I chuckled and shook my head. "It appears there was a misunderstanding."

James winked at me, then lifted each of the men one at a

time. Knox was first, and he came over and apologized for scaring me. He wrapped me in a big hug that was nice, but was more like hugging my brother. If I had one.

Daniel was next, and he said and did the same. Both of them were wonderful men, and I was happy that my friends found them.

Last was Derek. He stood and stayed where he was, far away from me.

I glanced in his direction, but he didn't make a move to speak to me.

Knox and Daniel moved toward the street, leaving Derek and I alone, with an audience of four.

"I'm sorry we scared you," Derek said. "I've done so many things wrong, but having you fear for your safety was never something I wanted for you."

"It's fine. I just panicked. I shouldn't have overreacted the way I did."

"No, you were right to. We were trespassing. I wanted to apologize. To do something that would make life easier for you. Knox mentioned those tracks, and I just thought it might be nice for you."

"It will be. I was just talking to the vet about the same thing."

Derek smiled. He took a step toward me. "I screwed up, Chelsea. When I didn't show up last weekend. I... I'm sorry. I can never make it up to you, but I wanted you to know I am truly sorry for how I made you feel."

"It's fine," I said quickly, swallowing past the hurt in my throat. "I should go. I, um—"

"I love you," he blurted as I turned.

I exhaled a laugh. I shook my head. "Don't do that, Derek. Don't tell me you love me to try to get me back. You said you can't. I'll keep my distance."

"I'm not telling you so you'll take me back. I'm telling you because you deserve to know the truth. Jude told me he loves you. That he wants you to be his mom. I freaked out. I just… It was…"

"Exactly what you didn't want."

He nodded. "He saw us. On the couch."

My eyes widened. I clapped a hand over my mouth.

"I told him I was going on a date, and he told me all of this. I couldn't do it. I saw us ending and Jude hurting, and it was all lies because I was afraid for myself even more."

"Why?"

"Because I love you. And I haven't let anyone in since Sasha. I used Jude as an excuse, but it was bullshit because I was the scared one. He doesn't remember his mom. I do. I remember the day she walked away. And it was easier to not show up last weekend than to imagine you ever walking away from us. It would break me."

"What about me? What about me sitting on my couch and worrying that something happened to you? Calling someone I don't know well to find out if you're okay?"

He nodded. "That's why I know I missed my chance. Because a decent man would never have done that to you. A man who deserves you would never have done that. I don't deserve you. But I will always love you."

He lifted his lips in a sad smile, then turned to go back to his house.

The four men at the curb just watched.

I stared after Derek with my mouth gaping. "Are you fucking kidding me right now?"

All five men froze.

Derek slowly turned to face me.

I stomped over to him and pounded on his chest. "You

tell me you love me, then you walk away without giving me a chance to say it back to you."

"You love me?"

"Yes, but you're an idiot, and you need to listen to me. If I give you another chance, you can't do this again. You can't decide what you think is right. You can't disappear and get scared and act like you're the only one who has big feelings. Because that's bullshit. I may not have been married. I'm not a parent. But that doesn't mean I'm not just as scared as you are. It doesn't mean I don't have a right to be just as scared."

"I know. You're right. I'm so sorry. I should—"

"I'm still talking," I barked.

The guys at the curb snickered. Derek zipped his lips.

"I sat on my couch and waited for you to show up. I was so excited to have unlimited time with you. To get to know you better and to feel like what we had wasn't something you wanted to hide."

He opened his mouth to argue, but I held up my hand.

"I'm still talking. Watching the clock and not hearing from you... That hurt. A lot. I won't ever do that again. If you're not going to show up, you will call me or text me. If you change your mind about us, you owe me a conversation. You don't get to take the easy way out and let someone else tell me you're not coming because you ditched me. I deserve better, and I demand better."

He drew a breath and slowly let it out. When I didn't speak for a minute, he asked, "Is it my turn now?"

"If you agree and don't do it, I will have James and Rowan arrest you for... what was it?" I glanced at James.

"Scaring the hell out of you, but we can come up with more," James said.

"For something," I said, glaring at Derek.

He smirked, then asked, "Now, is it my turn?"

I shrugged. "It can be."

"Then all I have to say is you're right, I was wrong, I'm sorry, and I love you."

I glanced past him to the other four. "Did they teach you that?"

Derek nodded.

"Smart men. You could learn a thing or two from them."

"I'm trying."

"Hey, Knox?" I called.

"Yeah, Chelsea?"

"Think you could come back some other time and finish the run for Dozer?"

"Whenever you want."

"Good. Bye!" I grabbed Derek's hand and dragged him toward my house with the other four cheering.

"I want to prove to you I want more than just sex," Derek said when we got inside and I made a move toward the stairs.

I looked back at him. "Are you willing to prove it later? Jude'll be home in an hour, and you owe me."

Derek smirked. "You're right, I'm wrong, I'm sorry, and I love you."

I snorted a laugh.

Derek chased me up the stairs, clothes flying as we ran to my room. "That works so much better than I ever expected."

"You're lucky I love you as much as I do."

"Say it again, Chelsea."

"I love you, Derek."

He let out a shaky breath. "I love you, Chelsea."

"Good. Now show me."

"With pleasure."

EPILOGUE
NATALIE

DAISY LOOPED HER ARM THROUGH MINE AND LED ME TOWARD the door to O'Kelley's. I wasn't a bar person. Or an adult person. I did much better with kids. Kids who looked up to me and respected me instead of judging me, like other adults always did.

"It'll be fine," Daisy said, her normal sunny disposition on full display with her bright smile and even brighter outfit.

"At least I know I won't lose you in the crowd," I teased her.

Daisy laughed, always one to find the humor in everything. She was wearing an electric yellow sweater with bright blue pants. I didn't know anyone else who could pull off something like that, but Daisy marched to her own beat and didn't care if you didn't like it. Or her.

I had been waiting for that confidence to rub off on me since we met. Unfortunately, I was still waiting.

"You're going to have fun. And we were invited. It's not like we're crashing the party."

I pursed my lips at her. "We happened to be at Serenity

Salon this morning when Chelsea and Haley were talking about Haley's engagement. We weren't invited ahead of time."

Daisy waved her hand. "It's fine. This is how we make friends. They are both kind and wonderful, and we agreed we would go to their book club and never did, so we're going to this."

I grumbled and let Daisy pull me inside the bar.

Holy crap, it was busy. Sure, it was Saturday night, but it was busier than I expected. Wall to wall with people and music and alcohol.

What was I thinking?

"There they are!" Daisy shouted so I could hear her. She grabbed my hand and pulled me toward the group of tables near the pool tables where Chelsea and Haley and a bunch of other people were gathered.

People I didn't know. People I wasn't friends with. People who were going to judge me.

"Daisy! Natalie! You came!" Haley gushed, getting up to hug both of us.

I let her pull me in and wondered if she was sincere. "Thanks for inviting us," I said.

"I'm so happy you're here. Come meet everyone." She took our hands and tugged us closer to the crowd. "That's Knox, my new fiancé. You guys know Chelsea, and that's Derek. Have you met Sofia?"

"I have," Daisy said, waving to the blonde woman I knew by reputation only.

"Okay, well, that's Sofia and Daniel," Haley continued.

The names went on and on. More than a dozen couples were at the table, and more were pointed out around the bar. So many people.

"Who needs a drink?" a man asked. Baseball hat, beard,

kind eyes that winked at one of the women. Maybe the guy who owned the bar?

Ugh. I was so bad with names. Almost as bad as I was with people.

"We both do!" Daisy answered for us.

The guy in the hat poured us drinks from the pitcher he carried to the tables, then handed them over. "Please let me know what you think. We're always trying out new drinks."

"Sounds good, Hudson. We will," Daisy said.

Another thing I envied about my best friend. She could meet someone once and know their name.

I smiled at the guy, Hudson, and nodded, knowing Daisy would handle any and all communication for me. Because I was barely functional.

"Are you okay?" Daisy whispered.

I nodded. Being there was important to Daisy. As a new business owner, she wanted to get her name out there. We catered to the same clientele, and I was positive the only reason my business hadn't already failed was because of her. She let me put flyers up in her toy store, and she talked me up to every customer.

Sure, it helped that what I was doing was filling a real need in the community, but I was awkward and struggled to explain myself to people in power. People who could make my business successful. Or not.

Daisy was the powerhouse. She dragged me along, kicking and screaming, to every networking event, every town meeting, every everything that could make a difference for the summer camp I was running.

My first summer was good, but I had plans to make the second one even better.

But first, I had to make it through the engagement party that I didn't want to go to for a woman I barely knew.

"Not your scene?" Chelsea asked from right next to me. Chelsea was my new stylist, a job no one had for the last few years. But I couldn't deny she was a magician and made me feel better about myself than I had in ages.

"No, but Daisy really wanted to come and support Haley." I was glad I ended up in the seat next to Chelsea, but I wasn't sure that was the right thing to say. Hopefully she knew me well enough to understand I was just awkward.

"That was nice of her. And nice of you to let her drag you here."

"I'm sorry. I don't mean to be ruining the night for you. I can go somewhere else so you can talk to others." I started to get up, but Chelsea put a hand on my arm.

"You're not ruining a thing. It took me a long time to feel comfortable with this group."

"I thought you grew up here."

Chelsea nodded, looking around. "I did. I've lived here almost my entire life. I love it, and I love the people, but it's not always easy to feel like you belong somewhere like MacKellar Cove."

"That's for sure," I said without thinking. The drinks must be stronger than I realized for me to admit something like that.

Chelsea chuckled. "This is a really great group, though. Women and men. Friendly and supportive. Some of them probably have kids in your camp, or considering it. Trent MacKellar..." Chelsea pointed to a tall, Black man with his arm around the woman who owned the romance only bookstore. "He invited all the kids to his house tonight. The older ones are keeping an eye on the younger ones, but there's about a dozen kids there right now. Could be good as counselors or campers for you."

I wrinkled my nose. "I'm not very good at talking people into things. Or putting myself out there."

"I get it. I have my job because I love making people feel good about themselves. I love giving people a new outlook and helping them to show the world the person inside. But there's only one salon in town, so if you don't want to have to drive, you have no choice but to come to Serenity Salon."

"Which is kind of the same for me. The Community Center has a program, but mine is bigger and gets the kids outside and doing different things."

"Colin Jones owns Jones Family Maple Farm and is married to my cousin. Could be a good person to speak to about field trips," Chelsea suggested.

"Really?" I asked.

Chelsea nodded. "And Ian Jameson owns Jameson Wooden Boats and might be able to do something. Melody Holland is a party planner. Elise, my cousin, is a tour boat captain and could do a private tour. James and Rowan are police officers. Piper, Gavin, and Zoey are all owners of MacKellar Inn, and Zoey's husband Sebastian maintains the lighthouse. They have three kids. And—"

"Okay, I get it. I need to get to know these people. But it feels slimy to talk to them because I'm hoping they'll send their kids to my camp or help me out in some way."

Chelsea smiled. "And the fact that you're worried about that tells me you would never do that. Let's start with Elise and Colin. She's my cousin. And they don't have kids so it's just you meeting some new people. Have you ever been on a tour boat or been to the farm?"

I nodded. "Both. The tours are amazing, and the farm is a magical place. It's stunning."

"Elise said the same thing the first time she went there. She felt comfortable there. Colin always made sure of it. But they're both just great people." Chelsea stopped in front of Elise and Colin. Both turned to her and hugged her, then she introduced me. "Natalie runs the new summer camp."

"Oh, I've heard great things about it," Elise said. "It was so needed for the town."

"I agree. That's why I was so excited when Amelia encouraged me to do it," I said, hoping I didn't sound too wooden. Or drunk. The room had definitely taken on a tilt.

"Amelia is the best. James is her son." Elise pointed to one of the men Haley pointed out earlier.

I looked at Chelsea, who grinned. "I didn't know that," I admitted.

"Small town," Elise said. "I think everyone either knows everyone or is related to everyone."

"Or dated everyone," Colin said. "I don't know if you do field trips from your camp, but I'd love to get the kids out to my farm and show them around. We aren't doing much in the summer, but we can set up a whole day for them so they can see how it works and what we do and give them some treats."

Chelsea nudged me. "I told you."

Colin and Elise looked between us while I struggled to find my voice. My cheeks burned, wondering if Chelsea set me up and prepped them before we walked over.

"Told her what?" Elise asked.

"Natalie doesn't want to seem like she's trying to get things from people, but I suggested the same thing. I thought maybe you could do a boat tour, too." Chelsea shrugged, keeping eye contact with Elise.

I was going to die.

"That's a great idea. Especially during the week. It's usually a little quieter, and we aren't always running all the boats. I'm sure we could make that work."

"I don't want to put any of you out," I hurried to say.

Elise shook her head. "Not at all. We love MacKellar Cove. And we love sharing it with others, but to be able to share it with people who live here? Maybe some kids who've never done these kinds of things? That's a truly special opportunity."

"Do you offer scholarships?" Colin asked.

I nodded haltingly.

"I would be interested in sponsoring a few kids, if you're open to that. We don't have kids and haven't decided if we're going to, but I know there are families that could use the chance to send their kids to camp but can't afford it." Colin pulled out his phone. "Do you mind putting your number in my phone and we can talk more next week?"

"I..." I looked at the three of them and tried to figure out if this was a dream. "Are you sure? I mean, it's really nice, but you don't have to do this."

Colin shook his head and smiled kindly at me. "I don't feel pressured in the least. I was not put up to this. I am asking because we've talked about things like that. Giving back to the community and helping others." He wrapped his arm around Elise. "We're very fortunate. I lived here when I was young, but my mother died and my father couldn't stay here. My grandmother died a few years ago and left the farm to me. It brought me back to MacKellar Cove, and the entire town welcomed me in without hesitation. I know it's not easy to accept when strangers are offering you something, but I know what you're doing is great for the people here. I just want to help."

"We both do," Elise said. "Chelsea probably told you I'm a smart-ass and don't take anything seriously, but kids matter. Kids need a safe place to be. Somewhere they don't have to do anything but be kids. And I know that's what you've created. We don't want to see that go away."

"Thank you," I said, my throat tightening with emotion. "That means a lot to me." I finally took Colin's phone and typed in my number.

"And for the record," Chelsea said, "I did not tell her anything besides you're my cousin. Haley and I have been trying to get Natalie and Daisy to come to book club."

"Oh, you definitely have to come to book club. We talk about relationships and eat cake and drink wine sometimes," Elise gushed.

"And read books," Chelsea added.

Elise waved. "Psh. Sometimes. The fun part is everyone getting together. Tomorrow night. Please come. It's at Book Boyfriends Unlimited at six. We'd love to have you both."

I nodded. "Okay. Thank you."

"Yay!" Chelsea said, hugging me. "I'm so happy you're going to come."

"Mind if I steal this one?" a Black man asked, wrapping his arms around Chelsea as soon as she let go of me.

"Derek, this is Natalie," Chelsea said.

"Natalie, nice to meet you. I've heard a lot about you. My son, Jude, was one of your campers last summer and will be back again this year," Derek said.

"Jude is such a nice kid. A true pleasure," I said, meaning every word. Jude was one of my favorites. He was never mean and helped the younger kids a lot, making sure no one was left out or left behind.

"Well, that's the best compliment a parent can get. Thank you."

I smiled at him, not knowing what else to say.

"We were just talking about having the campers out to the farm," Colin said.

"Jude would love that," Derek said. "He's so excited for Maple Weekend."

"Still a few months away," Colin said with a chuckle.

"Doesn't matter. Jude's ready," Derek said.

I excused myself from the two couples, needing a minute to calm myself down again. I spun my ring around my finger and wound my way toward the hallway that I hoped had bathrooms.

I pushed my way into the women's restroom and breathed a sigh when there was an open stall. I used the bathroom and took my time getting out of there. I washed my hands and walked out, only to have someone slam into me.

My arm hit the wall. I lost my balance and fell, scrambling for something to grab on to. Just before I hit the ground, my fingers dug into something. I squeezed, slowing my fall down enough that I ended up on my knees instead of sprawled on the floor.

"Ow! What the—?" a male voice growled.

Whatever I was holding on to moved, and I realized I grabbed a person. A male person. A very large male person, right in the twig and berries.

"Do you think you could let go of me?" he snapped.

I unclenched my hand and looked up. Into the face of the man who held my future in his hands more than any other I'd ever met.

"Mr. Mayor," I stammered.

His brow lifted. "Ms. Edwards."

As if that wasn't bad enough, a flash behind me said someone took a picture. Of me. On my knees. In front of the mayor of MacKellar Cove. As he tried to pull his pants back up.

Fuck my life.

THANK **you** for reading Chelsea and Derek's story! When we first met these two characters, I had no idea they were going to end up together. I knew they would each get a book, but finding out they were perfect for each other was news to me! I hope you loved their surprise romance.

The next book in the series is Natalie and Omar's story. Omar is starting his re-election campaign and does not need any distractions. But Natalie needs Omar's approval to do some work to the new rec center she buys for the summer camp. And the more time they spend together, the harder it is for them to keep their hands off each other. Preorder His Curvy Distraction now and start reading on September 10!

WANT MORE from Chelsea and Derek? Derek's finally on board with block parties, but he has a surprise for Chelsea. Bonus epilogue is only available to subscribers. Sign up now!

LOOKING for more secret romance stories? Addi has always been the reliable one who takes care of everyone else. But she's ready to have a little fun herself. When Joey presents himself as the perfect opportunity to let go, Addi believes it's just casual, but Joey sees Addi as so much more. Pick up your copy of Bulky & Beauteous now!

ABOUT THE AUTHOR

USA TODAY Bestselling Author Mary E Thompson spent most of her childhood wishing she had a few less curves. She hid in the pages of books because her favorite characters never cared what size her clothes were. Now, neither does Mary, and she writes stories that celebrate women like her. Real women who have curves, chase dreams, and find love, because we should all be happy, no matter our dress size.

Mary spends her non-writing time with her husband and two kids, watching too much TV, cheering for her hometown football team (Go Bills!), and hiding chocolate from her family.

Visit https://MaryEThompson.com/ to sign up for Mary's newsletter, **Romancing the Curves**. Subscribers get free ebooks and other fun stuff, like exclusive, members only content and giveaways, plus are the first to know about new releases and sales!

www.ingramcontent.com/pod-product-compliance
Lightning Source LLC
Chambersburg PA
CBHW060656190726
48289CB00002B/431